Cully had his back to her.

As he bent and splashed water on his chest, then used a towel to wipe it dry, the long, ropy muscles of his back flexed in rhythm. The muscles across his shoulders were more defined, but still suited his long, lean looks.

Seven months ago she'd let her hands explore and touch his back and shoulders, feeling those muscles through the fabric of his shirt, then flesh-to-flesh. Her palms almost itched with the longing to touch him, this instant.

Suddenly Cully turned his head, locking eyes with her. More slowly, he turned the rest of the way.

Jessa prayed he couldn't read her mind.

Dear Reader,

April is the time for the little things...a time for nature to nurture new growth, a time for spring to begin to show its glory.

So, it's perfect timing to have a THAT'S MY BABY! title this month. *What To Do About Baby* by award-winning author Martha Hix is a tender, humorous tale about a heroine who discovers love in the most surprising ways. After her estranged mother's death, the last thing Caroline Grant expected to inherit was an eighteen-month-old sister...or to fall in love with the handsome stranger who delivered the surprise bundle!

And more springtime fun is in store for our readers as Sherryl Woods's wonderful series THE BRIDAL PATH continues with the delightful *Danielle's Daddy Factor*. Next up, Pamela Toth's BUCKLES & BRONCOS series brings you back to the world of the beloved Buchanan brothers when their long-lost sister, Kirby, is found—and is about to discover romance in *Buchanan's Return*.

What is spring without a wedding? *Stop the Wedding!* by Trisha Alexander is sure to win your heart! And don't miss Janis Reams Hudson's captivating story of reunited lovers in *The Mother of His Son*. And a surefire keeper is coming your way in *A Stranger to Love* by Patricia McLinn. This tender story promises to melt your heart!

I hope you enjoy each and every story this month!

Sincerely,

Tara Gavin,
Senior Editor

Please address questions and book requests to:
Silhouette Reader Service
U.S.: 3010 Walden Ave., P.O. Box 1325, Buffalo, NY 14269
Canadian: P.O. Box 609, Fort Erie, Ont. L2A 5X3

PATRICIA McLINN

A STRANGER TO LOVE

Silhouette®

SPECIAL EDITION®

Published by Silhouette Books
America's Publisher of Contemporary Romance

To Cathy and John, who encouraged me to dive in
from the start.

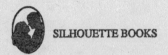 SILHOUETTE BOOKS

ISBN 0-373-24098-8

A STRANGER TO LOVE

Copyright © 1997 by Patricia McLaughlin

Books by Patricia McLinn

Silhouette Special Edition

Hoops #587
A New World #641
*Prelude to a Wedding #712
*Wedding Party #718
*Grady's Wedding #813
Not a Family Man #864
Rodeo Nights #904
A Stranger in the Family #959
A Stranger to Love #1098

*Wedding Series

PATRICIA McLINN

says she has been spinning stories in her head since childhood, when her mother insisted she stop reading at the dinner table. As the time came for her to earn a living, Patricia shifted her stories from fiction to fact—she became a sportswriter and editor for newspapers in Illinois, North Carolina and the District of Columbia. Now living outside Washington, D.C., she enjoys traveling, history and sports but is happiest indulging her passion for storytelling.

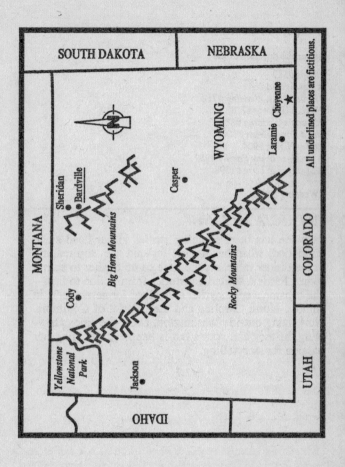

All underlined places are fictitious.

Chapter One

Sheriff Tom Milano glared at the computer.

He was too old for newfangled machines. He oughta be fishing or two-stepping with Rita. He stabbed one of three keys with an arrow aimed up. Words on the screen jumped and disappeared.

"Gol'durn it!" Rita didn't like him talking rough, but the following torrent constituted an avalanche of backsliding.

"Sheriff?" His open door framed the balding head and right shoulder of Deputy Russell Kasper. "Rita called."

Guilt jumped on him faster than a fly on road apples.

Kasper went on, "Said there's a disturbance at Jessa's."

Sheriff Milano frowned. Rita worked as a clerk at Jessa Tarrant's sundries shop. "What kind of disturbance?"

"Didn't say. Just said they had a situation—that's what she called it—and you oughta get over there."

Milano stood and grabbed his hat. "See if this contraption will spit out that report on paper."

"But the whole idea—"

"You heard me, Deputy."

"Yes, sir."

Tom Milano settled the well-worn hat into the groove in his gray hair and set out to restore the peace of Bardville, Wyoming.

"Let me get this straight," Sheriff Milano said. "Jessa, you were in back in the office with the door closed, while Rita was working the register. That right?"

Jessa Tarrant nodded. What did this matter? Who was where had nothing to do with what had happened or what would happen.

"And you were picking out things in the store, uh, Mr.—" The sheriff peered at his notes as if checking the name of the tall, lean man before him, though Jessa would wager a month's receipts Tom Milano knew exactly the identity of this man propping one hip against the wall, looking entirely at his ease. "Grainger?"

"Yes."

"Picking out some things, huh? You've got quite a collection there," the sheriff said with a nod to the full basket on the floor. "Why is that?"

"My nephew and I are staying at the Westons' for a few weeks." The sheriff's eyes went to the third person before him, a sullen-faced boy of about twelve. As far as Jessa could gauge through the mirrored sunglasses he wore, Cully Grainger didn't spare the boy so much as a glance. "Flew in today. We need some things."

"Westons' place, huh?"

The sheriff's vague question and the silence that followed were an implicit request for more information. For a long moment, Jessa thought the other man wasn't going to comply. Sheriff Milano waited with no sign of impatience or irritation.

The tight line of Cully's lips eased and one side lifted in the smallest, most reluctant of grins.

"I'm a friend of Boone Smith's. Came here last summer when he was visiting the Westons. Came back for the wedding."

As the sheriff damned well knew, Jessa thought. She shifted to her other foot and recrossed her arms at her waist. Tom Milano had been at the wedding of Boone Dorsey Smith and Cambria Weston ten months ago and at their combination belated reception and going-away party last October before they spent the winter in North Carolina.

Even if Cully Grainger hadn't been Boone's best man and among only a handful of guests from beyond Bardville, he wasn't someone you forgot.

He was nearly six foot four and rangy, with thick hair the color of walnuts. He moved slow, talked slower, and the sun could rise in the time it took his grin to take full effect. He presented an aura of supreme, imperturbable calm. Except for his intense blue-green eyes. And those he generally kept hidden behind mirrored sunglasses.

He hadn't kept them hidden the night of the going-away party. The night he'd insisted on driving her home. The night he'd invited himself in for coffee, and she'd said okay. The night she'd made one mistake, then almost made a much worse one.

She shifted her feet. "Sheriff, none of this matters, because I won't—"

"Hold on there, Jessa. From the way I hear it, with you in back and Rita up front, neither of you could rightly see what happened. Let me hear from Cully."

"When we first came in, I went down that aisle." Cully tipped his head toward the row of shelves behind him. "There were six of those fancy red pocketknives on the top shelf. While I picked out supplies, I heard Travis in that aisle. I heard scuffling, like objects rubbing against each other."

Jessa followed the direction of the sheriff's gaze to the bottom shelf, which held containers of cleansing powder.

The once-neat row looked like a line of soldiers about to allow the enemy to break through—or like a line of containers jostled by a shoe pushed among them so someone could stand on the shelf to reach higher.

"Then I heard rustling, like plastic."

On the second-to-the-top shelf, kitchen gloves, each pair enclosed in plastic, had tumbled from their usual neat stack.

"When I came around to see what was happening," Cully continued, "Travis was in the aisle, just taking his hand out of his pocket. There were five pocketknives on the top shelf. I asked Travis what he had in his pocket. He said nothing. I could see there was something. I asked again. He said nothing again. I decided to find out for myself. He had this."

Cully opened his hand to reveal a four-inch-long red-cased pocketknife, with enough gadgets and tools to replace a drawerful, and a price proportionately high. Because tourists liked the knives, they were among the few luxury items Jessa stocked.

She automatically took the end of the pocketknife he held out. He didn't immediately release the other end. She glanced up. He seemed to be staring at the knife. His face was unreadable. The sheriff cleared his throat, and Cully dropped his hand.

"That doesn't mean this knife came from here," she said. Something in her kept pushing to prove the boy's innocence. She didn't bother to wonder what it was.

"The price sticker is from your store," Cully said.

She gazed at the knife in her hand and the sticker that carried the name "Nearly Everything" along with the price. She wished she could make it disappear, along with the boy who tugged at her sympathies and—especially—the man who tugged at something else.

The sheriff looked from the pocketknife to the shelves to the boy and back to the man.

"You're a noticing sort, aren't you?" he said to Cully. "Heard you're in law enforcement back East."

"I was."

"Not now?"

"Not now."

Beneath Cully's even confirmation, Jessa caught an undercurrent. Boone and Cambria hadn't said much, but she'd gathered Cully might be leaving public police work. Though it hardly mattered. No matter how far from a uniform he got, anybody could see this man would forever be a cop inside. Look at how he reacted to his own nephew.

Sheriff Milano grunted an acknowledgment. "Know anything about computers?"

The question surprised Jessa, but Cully showed no reaction. That figured. He wouldn't care for the muddle of emotions, especially not emotions like surprise or confusion.

"Some."

"Good." The sheriff nodded, but returned to the main topic. "So, then what happened?"

"I asked Rita to call the sheriff's office so you could make an arrest."

Tom Milano's eyebrows rose until they disappeared under the sweat-stained band of his hat. "He's your nephew, didn't you say?"

"He stole."

The sheriff breathed out through his nose. Rocking back on the heels of his worn boots, he turned slightly to face the boy.

"What's your name, son?"

The boy didn't look up. "I'm not your son."

"You're right there, but you got a name. What is it?"

"Travis."

"Okay, Travis, you heard what your uncle here—" the boy curled his lip "—had to say. What've you got to say?"

"Nothin'."

Sheriff Milano didn't miss a beat. "He says you were taking this pocketknife. That so?"

It could be, Jessa thought, that Tom Milano had encountered this adolescent reaction a time or two before in his career. She allowed herself the first sliver of amusement she'd felt since she'd spotted Cully Grainger's long strides bringing him toward her store and had developed an urgent need to do work in back.

"So what. I wanted it. I took it."

"*So what* is it doesn't belong to you. It belongs to this lady here. And she works hard to put things in her store so people can buy them and she'll make a living."

"Big deal."

The sheriff looked from the boy's sullen face to Cully's set jaw to her. "You want to press charges, Jessa?"

Her arms tightened over where her white cotton blouse tucked into her khaki slacks. "No."

"It's your duty," Cully said flatly.

Jessa stared at him, seeing only the reflection of herself in his glasses. She looked shrunken and insignificant in the mirrored lenses. Like the child she'd once been. "I won't press charges."

"Then I will."

"He's a *boy*," she protested. "What is he—twelve years old?"

"What age do you suggest he start learning right from wrong?"

The calm, cool words felt like slaps against her face. Long remembered, and hated.

You're old enough to know right from wrong.

The sheriff cleared his throat. "Well, this being a first offense—"

"It's not," Cully interrupted without emotion.

"That so?" Milano looked at the boy thoughtfully. "Been causing trouble, have you? Got your ma and pa down to the police station to get you out of trouble?"

Jessa thought she caught a flicker of movement behind Cully's sunglasses, as if he'd closed his eyes.

"My father's dead." Travis spit out the words like a punishment. "And my mother can't be bothered, since she's panting after *darling Darryl*—"

"Travis." Cully's single word sounded a warning.

The boy didn't heed it. "And cops are all—"

Cully's hand shot out and grasped the boy's shoulder, not hard, but enough to turn them face-to-face.

Jessa didn't breathe as man and boy stared at each other, the man's eyes hidden, the boy's brimful of fury.

The muscle at the side of Cully's jaw flexed, then his hold eased. Travis jerked his shoulder free. He leaned against the shelving, a posture of complete indifference, except for his hands clenched into fists.

"Jessa—" Tom Milano started.

She shook her head emphatically. "I won't press charges."

She sensed curiosity behind the sheriff's professional calm. Most shop owners wanted shoplifting punished. But she had no obligation to explain. Her reasons were personal, and she didn't owe anyone an explanation. Including Cully Grainger, whose mouth and forehead were drawn tight in a frown.

"Well, here's how I see the situation. We got us a juvenile accused of shoplifting. He didn't leave the store, so that makes it a little shaky. But we got a witness saying he had the property hidden. And we got the suspect not denying the situation. Now, if the shop owner pressed charges—"

"I said—"

"I heard you, Jessa. I'm just telling you, hypothetical like, that if a shop owner pressed charges, most likely the boy would go on juvenile probation. They'd set him to doing chores for the county. Weeding that flower bed by the Welcome To Bardville sign, or dusting those magazine stacks at the library Wanda's always going on about.

Maybe they'd put him to work mowing and such on county property under Harry Banks. Fact, I think that's most likely, because Harry's been griping even fiercer than Wanda.''

Jessa frowned. ''Harry Banks hates kids. He's notorious. Yells at them all the time. You must have heard the tales. Why, he chased Will Randall with a shovel one time for cutting across the library lawn, and there's no nicer kid than Will.''

Tom Milano scratched his jaw. ''True enough, but Harry's been the board's squeakiest wheel a good, long time, so I suspect he's first on their list for oil—or elbow grease in this case. So that's the official way,'' the sheriff went on, ''if a shop owner or a concerned citizen pressed charges and we did this official like. Another possibility is to let the whole thing drop.'' He questioned Cully with a look.

''No.''

It was as final as a word could be.

''Didn't think so,'' Milano said philosophically. ''So, what I'm aiming for is something in the middle. A compromise, you might say.''

The look of bright expectancy he focused on Cully, then Travis, then her, didn't fool Jessa. Tom Milano was as crafty as they came.

''Like what?''

''Like the boy works for you instead of the county. This episode doesn't go on the books, so to speak, but the boy doesn't go sailing off like he's innocent as a newborn babe, either.''

Jessa eyed Travis. He wore a faded T-shirt several sizes too large over baggy jeans. Beneath a turned-backward baseball cap his hair had been shorn short in the front, with a straggle of longer hair at the back. The little she could see of his thin face as he stared at the floor revealed a turned-down mouth and a pugnacious chin.

He'd be more hindrance than help, since she'd have to

explain and supervise everything. That happened with any new employee. With this boy resenting every second he spent here, it only promised to be worse. Having him around would be like having a black cloud in the store.

Or like gazing into a twenty-year-old mirror.

If only Cully would change his mind...

She turned to him, and knew there was no chance.

His jaw was as pugnacious as his nephew's and his mouth, while neutrally straight, was as firm as an unshakable resolve.

She knew that look.

For all his slow talk and outwardly easygoing ways, this was a man who divided his world into right or wrong. Inside the law or outside. Saint or devil. Nothing in his world would dare to skip from one side to the other and back. Not even a twelve-year-old.

She knew that kind of man.

And she knew what it felt like to be a child ruled by that kind of man.

"How much would he work here?"

Tom Milano beamed at her, but the expressions of the other two males showed no sign of lightening.

"I'd say you and Cully need to work that out between you. Why don't I take Travis off your hands awhile? I'll show him 'round the sheriff's office and the town a bit. Rita can mind the store so you two can go off someplace quiet and talk. Maybe the café. Or there's a nice place out on the highway to Sheridan that Rita and I—"

"I don't think that's a good idea—"

Jessa's start on an objection was overridden by Cully's low voice. "I haven't said I'd agree to this."

"Why on earth not?" she demanded.

Instead of answering, he focused on the sheriff. "It shouldn't be a reward for stealing."

"I'd say whether it's reward or punishment depends on what you and Jessa come up with."

After a moment of strained silence, Cully turned to her. "You want to do this? It'll be a pain for you."

"Do I *want* to? No. But considering the alternative that your bullheadedness—"

"*Will* you do this?" The impatient words contradicted a slight easing around his mouth.

"Yes."

"Seven days a week?" Jessa tossed her hands up. "You're crazy, Cully. The kid won't have any time for fun."

"I didn't bring him out from North Carolina to Wyoming for fun."

"No, you brought him out here as punishment. I just don't understand why."

They stared at each other across Jessa's sun-drenched living room. At least she stared at him, and she presumed he stared back. She considered demanding he take off the sunglasses, except she knew from experience that his eyes could be more unsettling than the mirrored lenses.

She couldn't reconstruct all the conversation that had sent her and Cully here. Tom Milano had been suggesting places that would have made the thing seem like a date; she'd countered by proposing they talk in the shop's back office. There had been comments about it being small and not very private, and all of a sudden she'd been backed into a verbal corner of either saying outright she didn't want Cully Grainger in her house, or giving in as graciously as she could. She gave in.

"I brought him here hoping to make up for a lot of years when he never had to face the consequences of his actions."

"I thought you said you wanted to teach him right from wrong."

"That, too. But considering some of the stuff he's done, there might not be time to wait for him to learn that. So first thing is to make him know if he does wrong, there are consequences.''

Jessa looked at Cully, sitting there so at ease on her couch, and desperately wanted to think him smug and rigid. He'd walked into her living room and gone unhesitatingly to the couch, where he'd sat only once before, one night last fall. This time he'd dropped his jeans-covered fanny in the very middle of the three navy-and-yellow floral cushions. If she'd sat on the couch they would have been nearly hip to hip, like two lovers side by side.

She not only hadn't sat on the couch, she'd bypassed the upholstered chair at right angles to it and taken the straight-backed chair by the door.

That didn't seem to bother Cully any. He spread his long arms along the couch's back in a posture of relaxed possession. His body language screamed a man settling in and not about to be easily ousted. The disquiet she'd felt since that first glimpse of him deepened.

"Why'd you bring Travis here?" she demanded.

"Why not? Nice place. Lots of open space. Get him away from the troublemakers he's been hanging out with.''

"You could have done that in North Carolina. Taken him to the mountains where you and Boone grew up, where there are people you know, who know you. Why didn't you do that?''

"Boone knows me. Cambria, too. And the Westons know me some. They're here. You looking for a reference?''

She didn't answer. Because he clearly wasn't going to tell her what she wanted to know. Why hadn't he gone home when he'd faced trouble with his young nephew? It hinted at a vulnerability in him she didn't want to see. Vulnerability could be contagious.

Oh, yes, she wanted to think him smug and rigid. Except Cambria and the Westons would not have taken to anyone—best friend of Boone's or not—if he were smug and rigid. Besides, she kept hearing something in his words that prevented her from dismissing him so easily. Almost as if he were afraid. For Travis? Of what?

There might not be time to wait for him to learn...

"More iced tea?" she asked abruptly.

Before he could answer, she'd started for the kitchen. Cully followed.

At the narrow doorway, she turned and blocked his way. "I'll be right back." She didn't bother to sound cordial.

"You forgot the glasses." He held up the two he'd collected.

"I'll use fresh ones."

"No, thanks. I don't want any more tea." He stepped forward, and she could either back up or be a heck of a lot closer to him than Mrs. Palmer had allowed in eighth-grade dance class. She backed up.

He went on in, with her trailing behind. The narrow opening in the U-shaped kitchen seemed even narrower than usual with Cully in it.

He looked around the small area, his gaze seeming to rest on the green glass bottle on the sill with the impatiens cuttings she hoped would root, on the glass apothecary jars she used as canisters, on the vibrant geranium print of the hand towel looped over the oven door handle, on the white-painted metal cabinets and worn countertops. His circuit brought him face-to-face with her.

"It's nice."

She'd forgotten he hadn't seen this part of the house last fall. Only the living room. And the threshold of her bedroom.

She didn't want him in her kitchen. She didn't want him in her house. She didn't want him reminding her. Not of that night last fall, not of a more distant past, not of impossibilities.

"Thanks. It's nothing like the one Boone and Cambria designed for their new house up the mountain. That's going to be great, especially with the baby coming."

Nerves kept the spigot on her mouth open full throttle.

If she talked fast enough and long enough she'd forget how Cully had held her, kissed her. Forget how she'd felt when she'd told him to leave, and he'd turned away and left her at her bedroom door. Forget how many times she'd wondered what would have happened if she *hadn't* told him to leave.

"It's a good thing Cambria got past those rough early months. She could hardly stand to hear the word *kitchen*, much less think about designing one. But she sure got over that. She's been knee-deep in how-to and design books. I told her I didn't want to hear another word about triangular work stations or appliance ports or under-cabinet lights. Cambria showed me the plans and brochures. It's going to be great. Terrific.'' Finally, she stemmed the rush of words, ending with an anticlimactic, "But this is fine for me.''

He didn't answer immediately. She grimaced. Perhaps he was making sure he wouldn't be run over by another freight train of words.

"It's a lot like the kitchen we had when I was a kid,'' he said slowly. "Only a lot cleaner.''

There it was in his voice again, the note she couldn't pin down. The one that made him too human for comfort.

Then, before she could try to isolate that note and define it once and for all, he was speaking again. This time with no hidden notes.

"You're doing Travis no favors by being soft on him.''

Impatience flared in her, and she welcomed it. It was so much simpler than nerves and memories and questions. "Neither are you by being so hard on him.''

"He's got to take responsibility. He's got to learn his actions have consequences. Or he's headed for big trouble.''

"And you've decided you're the one to teach him, huh?''

He didn't blink at her sarcasm. "His father's dead. His mother gave up. Said he was incorrigible. His grandparents

aren't an option." She wondered if he hesitated only to
draw a breath or from another cause. "That left me."

"So St. Cully came to the rescue, riding in on his white
horse and taking over. Is that how you see it?"

"I see a kid whose father died and whose mother can't
be bothered because she won't risk the kid screwing up
her new life. That's how I see it."

He turned his back to her and with a quick motion up-
ended the glasses. The only sound was liquid and ice cubes
hitting the sink.

Jessa stared at his broad shoulders, taut under the plain
white fabric of his shirt.

She closed her eyes and drew in a deep breath, trying
to erase the picture of an emotionally deserted boy his
words had called up all too quickly. She knew the kind of
pain Travis must be feeling. She understood it. Hers was
an older pain and not as deep, perhaps, but still sharp, and
very personal.

*Face it, there's no way you can walk away from Travis
Grainger.*

She flopped back so her shoulders pressed against the
refrigerator. Okay, she'd do what she could to help Travis.
And she'd do her best to get along with Cully in order to
accomplish that. She would also be careful. Very, very
careful.

Air came out of her in a long stream. She opened her
eyes. "I'm sorry."

"What for?" He seemed to stare out the window over
the sink.

"The St. Cully crack."

"Forget it."

"It was uncalled for. I apologize."

"Don't." He turned slowly and propped his hips against
the edge of the sink, his hands at either side of him. "And
don't go ducking behind that ice wall again, Jessa."

His deep voice speaking her name seemed to reverberate

on her nerve endings, especially the ones up the back of her neck and into her scalp. *Careful. Very, very careful.*

"I don't know what you're talking about," she said.

"The hell you don't." The words had no heat, yet plenty of underlying steel.

"I'm simply trying to be polite instead of—"

"Instead of being honest," he said, supplying his own ending. "I don't want your apology, and I don't want your politeness. What I want is honesty. And I know you're capable of it. Remember, Jessa, I've seen you when that mask slips all the way off. Or nearly all the way off."

She'd known it was a mistake to have this talk at her house. It was sure to bring up memories of the only other time he had been here. Memories like the ones filtering heat through her blood and urgency through her breathing.

She could ignore his reference to that night, or she could face it head-on. He wanted honesty? Fine.

"I'd had too much wine."

His low voice sliced at her with a harsh edge.

"Or not enough."

Chapter Two

Mistakes.

Her life was littered with them.

That night last fall had been a mistake. A big one. You'd think she'd know better than to get into a situation like that.

Was this a mistake, too, thinking she could overlook six feet four inches of Cully Grainger to maybe, possibly, with a whole lot of luck, help a boy?

"Maybe this isn't a good idea."

"Probably isn't," Cully agreed evenly. "I'll tell Milano we couldn't work it out, and I'll handle Travis my way."

"By doing what? Throwing him in prison?"

"If he keeps on the way he's going, that's where he'll end up. Or worse. When you break the law—"

"Great, just great. Forget being an uncle to a boy, just be a cop. That'll cure everything."

"Quit making me an ogre, dammit. You don't—" He bit off the words with a mumbled curse. "What it is about you…?'' He rubbed his hand across the back of his neck, then straightened. "I shouldn't lose my temper. Sorry."

Reactions tumbled through Jessa. He thought that bit of barking equaled losing his temper? The man must have no temper or a cast-iron leash on it. Or he wasn't as impervious to emotion as she'd thought.

What it is about you…? Something about her? Something about her that what? Unsettled him? Anything like the way he unsettled her? And what of her feelings? Did she truly think he was an ogre? Or did she try to make him into one because it was so much easier?

Easier.

She pulled her thoughts up short. Easier for whom? Certainly not for Travis. That's who this was about, after all. Not about her, or Cully.

"Let's start over," she said slowly. "Let's sit down and work this out. For Travis."

Cully nodded. "All right."

Before they reached the living room she stopped. "Let's go out on the deck. It's, uh, such a nice day."

She thought for a moment he saw through her, saw she wanted to avoid the living room and its memories from last fall. And she thought he would object. He didn't.

They sat on chairs—not too close together—with their feet propped on the railing, and they negotiated in earnest how Travis would spend his next several weeks.

"Three days a week?" Boone repeated, offering Cully a beer he'd pulled from a cooler.

"Monday, Wednesday and Friday, starting tomorrow," Cully confirmed, taking the bottle before sitting next to Boone on a stack of lumber in front of the house Boone had designed and was now building. He'd driven up to tell his old friend he and Travis had arrived. And to tell Boone about the unexpected turn Travis's summer had taken at Jessa Tarrant's shop this afternoon.

He shoved his sunglasses to the top of his head and rubbed the bridge of his nose.

"You're worried, aren't you, Cully?"

"The boy's headed for trouble."

"You'll turn him around. You've done it with harder cases than a twelve-year-old."

"Yeah, I did a great job with my own brother, didn't I?"

Boone frowned at his sarcasm. "Cully, you can't blame yourself for that."

"Can't I? No, don't say it—we've gone those rounds before. Let's say I sure as hell hope getting away from North Carolina does Travis good. He's not exactly off to a great start."

"Guess not. Sounds like you're going to be spending a good amount of time seeing Jessa, though."

"That's not a selling point with me."

"Isn't it? I thought…" Boone didn't need to fill in what he thought.

Cully had thought the same thing at one time.

That first time he'd come to Bardville, and Boone had pointed out Jessa and Cambria. One look, and Cully had known his oldest friend was far gone. But on which one? Cully had to admit—to himself—to a wave of relief when he'd realized Boone's heart had fixed on Cambria, not Jessa.

He supposed Jessa Tarrant would dismiss her looks by saying she had dark hair, dark eyes, fair skin. She did.

Dark hair with a ruby's glow—not streaks or strands, but almost as if the shine came from inside. It brushed her shoulders and cupped her squared chin. Fair skin that set off decisive dark brows and full lips. Dark eyes that spoke of wariness and strength.

Not until Boone and Cambria's wedding did he get close enough to discover the scent clinging to her was jasmine— like his Aunt Philly used to grow in her garden—and he'd only been close then because he'd been best man and she'd been maid of honor. Cully had hoped he and Jessa could get to know each other. But, as Aunt Philly had said, if hopes were horses, nobody'd walk.

Jessa Tarrant had looked at him then—the few times her eyes came to rest on him—with the same cool, look-through-you lack of interest as this afternoon.

And the fact that she'd looked at him a different way that night of the party—at least for a while—provided final proof she was the last kind of woman he needed.

"Don't need that kind of complication in my life," he finally answered Boone. Someone steady, reliable, easygoing, that's what he needed.

"I don't deny falling in love is complicated, but it's worth it." Boone's grin had showed up a lot this past year with Cambria. It sure hadn't dimmed since he'd found out they would have a baby come October.

Maybe for you. "Nobody said anything about falling in love. Besides, I've got all the complications I can handle."

And that meant he'd better find a way to keep a cushion between himself and Jessa Tarrant. She'd crept into his thoughts over the past months despite fifteen hundred miles between them. Now that they were bound to see each other, he didn't want to take any chances. Because running up against her too often could fray his resolve, good sense and willpower.

"The job offer or Travis?"

"Both." Cully took a swallow from the beer bottle, then settled it in a hollow in the ground by his feet.

"Start with the job offer."

"I wouldn't call it an offer. More like they might be interested in having me apply."

"That's not too shabby considering the outfit."

"No, it's not." Former federal law enforcement agents had started a business fifteen years ago that combined being among the world's top security firms with going well beyond normal measures if the situation required. All but two operatives were former federal agents. They were talking to Cully about becoming the third.

"So, what's next?" Boone drained the last of his beer.

"I go to Washington, take some tests, talk to some people."

"How come you aren't thrilled?"

"I am."

"Bull."

Cully cut Boone a look. "It's a great opportunity. Good money. As much security as you get in my line of work. Why wouldn't I be thrilled?"

"Because you like police work better." Boone answered so promptly Cully suspected he'd been waiting for that opening. "Because you don't think protection should go only to people who can pay for it. Because you believe in *serve and protect*."

"Maybe it doesn't believe in me."

Boone gave a grunt of comprehension, though Cully wasn't sure himself what he'd meant. He took another mouthful of fast-warming beer and put the bottle back on the ground.

"Where's Travis?"

Boone's question returned the conversation to Cully's other complication.

"The Westons'. Irene put us in Cambria's old cabin. I left him unpacking his gear. And muttering. What I caught would make a drill sergeant blush."

Boone's sigh conveyed sympathy. "It's not going well?"

Cully snorted. "You could say that." He rubbed his hand across the back of his neck. "Fran said the last time the cops picked him up, he'd been drinking."

He could feel the weight of Boone's look. Without returning it, he knew it carried concern and understanding. One thing about a friendship nearly as old as you were, you didn't have to explain much.

"Did you tell Jessa about Manny?" Boone asked.

"No."

Boone's dark brows rose. "It might help Jessa understand Travis better."

"Travis has been *understood* right into the fix he's in. And he's used being *understood* to get his own way ever since he learned how to play that particular trump card."

"Still, I think—"

"Jessa Tarrant isn't interested in the Grainger family's problems. She apparently has a soft spot for a kid in trouble or she doesn't like cops."

Boone's gaze went to the valley below the house. Cully didn't believe a sudden interest in the view, spectacular as it was, explained this shift in attention. Or the sudden silence.

"Does Jessa Tarrant hate cops?" Cully asked.

"She's never said that to me."

"You sound like one of those contract lawyers you hire, Boone. Do you know if she has some reason to hate cops?"

That might explain some things. Like a woman who had been liquid fire in his arms one minute and iced reserve the next.

Boone met his look. "What I know or what I suspect is going to stay with me, Cully. To quote my wife, if she wants you to know, she'll tell you."

Cully stood, draining the half-full beer bottle in the dirt by his feet. "Fair enough."

Seemed he and Jessa Tarrant were bound to keep secrets from each other.

As much as she would have liked to, Jessa didn't see how she could stay in the office when she heard the old-fashioned bell announce the front shop door opening, followed by Cully Grainger's deep tones wishing Rita good morning. She heard no sound of Travis following suit.

Shaking off lingering sleepiness from a restless night, she smiled determinedly and walked briskly to the front of the store, where Rita had been washing the previous day's fingerprints from the glass door.

"Good morning!"

Cully echoed her greeting. Travis's mouth turned down.

"Rita, this is Travis Grainger. He's going to help us out three days a week for a while. Travis, this is Rita Campbell, my assistant."

"You call her 'Miz Campbell,'" Cully interposed. He was freshly shaved, with a navy plaid shirt tucked into his jeans, a pair of beat up athletic shoes and, of course, his omnipresent sunglasses.

She purposely looked away from him to the framed piece of quilting in the place of honor behind the cash register, beside a photograph of her with the Westons at the shop's grand opening. Since she'd found the quilting in an antiques shop as a teenager, it had been her talisman of calm. It had followed her from her childhood bedroom to college to apartments in half a dozen cities, then on to Bardville, Wyoming, and her shop.

"'Rita' is fine," Rita said.

"'Miz Campbell,'" Cully repeated.

"We're not formal," Jessa said. "I'm 'Jessa' and she's 'Rita.'"

His brow furrowed and lines showed beyond the sunglasses' frames. He was either frowning or narrowing his eyes at her. Maybe both.

"I'd like to talk to you, Jessa. In private."

"Fine. I need some information to keep the paperwork straight, anyhow," she said, preserving her cheerful expression at the expense of a strain on her facial muscles. "Rita, will you get Travis a cloth, and he can help you finish the door?"

"Sure thing."

"Then you can start Travis on the sweeping. We'll be in back," Jessa added. She headed for the office, with Cully following.

The door from the shop was marked Private and opened

into a dim, narrow hallway. On the left, floor-to-ceiling metal shelving held neatly labeled cartons. A wooden stairway led to a small loft with more storage. The edge of the loft was protected by a wooden railing. Near the foot of the stairs rested more cartons, labeled by holiday: "Halloween," "Fourth of July," "Easter," "Presidents' Day," "St. Patrick's Day," "Thanksgiving," "Christmas."

Having the loft overhead had never made her feel closed in, because it was twelve feet above the main floor. But the hallway had never seemed as narrow or as dim as when Cully pulled the door closed behind them. For an instant Jessa froze. He was right behind her, close enough that she smelled a faint tang of soap, close enough that she felt his breath stir the fine hairs escaping from the barrette behind her ear.

A shorter row of shelves to the right created a doorway of sorts. Jessa went through it in a hurry, with Cully following more leisurely into what served as her office. A metal desk, two wooden chairs, a telephone, computer, printer, fax machine and filing cabinets filled the space.

She took the chair at the desk and gestured to the other. "Please sit down. The first thing—" she opened a drawer and pulled a form from the folder, thanking the Fates she got the right folder and the right form "—is Travis's Social Security number."

"What for?"

She noticed his nostrils flare slightly, as if drawing in a scent. Or as if he were angry. She'd lay odds which it was.

"For the government forms," she answered. *With saintly patience,* she added to herself.

"What government forms?" Cully seemed to only half listen to her. The other half of his attention he devoted to studying his surroundings. When he finished he could probably draw a detailed map and provide a more accurate inventory than the one she'd be doing in a few weeks.

Predator's eyes, she'd told herself the first time she'd seen him. But even a year ago, she'd known that wasn't right. That night last fall, he'd danced with her at the party for Boone and Cambria and then he'd driven her home. But not until they sat on the couch in her living room did she see what made his eyes so distinctive. A band of bright blue-green inside a dark rim, all enclosing a paler halo around the pupil. A gradation of colors that seemed to bore into you, into your mind, into your heart, into your soul...

She jerked herself away from such foolish thoughts. No one could read her mind or her soul, not with the most compelling pair of eyes.

"The forms I need to fill out in order to pay him."

That got Cully's attention. "Pay him? You're not paying him."

"Of course I am. He's an employee. He's—"

"He's no employee. He's working because he tried to *steal* from you, remember?"

"He didn't steal from me. And—"

"Because I stopped him."

"Even if he had, he'd work off the knife's value in a few days. After that, he should get paid."

"After that, he can start working off the misdemeanors he's piled up the past year."

"I won't have him working here for nothing."

"I won't have him getting rewarded for trying to steal."

She sat back in the chair, oddly deflated. "We could call Sheriff Milano and tell him the agreement's off."

His lips tilted into a faint, lopsided grin. "He'll tell us to work it out ourselves."

She smiled at him. "You're probably right." He had a wonderful mouth. You didn't notice it in general, because his other features were so strong. But he had perfectly formed lips, wide, even generous, with a fuller lower lip. *And he knew how to use those lips, especially the lower one.*

That thought pulled Jessa upright, jump-starting her problem-solving ability like a jolt of adrenaline. She needed to get Cully Grainger out of this tiny office. *Now.*

"How about if I put the money in a special account and he can claim it when you think it's okay?"

"How about if you give it to charity?"

"In Travis's name," she countered.

"In Travis's name," he conceded. "To the Police Athletic League."

She'd started to jot a note, but paused.

She didn't look up, and all he said was, "It's a league the cops run for kids."

"Okay. You can pick Travis up at four o'clo—"

"I have something to say."

She'd started to rise. His words brought her back into the chair. Her muscles didn't relax. "Oh?"

"You're not going to do him any good trying to be his pal, Jessa. And—"

"If you're talking about having him call Rita 'Rita' and me 'Jessa,' most kids do."

"And," he repeated more firmly, before going on, "you might do him harm."

"Harm?"

"Yes. He doesn't need pals. He's had those—well-intentioned adults who've been his buddy and let him get away with being a punk. What he needs are people who make him do what he's supposed to do. He needs the security of rules and having them enforced if he breaks them."

You know the rules, and you broke them. That's the end of it.

But, Dad—

No "buts" about it. I thought you were a good kid. I was wrong.

She stood, nearly trembling with something that might have been anger. "We don't have a lot of rules around here."

"Maybe you should get some."

"And we've done very well without their *security*."

"Maybe so. Maybe not. What matters—"

"You can say you don't want your nephew around here, but you can't dictate to me how I run my business or my life!"

"I didn't mean—"

"The hell you didn't!"

Cully sat still and silent. He watched her intently, and he wasn't one to miss a thing. Not the way she blinked hard to hold the tears from flowing. Not her knuckle-whitening grip on the back of her chair.

She forced herself to speak slowly and calmly. "You've got a choice, Cully. You can leave Travis in my care for these three days a week the way we agreed and take a risk that I'll do my best for him, or we can end the agreement right here."

Hands on his thighs, he leaned forward and, even with him seated and her standing, Jessa felt as if he loomed over her.

"I don't," he said, spacing each word, "go back on my agreements."

"Okay." She consciously opened her fingers from around the chair back, extending them to ease the tightness. "I don't, either."

A crash followed by a sustained chorus of metallic ringing ended the conversation.

With Cully on her heels, Jessa rushed into the shop.

"What—?"

Before she finished, she saw *what*. A freestanding card-board display that held scores of small cans of cat food at the end of the far aisle was neither standing nor free. Around the dented and collapsed cardboard, a mountain of cans still let loose a metallic avalanche or two.

Travis stood by the mess with a push broom in hand. Cause and effect were not hard to guess. Rita bustled over from her position by the cash register.

Cully's mutter linked Travis's name and a curse word. His shoulders tensed, and he made a move in the boy's direction.

Jessa placed a hand on his upper arm. Beneath the soft cotton of his shirt, her touch encountered hard, warm flesh.

He stopped immediately and looked down at her. Behind or around or through the mask of his sunglasses, she thought she read surprise.

"It's my store." She kept her voice low, though there wasn't much chance of the shop's other two occupants hearing, not over Rita's chorus of "Oh, dear," and Travis's litany of "It's not my fault."

Cully's shoulders eased, and he stepped back. "Yes, it is."

She started forward. This time his touch on her arm stopped her.

"Jessa, I know you'll do your best for Travis. I don't worry about that. It's the risk that what you *think* is best for him isn't."

"And what if what *you* think's best for him isn't best?"

His mouth went into a grim, flat line. "That's a risk I have to take. I've got no choice."

"Neither do I."

She met his look for an extra moment before she turned and headed for the mess two aisles over.

Cully walked out of Jessa's shop and headed east.

He could have almost felt bad for her. A day with Travis could wear down a smile made of granite. And that's what hers had looked like when she'd first faced Travis this morning. She'd wanted it this way. Not him. This was her idea of how to handle Travis.

If she changed her mind, he'd step in. But not until then.

Suddenly, the image of her smiling at him when he said something about the sheriff suffused his mind. A genuine smile. A smile made of blue sky and fresh air, not granite.

That smile had ended too quickly, and for no reason he could figure. Later, when amusement flickered deep in her eyes, he'd caught himself before he grinned back and triggered another unexplained retreat. It was near impossible to completely shut out someone when you shared their humor. But he'd let that possibility rest.

At the next corner he turned north, onto Bozeman Avenue.

One good thing came of this encounter. He might have spotted a way to keep a cushion between them. He'd need to look closer when he picked up Travis this afternoon.

Another block down he found the square, brick building that housed the town offices, magistrate's office, sheriff's department and, in a one-story addition, fire department.

The entrance to the sheriff's department was to the left, just inside the main door. Behind a long counter, desks neatly squared off in two blocks of four, each with a computer. A young woman typed into another computer atop the counter.

When he asked for Sheriff Milano, she opened a gate in the counter and gestured him through. Two more steps and she stuck her head into an open doorway.

"Sheriff? Cully Grainger's here to see you."

He hadn't given his name.

From behind his desk, Tom Milano grinned. "Have a seat."

The young woman departed without closing the door. Cully glanced over his shoulder as he sat, and the sheriff chuckled. "You're right. Open doors are part of how people 'round here know things like a man's name. Closing doors doesn't slow 'em much and it only makes 'em more curious. Only way to keep a secret is to never speak it. Otherwise, might as well tell everybody."

"Then I'll tell you straight out. My nephew's been in trouble in North Carolina."

"Has he, now?"

"Shoplifting. Smoking and drinking. The police there thought vandalism, too, though they didn't have evidence to make it stick."

The sheriff nodded. "Any violence? Weapons? Drugs?"

"Not that I know of."

"Good. That's good."

Cully thought it was a long way from good. He'd seen too many kids follow the path that led to violence and drugs.

"You'd think a place like Bardville wouldn't have any of that," the sheriff mused, "but we have our share. There're a couple young folks we keep our eye on. A couple older ones, too."

"Travis'll be mostly at the Westons' ranch, besides his days at Jessa's store. But I can't lock him up twenty-four hours a day."

"He wouldn't learn much if you did."

Ignoring that, Cully went on. "I'd appreciate it if you kept an eye on him."

"To prevent his getting in trouble or to catch him?"

"Both. If preventing doesn't work, he's got to learn doing wrong'll cost him."

"Okay. Be happy to."

"Thank you." Before Cully could do more than put his hands on the chair's arms in preparation to stand, however, Milano's voice stopped him.

"Now, I got a couple things to ask you."

"What?"

"Well, I know you grew up in North Carolina. Oldest of four kids. Joined the army with Boone out of high school. But you stayed longer. Went into the military police, got a degree. Five years ago, you got a job with the police in North Carolina. After eighteen months, you went on to Atlanta. Spent a little over eighteen months there."

Cully was impressed, and he let that show. He was also a bit uneasy. That he wouldn't allow to show.

"You didn't hear that by listening at open doors."

Milano chuckled. "Nope, though you could say keeping doors open over the years has helped me find out some of what I want to know."

Cully knew what he meant. Connections, friends, contacts—those could be an investigator's most powerful tool.

He mulled over what Milano had said. "Some of what you want to know?"

The sheriff's nod seemed to indicate he appreciated Cully picking up on that point. "I got the résumé. What I don't have yet is the man."

"The résumé is the man."

"Nah. Don't work that way. Take for instance, you leaving North Carolina. All the résumé says is you piled up commendations, got promotions, then left sudden like. Now, folks I talked to, they say you got a case where a small-time drug dealer killed a kid in a hit-and-run. You had the evidence. You found the guy. You brought him in. Then he turned state's evidence on a bigger fish, and got a soft sentence on the hit-and-run. You resigned."

Milano had very good connections, indeed.

"What I'm wondering is what makes a man resign like that. It sure isn't the first time in police work something's happened like that. Won't be the last."

If Cully's lack of response disappointed Milano, he didn't show it, as he started off again.

"Or take Atlanta. Made detective, more commendations. And then you're gone. Way I heard, it had to do with an arrest a senior detective made on a rape case. Seems another jurisdiction arrested a guy who copped to a series of rapes, including the one that senior detective pinned on someone else. And it seems that senior detective wasn't about to shake loose his arrest, because he'd gotten a lot of press for catching the rapist. Could've gone on quite a while, 'cept somebody leaked the story about evidence showing the other guy did the crimes. The first guy's lawyer got him sprung. That senior detective accused you of leaking the information. As the reporters would say, you wouldn't confirm or deny. But you did resign. Now, I find that real interesting."

"Do you find it interesting they promoted that detective?"

"Don't find it real surprising, considering how things work."

"How things work?" Cully repeated. "How about the fact that that boy he locked up was innocent, and he damned well knew it. It was politics, all about making his squad look good."

Sheriff Milano nodded, as if he'd expected that. "We still haven't gotten to my question. To start, what're you going to do now?"

"I'm deciding that."

"You left Atlanta near two years ago. You've worked a few private jobs. Some routine, though there was something about going to Mexico after a young girl...." Milano studied him. "What I want to know is if you're going private or if you're gonna give public work another try."

"Haven't decided."

"Fine, that's fine." Milano's heartiness seemed an extreme response to Cully's terseness. "That brings me to the second thing I want to know."

Cully waited.

"How'd you like to help us out 'round here?"

This time Cully didn't hide his surprise. He stared at the sheriff, then glanced over his shoulder toward the nearly empty main office. "Doing what?"

The sheriff chuckled. "Don't worry. I'm not looking to send you to settle disputes over broken fences or water rights. Not even to the Back Bar to calm the occasional fisticuffs. At least not yet," he added obscurely. "What I had in mind was you helping with these blasted computers."

The machine set at right angles to Milano's desk wasn't turned on. In fact, the unplugged cord trailed across the plastic-covered keyboard.

"I'm no technician."

"You can use the danged things. I hear you were real good. All I'm looking for is somebody to set up a system so it makes sense and give us pointers on how to use the things.''

''Us?''

The sheriff's thick, gray eyebrows clamped down at the note of amusement in Cully's voice, but his mouth quirked with humor.

''All right, give *me* pointers. I need somebody to translate the blasted machines into human talk, and I can tell you it doesn't do for a sheriff to be begging his deputies for help.''

How could one boy be so exhausting?

Jessa couldn't decide which was more energy sapping: the necessity of finding things for Travis to do, of explaining everything in detail and of more often than not making him redo each task, or the self-imposed requirement of remaining cheerful in the face of his Edgar Allan Poe-like gloom.

She rested her head against one fist as she sat at her desk, contemplating the apple, cheese and carrots she'd brought from home for lunch. It was long past lunchtime and she hadn't eaten, but she wasn't hungry. She was way past that.

She'd told Rita to take an extralong lunch hour, since the older woman had seemed frazzled after Travis had broken the second bottle of perfume while dusting the small cosmetics display. The air in the shop was rather thick after that. Enough to give anyone a headache.

Rita had returned looking so much more fortified that Jessa took her up on the offer to spend a quiet hour in back catching up on paperwork.

She glanced at the stack of invoices under her elbow without interest.

Maybe she'd rest her eyes first. She folded her arms on the invoices and put her head down. A few minutes. She was so tired.

And whose fault was that?

Cully Grainger's.

If she hadn't been thinking about his bringing Travis today she would have slept earlier.

If she hadn't been dreaming about his kissing her and touching her, she would have slept better.

If she hadn't jerked herself awake when she started to dream about what would have happened if she hadn't turned him back at the threshold of her bedroom, she would have slept longer.

It was his fault. For kissing her.... And holding her.... And touching her.... Yes, just like that.

Chapter Three

Cully couldn't remember when he'd realized he had an unsettling effect on people. All he knew was he'd been young, real young.

He figured a lot of it had to do with his eyes.

Eyes of a zealot, his mother called them. That and worse things when he was pouring her stash down the drain. Eyes of a prophet, Aunt Philly used to say, putting the best face on things she could, as always. A quirk of pigmentation, he called it, now that he knew better.

He'd taken to wearing sunglasses unless he was with people who knew him real well. Or unless he wanted to make a point with a suspect or an informant. Someone he wanted to lean on.

He'd taken them off for this interview.

He had an idea of how to build that cushion between him and Jessa Tarrant.

Problem was, as he stood at the doorway of her office and considered her, apparently napping with her head on her folded arms on the desk, he wanted nothing between them. Nothing between them, except heat and desire.

"Oh!" Jessa sat up, saw him and blushed, as if he'd caught her doing something illegal. Or as if she'd read his mind. "You."

"Me," he agreed. Was it his memory or his nose that was picking up the scent of jasmine?

She started to stretch. She either didn't see, or chose to ignore, his blatant survey. He'd put his money on the latter.

His odds improved when she cut the stretch short, as if she was self-conscious. That was the result he'd hoped for when he made his stare so obvious, to get her to stop stretching and stop tormenting him; so why wasn't he happier?

She frowned. "I didn't hear the front bell."

"I came in the back."

"It should have been locked."

"It's not much of a lock."

"It's fine."

Jessa's shortness didn't bother Cully. He just wished he were immune to other things she did. Like breathe. And smell. And move.

She uncrossed the legs she'd crossed two sentences ago, and his focus sharpened. He told himself it wasn't at the sleek line of legs encased in worn-to-smoothness jeans.

"It would be a piece of cake," he stated deliberately, "for anybody to break in here."

It was meant to provoke and it did.

You could learn a lot about people when they got riled. Not just what they said, but what made them lose control and how they went about restoring it—or whether they didn't bother.

Jessa sure did. She held on to control the way a corporate executive held on to a corner office. What slipped into her expression sparked of pure annoyance, but other than that one movement of her legs—pleasant to watch, but more a nick in his control than hers—she remained reserved.

"This is Bardville, not the Bronx. We don't need bars on the windows," she said smoothly. "And most people are polite enough to come through the front door."

"It only takes one perp to happen by."

"Spare me the police jargon."

He ignored that. He turned so he could lean against the shelving unit framing one side of the office doorway. Arms folded over his chest, he studied the outside door's latch. Next he skimmed over the frame. He slowed and looked again. *Son of a*— Moving quickly, he opened the door and looked at the outside.

He hadn't noticed coming in because his mind had been on other problems, more personal than professional. Any B-and-E pro would spot it right off and rub his hands with glee.

His abrupt motion must have caught Jessa's attention, because when he reentered from the alleyway behind the building, she was standing at the office doorway, watching him. Her hair was mussed from her nap, her cheeks still flushed.

She'd looked like this that night last fall. Only, her hair had been mussed from his hands, and her cheeks had been flushed from kisses and caresses they'd shared.

The temper he liked to think he'd conquered spurted to life. What the hell was she doing taking risks like this?

"Not even a piece of damned cake," he said. "Anybody who wanted to get in, anybody who wanted to steal from you—hell!—anybody who wanted to get to *you*—it's like an open invitation. God Almighty, woman, what are you thinking to—"

One look at her face stopped his words like a punch in the stomach. His anger evaporated.

All her flush had disappeared. Her eyes were huge and staring. She appeared both haunted and angry as hell.

"Jessa, what is it?"

His first touch to her arm galvanized her. She jerked away. Color flooded back into her cheeks.

"I don't care if the door's wide open. No one has a right to steal from me or anyone else."

"No," he agreed slowly. "But there's a long way between what's right and what happens. It makes sense to take precautions."

"Thank you for your professional concern, but there's no need."

"The hell there's not."

She blinked, her ice-cool presence apparently nicked by his intensity. Good. She needed to be shaken up. She recovered to say, "We've never had any trouble."

"With luck like that you should play the lottery every day. Have you ever looked at this back door?"

"Of course I have. I told you—it's usually locked. I'll make sure from now on. There's no need—"

"There's plenty of need, because the best lock in the world—and this one's far from it—wouldn't help when all somebody needs to break in is a screwdriver and a hammer. The damned hinges are on the *outside*."

"Oh." It was more a sound of deflation than a word. "I'd forgotten."

"You *knew*?"

"They switched the hinges when the shop was being renovated, to move in the fixtures through here—there isn't clearance for the door to swing all the way open with them on the inside."

"Well, you're going to have to find another way to get things in and out, because those hinges are coming back inside as soon as I get back from the hardware store."

"Cully, that's not nec—" she began placatingly.

He wasn't going to be placated. Besides, he might as well start building that cushion.

"Jessa, don't even try. It would take an arrest warrant to stop me, and once I showed Tom Milano where those hinges are, he'd be helping me instead of arresting me."

She stared at him for a moment, and he stared back.

And then Jessa Tarrant surprised him.

"Okay," she said simply. "Tell Al at the hardware store to put it on the shop's account. And thank you."

No argument. No scene. No excuses. She knew he was right about this and she didn't mind admitting it.

It was hard to remember at the moment exactly why he wanted to keep distance between them.

"How's it going having Travis Grainger working off his debt to society at the shop?"

"Fine."

Cambria Weston Smith, Jessa's best friend in the world, considered that answer for about a quarter of a second before grimacing back at her.

"Yeah, it sounds like it." Cambria settled into the other chair on Jessa's deck, patted her five-months-pregnant rounded belly and leveled a no-nonsense stare at Jessa. "Okay, now, tell me the truth."

"All right. It's lousy. It's exhausting. Travis is sullen on his good days. Rita's on edge because she's not used to boys who think they're punks. I'm constantly trying to find things for him to do that will keep him out of her way, keep him out of temptation's way and keep him out of customers' way, because one look at his face could have put Imelda Marcos off buying shoes for life."

"That bad, huh?"

Jessa, slouching in the chair with her eyes closed, merely grunted.

"Why not talk to Cully about it, then?"

That opened her eyes. "I don't think so."

"Why not? Travis is his nephew. And from what I've heard, Cully's spent most of his life looking out for his family. If he didn't care, he wouldn't have bothered to bring the kid out here to try to straighten him out."

Jessa snorted. "More like he's trying to protect society from the hideous dangers of one twelve-year-old boy."

"Well, from what you've said and what I've seen of him, Travis isn't going to get any merit badges for deportment anytime soon. You should have heard him giving Irene a hard time about not being able to see MTV here. And when he realized the only TV was in the main house and he'd have to share it with everyone else, I thought he'd explode. Pete was about ready to deck him for talking to Irene that way, and a fun time was had by all."

"I'm not saying he's an angel, but that doesn't mean he's a bad seed," Jessa said stubbornly.

"Is that all there is to this?"

"This what?"

"This coolness between you and Cully. Or maybe I shouldn't say coolness, because it's friction, and friction definitely causes heat."

Jessa glanced over at her friend, and met a narrow-eyed, concentrated stare. She immediately looked away. "Of course that's all there is to it. Cully Grainger and I are simply on opposite ends of the spectrum when it comes to dealing with a kid who isn't perfect. He would have fit right in with the folks Dickens used to write about who believed in flogging and sixteen-hour work days in the mines as proper treatment for kids, and I take a more humane approach."

"Uh-huh." Cambria's disbelief was heavy enough to outweigh a sumo wrestler. "What happened between you two?"

"We disagreed over how to deal with Travis's shoplifting, that's all."

"That's not all." Cambria tipped her head and pursed her lips in an apparent effort to aid her memory. "You've been edgy around Cully since the first moment he showed up here last year to see Boone."

"That's not true. I've always been polite to him—"

"Sure, when you couldn't manage to avoid him. But mostly you avoid him. The way you used to avoid all eligible men. I thought you'd gotten past that. You've been telling me what happened in Washington isn't still bothering you.''

"It isn't," Jessa said quickly.

"You're not open with guys."

"I get along fine with Boone," she argued. "And I have from the start."

"That's true. In fact, there was a time when I thought Boone might be just the guy for you."

Jessa smiled. "Only while you tried so damned hard to deny that he was just the guy for you, Cam. Besides, it was clear to anybody with eyes—he wanted you and no one else.''

Cambria grinned back at her a little dazedly for a moment, then visibly caught herself. "We're not talking about Boone and me. We're talking about why you—" Cambria abruptly sat up straight. "Of course. That's why you've been so at ease with Boone. You've thought from the beginning that he was taken, and therefore safe."

"That's ridiculous."

Cambria wasn't listening. "And that's why Cully makes you so *uneasy*—because he *isn't* safe. Oh, this is great. This is wonderful. After all the pushing you did with me last spring when Boone showed up, now I get to give you a shove!"

"This is not an attractive side of you, Cambria." Jessa tried to keep her tone light, but she felt like a fox with the hounds on its trail.

Jessa parked in the deep shadow of a big RV belonging to a guest of the Westons' bed-and-breakfast, well out of sight of the main house, turned off the engine and pulled the key out of the ignition.

Her hand was shaking.

This was plain stupid. Why should her hand shake just because she'd come looking for Cully? Cambria's speculations echoed around in her head with a taunting quality. *Ridiculous.* She'd been attracted to Cully Grainger last fall, but she'd recognized the folly in time, and now felt only frustration at his stubborn, misguided treatment of Travis.

Besides, this wasn't a social call. She wouldn't be looking for Cully at all if she hadn't overheard Travis's phone conversation this afternoon.

She would have asked Cully to step into her office if she'd caught him when he'd picked up Travis. But he hadn't come inside.

Not that it mattered. There was no reason he had to come inside the shop.

She supposed she could have called instead of driving out here to the Westons'. Why hadn't she?

Because she hadn't wanted to have whichever Weston happened to answer the phone or happened to listen to her message on the machine know she'd sought out Cully.

Pretty darn silly.

Because she had to see his face when she talked to him about this.

Pretty darn stupid.

What did she hope to see? Cully allowed his face to reveal no more than he wanted. And to this point, she'd studiously avoided searching out flaws in his mask of absolute calm.

She knocked on the screen door of the cabin Cully and Travis were using. It had been Cambria's from her return to Wyoming a couple of years ago to run the Westons' bed-and-breakfast operation until she and Boone had completed enough of their house to move in. The cabin sat away from the ones for the B-and-B guests, and by a creek Jessa could hear mumbling in the background.

The inner wooden door was ajar, but no lights showed in the cabin.

"It's open."

Cully Grainger's disembodied voice, deep and slightly raspy, came out of the shadows like a night wind. She fought down the impulse to shiver and went inside. After the lingering twilight, the room seemed as dark as a cave.

She stopped so close to the door the screen brushed her fanny.

Cully rose from the couch halfway across the room. For a suspended moment she thought he was naked.

Her heart stuttered to life again. He was bare-chested, but he had on running shorts, and what looked to be a T-shirt slung around his neck.

"Travis isn't here. Irene and Ted took him to Pete's baseball game."

"I know. I wanted to see you."

An extra beat of silence told her she'd surprised him. He recovered quickly.

"You're in luck, then." He pulled the T-shirt from his neck and used it to wipe his shoulders and down his chest. She followed the motion. Dark hair spread between his flat, brown nipples, then followed a line down the center of his muscled chest. "Irene and Ted asked me to go, but I figured Travis wouldn't view it as much of a treat with me along."

"If you'd let up on him now and then—"

"What can I do for you, Jessa?"

Her throat closed, stopping her words more effectively than his interruption. Damn her imagination, reading a different meaning into those words, fed by his movements as he twisted his torso to slip first one arm, then the other into rolled-up sleeves of a sport shirt.

"I want to talk to you. About Travis."

She caught a flash of white teeth as he grinned. The grin didn't do much to soften the sarcasm. "That's a surprise."

"He called his mother today. I overheard some of the conversation."

"From your store? I'll pay for the call."

"That's not the point."

For an instant she wished he were close enough that she could beat on his chest—it must have been some atavistic instinct to get through to him, if only physically. Then he moved, and she prayed he wouldn't come closer.

He cut the eight feet between them to five, then stopped, propping his shoulder against the wall, apparently totally at ease.

"What *is* the point, then?"

"What Travis said—that's the point."

He sighed. "He begged his mother to come get him and take him home. He swears he'll be good. If she'll only give him another chance."

"How do you...? He's done this before?"

Cully nodded. "His second chances are up to triple digits. It's his MO. His and every other kid who gets in trouble. Say they're sorry when they're not, beg for another chance when they only want another chance to do what they please, then take advantage when someone's softhearted enough to listen."

Behind his cynical weariness, Jessa thought she heard something more. But maybe it was her own chilled heart, cracking a little. This was how people who saw only black and white viewed those who strayed into the realm of gray.

She'd been judged that way and she'd been found wanting.

For herself, she would have turned and walked out. But there wasn't only herself to think of.

"Travis told her he hates it here."

"He hates it because he has to do what he should do."

She shook her head in frustration. "It is not cut and dried. Dammit, why can't you see that?"

"Nobody's mistreating him."

"That's not the point. Whether he's done this before, whether a million kids have done this before, it doesn't change what he's feeling. He's lonely, Cully. And he's scared."

"He's not a baby. In some states he could be tried as an adult."

"*Tried?* Listen to yourself! This isn't about a court case or a trial. This is your nephew, your family. And it doesn't matter how old someone is, they can still be lonely and scared. They can still need family. They can still be wounded by having their family turn away when they need help."

For a moment, while her heart thundered with emotion, she feared she'd said too much. He stood there, still and quiet, and she thought that even in the dark he could see past her fears for Travis right into her old fears for herself.

"So, what do you suggest I do?"

"Talk to him."

"About what?"

"Anything other than what he's done wrong lately. That would be a major improvement."

He leaned against the wall, arms folded over his chest, head tipped back. "You're going to have to give me something more specific than that."

She glared at him, but didn't let his baiting tone sidetrack her. "Talk to him about what twelve-year-old boys are interested in."

"Like?"

"Baseball, bikes, movies, computers. Try some of those. Look for things you have in common."

"Like?"

"I don't know." His skepticism was a stone wall. "You come from the same family, the same background. Surely you had experiences at his age similar to what he's going through. You might be able to help him understand what's been happening and how he's feeling."

Her words trailed off as she sensed a change in him. His face remained impassive. He still leaned against the wall, seemingly at ease. Then she looked more closely. His fingers flexed hard, digging into the flesh above his elbows.

"At the very least," she added slowly, "he'd know he's not the only one who's felt these things. He'd know he wasn't alone."

"Sounds like the kind of psychobabble people on the talk shows dish out. Emotional mumbo jumbo."

She knew she'd hit a nerve, or his answer wouldn't have been so harsh, his voice stripped of its slow charm. But he had hit a nerve, too. And it jangled so loud in her head she couldn't stop the words from flowing.

"Not all psychology is babble, Grainger." She yanked the car keys from her jeans pocket. "And emotions aren't mumbo jumbo. But I could see why you have trouble with them. They don't come in simplistic black and white—they come in complex Technicolor. Well beyond your scope."

"Jessa."

The single word stopped her at the door, but she didn't turn around. "I have to go."

Before he could say anything more, she left. As she drove back to town, the scene played over and over in her head. And the thought rolling through her mind was: one of them was slipping.

Either he had allowed more reaction to show through, or she had picked up on subtler signs.

Definitely, one of them was slipping.

Or both of them.

Life settled into a routine. Cully dropped Travis off at the shop, without coming in, and picked him up, without coming in. In between those two events, Travis did what he was told. Certainly no more, occasionally somewhat less. He didn't talk much and he smiled infrequently.

It was starting to get to Jessa.

A couple of times Travis had actually edged near to opening up to her. A few comments about his old school. A couple of references to North Carolina. An occasional time when she didn't feel as if he'd lumped her into the "them"—presumably all adults—he spoke of with disdain.

But most times it was like hearing a long-forgotten recording of herself. The same anger stemming from the same confusion. The same isolation stemming from the same loneliness. Only, hers had been kept inside and no one had ever recognized it. She couldn't help wondering what would have happened if somebody—anybody—*had* recognized it.

That was why, she told herself, she'd followed an impulse and accepted the invitation to the Westons' ranch for Tuesday supper. Her brain had said "No," but her mouth said "Sure."

Cully would be at the Westons'; that was unavoidable.

Not that she doubted her ability to make it clear she wasn't interested in him, despite that one slip last fall.

It was what was going on inside her that rubbed her nerves so raw. So he was attractive. So she dreamed of the way he'd kissed and held her last fall even now, seven months later. That didn't even make a dent in the incontrovertible fact that he was the precise type of man designed to make her most miserable.

Unless, a small voice inside her suggested, he wasn't really that type of man. He was truly and deeply worried about Travis. She'd heard that in his voice several times. And there'd been that other element in his voice last week at his cabin, a sort of closed-off sadness. It hinted at other dimensions to Cully Grainger. It made him a little too human for comfort.

There, that was what made her uneasy about this whole arrangement. Two weeks and already insidious hope tried to tempt her into ignoring facts.

Dangerous. Very dangerous.

Maybe she shouldn't go to the Weston ranch, Travis or no Travis.

Closing the shop at five Tuesday afternoon, she was reconsidering. The second-guessing had jumped to double digits. She put the key into the shop's front door, preparing to reopen long enough to call Irene Weston and say she couldn't make it after all.

Then Cambria arrived.

"Oh, Cam, I'm glad you stopped by. Would you please

tell Irene I'm sorry to back out of dinner at the last minute, but I've got so much to do—"

"You've got to come," Cambria interrupted. "Boone dropped me off a few hours ago so I could go to the dentist, then go get my hair trimmed. I told him I could get a ride with you." She paused. "Unless you're reluctant to come to the ranch for some reason. I know it's not Boone or me or my family. And you seem to get along with Travis, so it would have to be Cully. Is that why you don't want to come?"

"Of course not. I just—"

"Good, then let's go."

Left no choice by her decisive friend, Jessa reminded herself of the possible benefits of seeing Travis in different circumstances.

The Westons' seventeen-year-old son, Pete, would be there, and probably Will Randall, a fifteen-year-old from the neighboring ranch who Cambria said had been helping out this afternoon. They weren't exactly Travis's contemporaries, but they came considerably closer than she and Rita did. It would be interesting to see how he interacted with them.

When she and Cambria arrived, Travis wasn't interacting with anyone.

He sat with his back propped against a corral post and poked at the dirt with a stick.

Jessa and Cambria exchanged a look as they got out of the car, and walked toward the boy of one accord. Cambria got there a step or two before Jessa. She scanned the dirt in front of the boy, then tipped her head with a quizzical lift of her eyebrows. Jessa moved around so she could see. Travis had been tracing rude words in the dirt. The spelling wasn't great, but he got his point across.

"Hi, Travis. How come you're here alone? Where is everybody?" Cambria asked.

Travis gave an uninterested shrug.

From her experience with Travis in the shop, Jessa took

a more specific approach. He gave no more information than the questioner asked for, and often less. "Where's Irene?"

"In the house, I guess."

"What she's doing?"

"Cooking something."

"Where's Ted?"

"He took the pickup."

"Toward town or on a ranch road?"

"Ranch road."

Picking up on the technique, Cambria added, "Where's Cully?"

"Boone's showing him something about some cabin." His uninterested wave indicated the cabin Boone had designed the previous summer from the remnants of an older structure.

Jessa exchanged a look with Cambria.

Boone and Pete had grown close during the weeks they worked on it. Then they nearly lost their friendship for good when first Cambria, then Pete, discovered Boone had come to the ranch in the first place because he was Pete's biological father. Boone eventually came to accept that his only role in Pete's life would be as his brother-in-law, but that cabin still had bittersweet associations for him and Cambria and all the Westons.

"Didn't they invite you?" Cambria asked.

"Why would I want to see a dumb old cabin?"

Taking that as a rhetorical question, Jessa finished the roll call. "How about Pete and Will—where are they?"

"They're riding. Said they were going to help Ted with some stupid calf."

"And they didn't take you?" Cambria asked.

"No."

"They didn't ask you?" Jessa pursued.

"They said I could go if I wanted. I didn't want to."

At his sneering tone, Cambria raised her eyebrows at Jessa. Jessa shrugged.

"Don't you like horses?"

"They're okay."

"Do you ride?"

Jessa admired Cambria's offhand tone.

"People don't have to ride horses anymore where I come from," Travis said, the sneer thicker than ever. "They have cars."

"I could teach you," Cambria replied casually.

Travis looked up for the first time. "Yeah?"

"Yeah. If you'd like to learn."

Travis's cool never slipped enough for him to come out and say learning to ride a horse would thrill him, but it clearly did. Thrilled him enough that he initiated a conversation with his uncle, telling him of Cambria's offer when they were all seated at the big, round wooden table in the Westons' kitchen.

"That's real nice of Cambria to offer to teach you to ride," Cully said, with a slow smile to Cambria. "'Course, you've still got an obligation to Jessa…"

Travis's mouth, shaped remarkably like his uncle's, started to turn down and take on a mulish cast.

Jessa parted her lips, but a sharp look from Cully surprised her into silence.

"I guess it'd have to be on the days I'm not working at the shop," Travis said, with ill grace.

"If…" Cully prompted.

"If that's all right with Cambria," the boy rasped out. "Would it be?" he added more naturally.

"Something can be arranged, I'm sure," Cambria said. "Besides, this time of year there's enough light we could ride after you finish at the shop, too."

Travis brightened. "Yeah. That's right. I'll practice every day and I'll get so good I'll be riding every horse in the stable."

"Every horse but Midnight," Pete said, then chuckled. "Only Cam rides him."

"That's because no one else has taken the time to earn

his trust." Cambria gave her brother a pointed look. "You could. If you took the time."

"Hey, I've got better things to do this summer than coddling a devil of a horse."

The glint in Pete's eyes indicated he was more intent on bedeviling his sister than really making a point. Although Jessa knew Pete did have a full calendar this summer, his last before leaving for college. Along with working on a highway construction crew, helping Ted with the ranch work and playing amateur baseball, he had a steady girlfriend.

"He's not a devil. He's young," Cambria protested. "And he hadn't been treated right until we got him."

"Yeah, your pet juvenile delinquent," Pete teased.

Across the table, Travis stiffened, and Pete flushed. "I mean— I didn't me—"

"That's quite a privilege getting to ride a horse, Travis." Cully's low, calm voice caught his nephew's full attention and slid right over Pete's embarrassment. "Privileges don't come free, though. Usually, a privilege comes as a reward for hard work. This time you've gotten the privilege first. But you still gotta earn it. You know how?"

Travis had been watching his uncle with the wariness Jessa reserved for snakes.

"Responsibility," he said with less than enthusiasm.

Cully nodded. "That's right. Maybe Cambria has something for you to do to help her out, since she's going to help you out."

"Riding a horse is a lot more than sitting on his back and letting him take you places, Travis," Cambria said.

She glanced at Cully. Jessa thought a silent communication passed between them. Would she ever find such accord with Cully?

Cambria continued with assurance. "You're responsible for that animal. For his well-being and health and safety. To start, you could help Pete clean out the stalls. Then some feeding, and along the way we'll get your help with keeping up the tack.''

"Tack?"

"Don't worry, Travis," Pete said. "I'll help you. Cambria can be a slave driver, but I survived. So will you."

Travis did not look entirely reassured, yet seemed to appreciate the older boy's offer.

"I think you'll do more than survive, Travis," Cully added. "I think you'll become a darned good horseman."

Travis stared at his uncle for a moment, then colored up as the conversation took another turn.

Jessa blinked rapidly. Did the threatening tears stem from Travis's seeming so dumbfounded by that expression of confidence in him or from Cully's thinking to say the words?

Intent on a discussion with Ted and Irene about the history of the sheriff's department, Cully presented her his profile. The strong bones of brow, cheeks and jaw reminded her of the cliff that rose behind where Boone and Cambria were building their house. Not so much the cragginess—though Cully's face was far from the smooth flow of boyhood—but the impression that time and storms had worn away whatever was weak, leaving only strength and durability. Except, perhaps for his mouth.

The sensation of being watched prickled at Jessa. She glanced around, to meet Cambria's speculative look.

Immediately, Jessa lavished undeserved attention on the green peas on her plate.

She was careful to not look at Cully, simply as a precaution against Cambria's getting any wild ideas. By the time they had cleared the dishes, she'd begun to relax.

"Oh, drat!" Cambria slapped a palm softly against the counter. "I forgot."

"Forgot what?" Irene asked.

"That special cookie selection I ordered from the catalog came in and I meant to bring it for dessert tonight."

"I thought you were going to freeze those," Boone said.

Cambria glared at him. "No. I wanted to bring them tonight and let everybody try them. I'm going to dash up to the house and get them." She already had her car keys out. "Why don't you come with me, Jessa?"

"It's such a big box you need help?" Jessa could smell a grilling coming, and she would just as soon avoid the flames.

"Of course not," Cambria said sweetly—always a sign of danger. "But I thought you'd like to come along."

"But we're all going to help Ted get the old pickup up on blocks so he can fix it."

"Oh, don't worry about that," Irene said. "The boys'll be plenty of help for him. You and Cambria can help me with the dishes when you get back. It's worth going up nearly every day to see what Boone's done to that house."

"It's been so long since you've been up," Cambria added pitifully, "I thought for sure you'd like to see the progress we've made. Aren't you interested?"

And there was no way out after that. How could Jessa say she wasn't interested in the house her best friend and her husband had designed and were building with such love and care?

She couldn't. And in two minutes she was seated beside Cambria in the truck Boone had driven to the Westons'.

They followed the highway for a short while before turning off onto a drive Boone and Cambria had improved from a two-rut lane, but not by much. If the suspension hadn't demanded it, the twists and turns would have required that Cambria slow to a more sedate speed than was her custom. But the view at the top was worth it.

The house rested on a huge outcrop, practically hanging over the canyon that cut into the eastern edge of the Big Horns. It looked up to the mountains and down to the valley ranched by the Westons.

On the ride up, the talk was of the house. The frustration of the slowness of construction, the satisfaction of each small step's completion, the pleasure of molding a dream into reality. When they pulled up, the massed windows reflected the Big Horn Mountains, while the stone and timber construction echoed the surroundings.

"Look around," Cambria invited when they stepped inside. "I'll just be a minute."

So far this glass-, wood-and-stone living room and a bathroom provided the only habitable space. Besides a couch and two chairs by a stone fireplace, the room had an iron bedstead behind a screen, a drafting table by a window, a corner set up as a minikitchen, a wall of books and a grove of framed photos atop a beam mantel.

Cambria was true to her word. They returned to the truck and started down the hillside, while Jessa still enthused.

"It is great, Cam. It's even better than I envisioned. I can't believe how much progress you've made the past couple weeks. When you guys are done it's going to be spectac—"

"I was teasing you before. Now, I want to know, Jes— are you interested in Cully?"

Jessa had been expecting this, but it still caught her off guard. She'd hoped the house might be the one subject designed to deflect Cambria Weston Smith.

"What? What on earth makes you ask that?"

"Don't look so outraged. It would be only natural."

"Natural?"

"Oh, come on, Jessa. Don't be dense. He's a damned attractive man. That slow grin. Those wicked eyes. And that even more wicked body."

"Cambria!"

"Don't sound shocked. I'm married, not blind. And you're not either one. On top of that, you're spending time with him because of Travis. And you could do a whole lot worse. He's a good man. You know he and Boone have known each other since they were kids?"

"Yes."

"Neither had the easiest childhood. Maybe that's why

they're close. I got to know him this winter in North Carolina, and he's a man I'd trust, and you know that's not my strong suit. I don't understand why you're so opposed to—"

"He's a cop, Cam."

"Not now he isn't. Though Boone thinks he'd be a lot happier if he was."

"Not being on the force now, or ever again, makes no difference. It's not the uniform—it's the state of mind."

"I don't know that Cully's like that. He's—"

"*I* know he's like that. Look at how he deals with Travis."

"He's strict, but he's not unreasonable," Cambria objected.

"Yeah, as long as Travis toes the line. But let him make one mistake, break one rule, and Cully would punish him to the full extent of the law." She'd purposely pushed the conversation toward Travis and away from herself. "It's the mind-set."

Cambria didn't follow the detour. "I think Cully's a man who would always be there for you, Jessa."

"I'm not looking for a man to be there for me, Cambria. Not Cully Grainger or anyone else."

In profile, Cambria's mouth pursed. Jessa's spirits sank. If she knew her friend, this was far from over.

"You've told me over and over that you're not shutting out the possibility of meeting a man—though you sure don't do anything about it," Cambria inserted in a tart tone. "And some of the looks Cully sends your way could ignite a fire extinguisher. Not to mention what I saw on your face tonight."

"That's ridiculous."

"It's not ridiculous."

"If I were to get involved—"

"When," Cambria amended.

Jessa sidestepped an argument by ignoring the distinction. "It would not be with someone like Cully Grainger."

Her friend studied her with that intent expression that always meant Cambria was trying to see deeper than the other person wanted to be seen.

"Then who would it be like?"

Jessa hadn't expected that question. She'd tensed to deal with more *Why not Cully Grainger?* interrogation. And not having an answer to that question that would satisfy Cambria didn't mean she liked this one any better. "Who?" Jessa repeated, stalling for time.

"Yes. Who?"

"Uh, somebody like, um, Dax Randall."

"Dax Randall!"

Dax owned a neighboring ranch to the Westons, which he ran with his teenaged son, Will. He was good-looking, polite, unattached and phobic about dating.

"He's a very nice man." Defensiveness wasn't a good tactic with Cambria. Jessa shifted to defiance. "And a hunk. He's got a great body—I've heard you say so yourself. Besides, he's someone I could feel comfortable with."

"I can't argue about Dax's looks or body, but the reason you could feel comfortable with him is he'd be three states away if he had the slightest hint you might be interested in him. Good heavens, Jessa, the man's got fear of commitment down to a science."

"I'm not looking for commitment. Not now," she added hastily, before Cambria could launch into her standard lecture. For the past couple of years Cambria had been pushing Jessa to get back into dating. In the year since Cambria had met and fallen in love with Boone she'd gone from pushing to shoving.

"You know what Irene says about fear—"

"Yes, I do."

That didn't stop Cambria from repeating it. "You can't let fear rule your life or it's not living. I found that out with Boone. Isn't it about time you did, too?"

"I'm not on a schedule," Jessa snapped. Then she

sighed. "Sorry. It's just... Look, Cam, it's like someone who's been afraid of flying and just passed the course to get over that. You'd send that person out on short flights, letting them get comfortable before you'd try to ship them out for a long haul. I mean, you wouldn't send them to Australia on their first flight."

"Oh, I don't know. Once you got them on a plane they'd have to give flying a fair chance. And if they wanted to get home anytime soon, they'd have to take the return flight, too. With something like that, I'm a firm believer in diving right in instead of trying to ease your toe in to test the waters. It's the sink-or-swim approach."

"Not the best image when we're talking about transpacific flights and fear of flying," Jessa said wryly.

Cambria didn't crack a smile as she parked the truck by the Westons' back door. "Oh, but that's not what we're talking about. We're talking about Cully Grainger and your fear of feeling."

Might almost be a trip to an local with Travis," Irene to roll as it for another at sea... Cully went in by something that they had made a hook now and then. It's just the fact... come in your house, by the way not that.

Jessa ached a long time, hands a graded to the "You still can inane in as in the attraction, so with Pete in hide, she scrupled. The other across tournament to water...and Jessa thought bear, and Phil went to work that Pete wanted to vary off a college at night... By the Traders Sea say.

"I'm afraid shore is like me too blame," Cambricant, as she came the chair, as thing up for the fact she said in it. "Traders? who you have.

Chapter Four

"**I** think it'll be great for Travis to learn how to ride." Jessa took a just-washed salad plate from the drainer, where Irene had placed it. Jessa had come inside before Cambria could resume her grilling. Now Irene's presence offered some protection. "That was nice of you to offer, Cambria. You've all been so nice to Travis."

"Nonsense," said Irene. "Just doing what anyone would do for the boy. It's natural."

Jessa and her fellow dish dryer, Cambria, exchanged a look behind Irene's back—it wasn't "anyone" who would help out a troubled boy, but it *was* natural for Irene.

"From what Travis says," Jessa went on as she put the salad plate in the cabinet and went for another wet plate, "it sounds like he spends a lot of time with you folks instead of his uncle."

"That's natural, too," Irene said. "Cully's got a hard row with the boy, teaching him discipline when he hasn't had much all his life."

"Cully doesn't have to be so harsh with Travis."

Irene looked over her shoulder at her. "Cully's got to be consistent, but any boy needs a break now and then. It's best the lessons come in short bursts. So this works out fine."

Jessa noticed Irene hadn't really responded to her.

"Ted and I are happy to have the extra company, with Pete so busy this summer." The older woman sounded a bit wistful, and Jessa thought Irene and Ted would sorely miss Pete when he went off to college in the fall. "Besides, Travis is a nice boy."

"I think 'nice' is going too far, Mama." Cambria turned to Jessa. "Actually, I would've given up on the kid the first day if it hadn't been for you, Jessa."

"Me?"

"Sure, Cully told us how you stuck up for Travis—"

Startled by the spurt of warmth filling her, Jessa recovered to answer dryly, "I'm sure that's how he phrased it."

"Not in those exact words," Cambria admitted, grinning. "But that was the gist of it. So, I figured if you saw something good in the kid, he had to be basically all right."

"Yeah, like I'm such a great judge of character."

Cambria frowned at her. "You are. You're a terrific judge of character. You're not still kicking yourself over Glenn Kaye, are you? There was no way you could have seen that coming. Nobody could have."

"Cambria." It was a one-word warning. Jessa tipped her head to where Irene calmly washed the last dinner plate.

Cambria mouthed, "Sorry."

Without turning around, Irene said serenely, "If you mean that stalking business, Cambria, you're absolutely right. There's no way Jessa could have known that man would do such a thing."

They looked at each other, then stared at Irene's back

before Cambria asked, "How did you know about that, Mama?"

"Well, it didn't take a genius to guess it took more than a whim for Jessa to give up a successful job in Washington and move herself to Bardville, Wyoming, to open a store." A trace of tartness had seeped into Irene's voice, the kind that made an apple pie perfect. "Of course, I knew you came back, Cammy, because you thought we needed the help with the bed-and-breakfast—well, to be totally honest, because *I* needed the help. But Jessa wouldn't have come just to keep you company."

"But when did you find out about the stalking?"

"Oh, not until this past winter. Not for sure. I had an inkling from things you said. Then Wanda started teaching me about using the computer at the library over the winter."

"You've known since winter and you haven't said anything?" Jessa had seen the Westons at least twice a week; Irene had given no indication of knowing that piece of her background.

"There's no cause for you to keep it a secret like it's something to be ashamed of, but it's not my place to say anything, Jessa." Irene turned to Cambria. "Ted and I thought we'd get a computer this fall when Pete goes to school and you and Boone head back to North Carolina. I like that e-mail. It's not nearly as good as being together or even talking on the phone, but it'll help from missing you all so much."

"That's great, Mama. That's a wonderful idea. I'm sure Boone—"

"Wait a minute." At the moment, the Weston family's communication plans didn't interest Jessa. "How did you know about the stalking?"

"Oh, that. Well, I was surfing the Internet one day and found a bulletin board talking about computers and durability and repairs and such. And someone mentioned a man who'd been a computer repairman who was sent to prison for stalking. That message mentioned he'd stalked a woman who'd worked at the firm Jessa worked for. I asked a few more questions and all the details fit, so I figured... What on earth are you laughing at, Jessa?''

She held her side and gasped for air before she could answer. "The way Cambria looked...when you said... 'surfing the Internet.' It was...priceless.''

Irene started to chuckle, too, and then all three were laughing tears-in-the-eyes hard.

"What's going on here?'' Ted demanded from the doorway, a grin already lifting his mouth. Behind him came Boone and Cully, then Pete, with Travis trailing.

"It's too hard to explain,'' Irene said between laughter. "One of those you-had-to-be-heres.''

Jessa knew the older woman was protecting her privacy by sidestepping the cause of their laughter. She appreciated that. She'd told herself it was over and forgotten. She'd left all that behind her in Washington. Still, it would make her feel exposed, a little more vulnerable, if Cully knew.

She turned and locked looks with Cully. With the masking sunglasses pushed to the top of his head and the empathetic laughter folding lines at the corners of his eyes, Jessa realized it wasn't only secrets being revealed that could make you feel vulnerable. It was darned hard to keep your defenses up while laughing.

Any hopes Jessa had held that Travis's interest in horseback riding might mean a difference in his attitude ended with his arrival at the shop the next day.

"Good morning, Travis. Good morning, Cully.''

Cully, looking rather grim, nodded but said nothing.

Travis made up for that.

"It's not a good morning. It's a sucky morning. Every morning's a sucky morning I have to come to this stupid place and work like a slave for nothin'. I didn't even want the stupid knife. That knife sucks. There are lots better knives around.''

Cully's expression convinced Jessa this was a complaint Travis had voiced before, probably all the way in from the Weston ranch. She gave him a look of sympathy. His mouth twisted slightly. He crossed his arms over his chest and leaned back against the counter that held the cash register.

"It's probably against the law," Travis went on. "Making a kid work for nothing—that's gotta be against the law. Child abuse or something. Just because you've got this stupid old sheriff in your pocket doesn't mean I can't turn you in. Besides, you've practically kidnapped me. I should call the FBI—"

"I have your mother's permission, Travis, remember?"

The boy's face darkened with anger, and possibly pain. He was probably remembering that not only did Cully have his mother's *permission* to take him off her hands, she had refused his own, more recent pleas to be allowed to go home.

"She's a witch."

"Travis!" Cully's voice cracked out without being raised. It made Jessa jump, as well as Travis. "You don't talk about your mother that way. You don't talk about any woman that way. Understand?"

Travis remained sullen and Jessa fervently wished she hadn't told Rita to take the morning off.

"Do you understand?" Cully repeated, evenly spacing each deliberate word.

"Yeah," came back the barely audible mumble.

"Good." Cully sighed, then added more naturally, "Your mother hasn't had an easy time of it. Losing your dad and all."

As an attempt at conciliation, it failed miserably. Defiance and anger flooded Travis's face as he stared at his uncle.

"Yeah? Where were you when she was having such a tough time, huh? Didn't see you around anywhere. Dad always talked about how tight you two were, how great it was to have a brother like you. How when I had a little brother I should try to be just like you." Despite the sneering sarcasm, his voice trembled slightly beneath the pain. "Then he died, and I saw he was wrong about all that. You didn't even care enough to stick around after they buried him."

Travis fled down the aisle. The slam of the door to the storage area started Jessa breathing again. Cully hadn't moved. Deep brackets around his grimly set mouth told his reaction.

Whatever their differences about Travis, she wouldn't—couldn't—deny the pain he must be feeling at his nephew's harsh words.

Jessa put her hand on his forearm. It was startling that someone who moved and talked with such languid ease had such urgency of heat in his skin. The warmth seemed to travel from his skin into her fingers and palm, then deeper, into her bloodstream.

"He's a boy, Cully. A boy who's lost his father and who feels abandoned by his mother. He's hurting, and he's lashing out any way he can."

"Yeah? Well, he knows where to lay that lash. He's a master."

"Don't let it cut too deep."

His head dipped slightly, and she thought he was looking at her hand, still resting on his arm. Then he raised his head, and enough light reached through the tinted lenses for her to know he was looking directly at her.

She hurriedly removed her hand.

"With some things," he said slowly, "you have no say in how deep they cut."

"No, I suppose not. But you have a say in how you react to them."

Were they talking about Travis still? Or something entirely different? Was he saying she'd hurt him last fall?

She pulled her thoughts up short. That wasn't the issue.

It hadn't been then, and it certainly wasn't with Travis in the picture.

"Cully, there's more to it than teaching a kid right from wrong. You've got to show him how to deal with the consequences when he does do wrong. Because he's going to. Just like adults. Unless you're dealing with saints."

"No danger of that. The Graingers run more to sinners than saints."

"So, you've got to let him know one slip doesn't make him permanently a sinner. Or why should he even try to be better? In fact, why shouldn't he give up entirely?"

She knew immediately she had somehow said the wrong thing. He jammed the sunglasses on more firmly. His jaw hardened and the lines beside his mouth etched deeper.

"I've gotta go. Got some things to pick up."

"Cully, wait—"

Her hand on his arm halted him after one stride. If she'd used every muscle in her body she couldn't have stopped him by dragging with all her might, but that touch had. That terrified her. She didn't want that sort of power over him. She didn't.

She pulled her hand away. While her heart hammered at her breastbone, he stared down at where her hand had rested twice within the past minute.

When the silence pulled tight with tension, he gave her a dry grin.

"See you later, Jessa."

The sheriff's car stopped in front her house while Jessa was sweeping the front steps that evening. She crossed the grass to meet him.

"Good evening, Sheriff. Is something wrong?"

"Not a thing, not a thing. Thought I'd swing by and check with you on how young Travis's doing."

"He's doing okay," she answered. "Now, why are you really here?"

"What do you mean, Jessa?"

"I mean you stop by the shop every day, usually two times a day on the days Rita is working, so you could have asked me about Travis anytime. And that's if you needed to ask me at all, since I'm sure Rita can—and does—give you a full report."

He shook his head. "Now, that's somethin'. I never thought of that. Just goes to show what I've been thinkin' lately. I'm getting too old for this job. Entirely too old. I'd be thinkin' of retirement this minute if I had the right one to replace me. I could do some fishing, more hunting. Take Rita dancing. Catch up on the books I've been meaning to read—love those mysteries, even if I don't ever figure 'em out. But I can't up and retire and leave Bardville in the lurch. It would need someone special like to come in as sheriff. Someone with the right touch. Someone who cares about the law and cares about the people, and can balance the two."

"Have anybody in mind?" As if she didn't know.

"Thought this Cully Grainger could be worth taking a look at."

"Then you thought wrong, Sheriff. Wouldn't you say dealing with people is mostly wrestling around in the gray area between right and wrong?" she challenged.

He conceded with a grave bowing of his head. "I'd have to say it is."

"Cully Grainger doesn't believe in gray. He might know law, but when it comes to people, all he sees is right or wrong. He'd make a terrible sheriff. Besides, I think he's talking to some big security firm back East."

"That don't worry me none. And as for the other, well... You see these boots?" He rocked back on his heels to show off his scuffed, sturdy footwear. "These boots were the stiffest cusses when I first got them. Took time and patience to break 'em in, but since I did, they've served me well. They've lasted me a good, long time and I expect 'em to keep on lasting. Worth that time and pa-

tience, because they're made from good material. Quality.
That's what counts.''

"You're comparing a man to a pair of boots?''

"Yep,'' he said, unabashed. "They're not so far apart.
Bad pair of boots, a bad man—either one can make your
life miserable.''

"Fine. Well, you asked my opinion of Cully as a can-
didate for sheriff and I gave it. You've got what you came
for…'' And started something churning in her stomach at
the prospect—unlikely as it was—of Cully Grainger stick-
ing around Bardville for good as its sheriff.

"Oh, that's not why I came. I came to tell you a story.
Here, let's sit on the steps and enjoy the last of the day's
sunshine. You see, there was this young man who went
into the army and joined up with the military police. Happened to be from North Carolina this young fellow I'm
talking about.''

"Sheriff Milano, I don't—''

"Hush now. I'm telling this story. You're listening.''

"It's about time you got back.''

Hands on hips, Jessa glared at Cully Grainger as he
stepped from the shop to the back area and closed the door
behind him.

She'd expected him to show discomfort or guilt or
something. Instead, he looked totally at ease. It made her
madder.

His expression remained deadpan. "I was just down at
the hardware store, but it's nice to be missed.''

If it made any sense, she'd think he was deliberately
goading her. Or perhaps she was reading her own feelings
into that.

After seeing him yesterday morning—an uncomfortable
start to an entire day of Travis at his most sullen—Jessa
had found herself thinking of Cully too often and too sym-
pathetically. Tom Milano's visit last night hadn't helped.
He'd told her about Cully's background in police work.

His departures from the two police departments reflected an honorable man's frustration with a far-from-perfect system.

"That's all very interesting," she'd told the sheriff, "but as I said before, it looks as if he's going into private security." She hadn't asked the sheriff why he was telling her all this—she'd been afraid he'd tell her.

"That'd be a real shame, because he could be the kind of man Bardville needs. And he won't be happy in private security. Maybe," the sheriff had finished with a sly look, "all he needs is a little breaking in. Patience and time and breaking in."

Just because Cully could be hurt by his nephew's sharp words and just because he might be happier staying in public police work didn't mean she should get involved with his problems. Trying to help Travis was enough of a project. Besides, she had her own problems. And her hormones' insistence on ignoring how wrong Cully was for her happened to be one of them.

Being irked at him had its good side, she thought now.

"Missed like a toothache, Grainger. What do you think you're doing making changes around here? It's high-handed. It's arrogant. It's an *intrusion* in my business and in my life, and I don't appreciate it."

Usually, she took Thursday afternoons off, but she'd come in to catch up on the paperwork she'd fallen behind on lately—and whose fault was that?—and she had found the storage area looking as though an electronics security conference had moved in.

When she'd stormed up to Rita, demanding to know what was going on, that kindly woman had appeared first astonished, then flustered.

"Oh, dear. Oh, dear. Cully said he'd finish up the work he'd started when he changed those hinges last week. That seemed to be all right with you, so I thought this was okay, too. I should have checked with you. I'm so sorry. Oh, it's my fault. Oh, dear."

There was nothing to do but reassure the clerk that no, it wasn't her fault. No, Jessa wasn't angry at her. No, there wasn't anything else Rita could have or should have done. No, nothing was the matter. Jessa would wait in back for a little talk with Cully.

And while she waited, with the culprit nowhere to be found, she was going to consider ways to make him pay.

She hadn't yet settled on appropriate retribution, when he came strolling back in with his hot grin and his unconvincing act of ignorance and innocence.

"You talking about something in particular?" he asked blandly.

"Yes, I'm talking about something in particular. I'm talking about automatic lights at the shop's front door. I'm talking about the battery of lights at the back of this building that could light up a football field."

"Oh, that. Few precautions, that's all. Just like the hinges."

"It's *not* just like the hinges. For one thing, I knew about your changing the hinges, and for another thing, I thought that needed doing, too. All this—" She waved her arm at empty electronic boxes and a stack of manufacturers' warranties on her desk.

"The boxes? I left them so you could get serial numbers. If they're in the way I'll get them out of here."

"I *don't* mean the boxes. I won't have—"

"Just the start, really."

"You making— What?"

"Just a start, those lights and such. Basic. Anyone with a lick of know-how could get past them. Besides, it was my job."

The flare had gone out of her anger, and he seemed to sense it. He turned away to fiddle with wires in what looked like a control panel, but not before she caught a twitch of a grin on his lips.

"Your job?"

"Yeah, I'm sort of a consultant for the sheriff. Security for local businesses falls under his watch."

"How about *buying* security equipment for local businesses and installing it?" He kept his back to her and said nothing. She read the body language loud and clear. "Ah, or is this the only local business the, uh, *sheriff's* department has taken an interest in?"

"Sort of a pilot program."

"So I should reimburse the county for all this expensive equipment, not to mention your time?"

He shook his head as he let a wire down the side of the door frame. He shifted for a better angle on the wire, and his muscles flowed under his shirt.

Damn Cambria. Why did she have to say all that stuff about Cully Grainger's body Tuesday night? She'd been doing pretty well putting that out of her mind—until Cambria had gone and reminded her.

"No reimbursement expected. In fact, it wouldn't be accepted. It's a sort of a grant."

"I think I'll ask Sheriff Milano about this pilot program nobody seems to have heard of."

"It's secret, so he can't tell you about it. But he'll back me up about the shop needing this equipment—and if he doesn't," he added in a mutter, "he'll never find his records in that computer."

For some reason her anger, usually banked low, bubbled closer to the surface when it came to Cully. Right now she wanted to be angry at him—she *had* been angry at him. Red-seeing, fist-clenching furious. Who did he think he was, barging in here and unilaterally making changes in her store—*her* store!

She didn't want to be amused. She didn't want to smile. But she was, and she did.

"It's very nice of you, Cully, but—"

"No, it's not."

"It's not?"

"No. Definitely not."

"It looks nice to me."

He shook his head as he threaded the wire through a hole in the exterior wall. "I learned a long time ago to head for the hills when a woman said something I did was nice. It was even worse if she said *I* was nice."

"Oh, I didn't go that far," Jessa murmured.

"No, and I'm grateful," he said, deadpan.

"Well, if this isn't nice, what is it?"

"Selfish."

"Selfish?"

He opened the back door and used a small hook to fish out the wire from the hole on the outside. "Selfish. I'm thinking of myself."

"How's that?"

"I'm thinking of Travis being here and what would happen if somebody broke in while he was working. What if he got hurt? I'd feel real guilty. Or what if you held him responsible? You could sue me. Or what if he chased the bad guy and somebody hit him with their car and it ruined their life, not to mention hurting him? Or what if—"

"All right, all right. I give. No more. I graciously accept your selfish and not-nice gesture of installing all these gadgets and gizmos and...and whatever those things in the box are—"

"Security lights."

"Security lights?"

"Yup."

She sighed heavily. "Security lights. Okay. Thank you very much. End of discussion."

"And you'll use them faithfully," he prompted. He crouched, one knee inside the door's threshold, the rest of him outside.

"Don't push your luck."

But he did. He pushed it, and it snapped the truce and her feeling of goodwill like a toothpick.

"The shop's lack of security truly was like inviting someone to break in, Jessa, and—"

"It's always the victim's fault in the end, isn't it? It wouldn't have happened if the victim hadn't been *asking for it*. Isn't that the phrase? Isn't—"

He turned his head and shoulders toward her. "That isn't what I meant."

"Isn't that what you people think?"

"*You people?* What people are those, Jessa?"

"I've known men like you all my life."

He stood and took two strides closer to her spot by the office doorway. For a second she expected him to loom over her, intimidating with his size and presence.

But he didn't move any closer. He simply stood there, looking at her.

"You don't know me, Jessa."

She could almost imagine a snapping sound of a connection breaking when she jerked her head away from his look.

"No, I don't. And you don't know me. So you have no cause for concern about my store's security."

She grabbed the first thing that came to hand, which happened to be a carton of bug repellent sitting on a nearby shelf. She counted the cans. Twice. Twenty-four, as the carton said. She put a big, black, officious check mark on the carton, as if that meant something. All the while he stood there staring at her.

"What happened, Jessa?"

"What do you—"

"When someone said that whatever it was that happened to you was your fault."

It just got out of hand, Dad. I didn't invite those people. It was just supposed to be a few people. I didn't mean for it to get like that—

You didn't mean for it to get like that? You didn't mean for it! That's no excuse. You brought shame on this family—you brought shame on me—that's what you did. My daughter with a record. You're a disgrace. I taught you the rules. You broke them. You're more at fault than those dope heads who brought their drugs into this house. You were asking for it. And you got it.

She suddenly became aware of Cully again. He was close. Too close. He leaned toward her, making her aware of his height, his broad shoulders.

But he wasn't intimidating.

She opened her mouth to answer him. Nothing came out.

"Jessa." His voice was slow, deep. Like a stream over rocks, deep in the woods. So deep in the woods that the stream sounded like the earth's pulse. It could lull her if she wasn't careful. "Did something happen to you? Did somebody hurt you?"

She looked into his eyes. They were intense, sharp, but she also saw a worry in them. The worry men got about their women.

Did he mess with you? Ten years later, and another encounter with the police, this time with her seeking their help instead of being turned in by irate neighbors, and that had been her father's first question. When she'd said no, a man was stalking her, tormenting her, shredding her life and her self-confidence, but he hadn't *messed with her*, her father's next question was, *What did you do to egg him on?*

You got it, so you must have been asking for it. That was the code she'd grown up with.

The code of a cop's daughter. A cop like Cully Grainger.

A tight smile stretched her lips without lifting them. "Did somebody hurt me? Not the way you're thinking. So there's no need to get all paternal and protective."

"You don't know what I'm thinking. It's like I said before, you don't know me." Two easy steps took him to the back door. He paused, then he looked back at her. "You don't have a clue what I'm thinking."

Chapter Five

"So," Boone ventured four days later as they put away tools after finishing up an afternoon of working on the house, "Jessa was irked at you for installing all that security equipment without checking with her first, huh?"

"You could say that."

You could also say his nonchalance and her sense of humor had gotten them past that—until he'd set off a second, more serious blast. He still wasn't quite sure how it had happened. He had some ideas, but no evidence. And it didn't look like he'd be getting any soon, at least not from Jessa.

Because he'd gotten his cushion and then some.

Jessa had resumed avoiding him full-time. And this woman didn't do a thing partway. If the United Nations ever put her in charge of embargoes against rogue nations, the troublemakers would crumble in a matter of days.

"Didn't you think about how she might react, Cully?"

He grunted in answer.

Boone placed a hammer in the toolbox and closed the lid. "It's not like you to do something without thinking of consequences. I can't think of a time you've ever done that."

Cully kept wiping his hands on a rag. "There's a first time for everything. Gotta go. Time to pick up Travis."

He'd reached the four-wheel drive he was renting for the summer, when Boone called his name. He stood at the open door and tapped his hand on the frame, waiting for his friend.

"What is it, Boone? I gotta get going."

"Jessa got in some drawing paper for me. Could you pick it up? I'll come to the cabin and get it later."

"Sure." He started to swing one leg in, when Boone's voice stopped him again.

"Cully, you had all sorts of advice for me a year ago when I came out here to find the son I'd fathered. And later, when I met the Westons and Cambria. And when things started changing between Cambria and me."

Cully snorted. "Yeah? I didn't notice you following a whole hell of a lot of it."

"More than you know. Anyway, it's my turn."

"Not the same situation."

"No, it's not. But I don't suspect the feelings are all that different, so—"

"And here I thought Cambria was breaking you of taking on the problems of the world. I thought you'd given that up."

"She is, and I am. That doesn't mean I'm going to stop looking out for my friends."

"Boone, I don't need anybody looking out for me."

"The hell you don't. Everybody does."

"Boone—"

"All right, all right. I won't push. Not now. But I am going to say one thing to you, like it or not."

"Not," Cully drawled.

Boone frowned, but didn't let the interruption stop him.

"I learned something last year, Cully. You can't put the different parts of your life in compartments and keep them separate from each other. I tried with my feelings for Cambria and the situation with Pete and it caused a hell of a lot more trouble. The other day you talked about having too many complications in your life already, with Travis and the job situation. I know you, Cully. And you think the best way to avoid having Jessa become a complication is to push her away. It won't work."

It's working just fine, Cully mentally disagreed.

"You've got to deal with all of your life at once, just the way it happens, messy as that gets sometimes. And that means you've got to face your feelings for Jessa— whatever they are."

"See, Boone, that's where all this advice giving of yours goes haywire. You're presuming I've got something going for Jessa. She's a fine-looking woman, and I surely appreciate fine-looking women. But that's all there is. Nothing more." He clapped Boone on the back and grinned. "Just because you and Cambria made a match doesn't mean the rest of the world marches two by two."

Boone stared at him for half a minute, then shook his head. "You are so full of it, Grainger. And you're in for one hell of a rough ride, let me tell you. I only hope you come out the other end of it half as well as I have."

Cully met his look, refusing to consider coming out the way his friend had, with a wife and family and home.

Boone drew in a breath. "You go in to her shop, you put in all the equipment, and you think—"

"It wasn't all."

"What?"

"It wasn't all the equipment. The rest of it's on order, along with the stuff you asked for."

Boone muttered an expletive. "Jessa's going to skin you alive." He shook his head and stepped back from Cully's vehicle, as if to say if his friend wanted to drive headlong into trouble, he couldn't stop him.

Cully thought about that as he drove down the steep, twisting dirt road and onto the highway toward Bardville.

He *was* driving headlong into trouble, but it was in order to avoid bigger trouble. In fact, he counted his high-handed maneuver a double success. First, her store would be a hell of a lot safer. Second, with Jessa acting chilly again, he wouldn't indulge in foolish hopes, like the ones pricking at him more and more often of late.

He couldn't afford those hopes and he couldn't afford to forget how they'd parted last fall, or how he'd felt walking away from her.

They'd danced at the combination belated wedding reception and going-away party the Westons had held for Boone and Cambria at the Back Bar in Bardville. They'd danced slow dances, close enough for the delicate jasmine scent she wore to seep into his head. Three in all, including the last dance. Then they'd joined the others in toasting the newlyweds with a final glass of champagne and walked out into the new-scrubbed freshness of a Wyoming night in October, with the stars trying to ignite their bed of black velvet.

He'd driven her home. He'd asked if she had any coffee. She'd said yes. They'd sat on the couch, sipping more wine instead of coffee, and talking about Boone and Cambria. How he'd known Boone since they were kids in North Carolina. How they'd joined the army, how he'd settled in with the military police while Boone finished his minimum hitch and started his business designing and constructing log homes. How she'd met Cambria through a seminar while they'd attended different colleges in Washington, D.C. How a summer rooming together in a Capitol Hill shoebox had cemented the friendship, even when jobs took Jessa to different cities. How they'd reunited in Washington several years ago, then both decided to move to Cambria's home state of Wyoming three years ago.

Jessa. He remembered saying her name before he'd brushed his lips across hers the first time. He remembered how he'd waited before the second time, waited for a withdrawal that hadn't come.

He'd kissed her, and she'd responded.

She'd opened to him. She'd kissed him fully, completely. They'd held on to each other there, on her couch. Held on as if letting go would mean sure drowning. He remembered the feel of her fingers, tight on his shoulder. He remembered the slope of her shoulder blade, almost fragile under his hand. The taste, even sweeter than the jasmine smell. They'd touched. Exploring, and pleasing.

Pleasing so much he'd thought he'd explode. But he'd been determined he wouldn't make love to her on a couch, not the first time, like a couple of kids with nowhere else to go. He wanted the first time in a bed. He wanted to give their start that bit of permanence. Oh, hell, he'd wanted to make love to her in her bed so every damned time she went to bed she'd remember him, the way he'd been remembering her since he first saw her.

He'd kept kissing her as they fumbled their way down the hall, stopping in the middle for a long, involved kiss that had left them both needing the wall's support. He'd found the bedroom door by luck. Then stopped for another deep, openmouthed caress.

One moment he'd felt her hands stroking his chest, bare beneath the shirt buttons she'd opened. The next she was pushing him away.

No. No, this is a mistake.

He released her and stepped back. *Jessa.*

No, this is a mistake.

He tried to talk to her, but that was all she would say. When he flipped on a hall light and saw her face, he had felt that punched-in-the-stomach feeling he used to get as a kid when things were going to hell and he couldn't stop them.

I'm sorry, she'd said, drawing her unbuttoned dress around her like a shield. *This was a mistake.*

Tell me what's wrong.

Please, go.

And he'd done the only thing he could do. He'd gone.

No, he thought as he pulled up in front of Jessa's shop, he couldn't afford foolish hopes. Not again.

He had his hands full—more than full—with Travis and the upcoming job interview. He sure didn't need a complicated woman like Jessa in his life…no matter how much he wanted to be in her bed.

So why the hell did he go into the shop to pick up Travis?

He had no answer.

But he had a number of added questions when he pushed open the glass door and found Jessa in close conversation with a rugged-looking cowboy. Not a dressed-as-a-cowboy type, but the real thing, from his worn boots with enough heel to stay in a stirrup, to his work-stained straw cowboy hat.

Jessa bent over something on top of the wood-and-glass counter that came from another era, standing next to the sleek computerized cash register that most definitely came from this era. The problem was that the cowboy bent over the same thing—so close the brim of his hat snagged strands of her dark hair, holding them out so they burned red in the afternoon sunlight pouring through the window.

Stopping dead, Cully felt as if the red burn had lodged in his gut.

"This has got to be it, Dax. It's perfect," Jessa was saying with enthusiasm when she looked up. She was smiling, and her brown eyes held added warmth. That faded beneath a cloud of wariness when she recognized Cully.

The cowboy, apparently sensing her distraction, also looked up. He straightened slowly.

"Uh, hello, Cully. I didn't expect you— I mean, is it time for Travis to leave already?"

"I'm early. I'll wait."

"No, no, that's all right. He can leave as soon as—"

"He's supposed to work till four. He'll work till four."

She stood totally straight. "That's ridiculous. A couple minutes won't make—"

"I'll wait."

They were glaring at each other when the cowboy touched Jessa's arm with his work-roughened hand. Cully turned his glare on the cowboy, especially when the look Jessa turned on the other man softened into another smile.

"I gotta go, Jessa."

"Of course, Dax. I'll place that order today if I can. Tomorrow at the latest. Okay?"

"Yeah. That'll be good."

"Okay. Let me make sure I have all the information...."

While she dug out papers from beneath the counter, the cowboy took a stride toward Cully and held out his hand.

"I'm Dax Randall. Neighbor of the Westons."

The man was about his own age, midthirties, he'd say. He had a well-muscled build and a craggy face. He met Cully's look without blinking.

"Cully Grainger," he responded. He made his handshake a shade harder than usual. It didn't seem to bother Dax Randall any, though one eyebrow rose a fraction.

"Figured," Randall said rather enigmatically.

Cully turned to Jessa. "Boone asked me to pick up paper you got in for him."

"It's in back. I'll get it as soon as I've finished with Dax."

"I'll get it."

"If you'll wait a minute—"

"No need. I'll get it." He nodded to Dax Randall. "Nice meeting you."

He took longer in back than he needed, even taking time to recheck the measurements of a beam for the placement of the alarm system he'd ordered. He figured he'd give Jessa and this Dax guy plenty of opportunity to say their goodbyes, if that's what she wanted. Or to make their plans, or set up their next meeting.

Because that was the element Boone had left out of his advice about how Cully should stop pushing Jessa away—Cully wasn't the only one doing the pushing. Jessa was shoving him away for all she was worth.

He should have realized that just because she thought it was a mistake for her to be with him didn't mean she felt that way about all men.

Maybe Dax Randall was the reason she'd felt what happened between them last fall was such a mistake that her hands and voice shook with it. Maybe Dax Randall was the one she wanted. Fine. He sure wouldn't stand in her way.

As he reentered the shop, he closed the door behind him hard. Hard enough to send a sound wave through the store. To warn Jessa and Dax they had company.

Jessa was alone. And as far as Cully could tell, his warning had succeeded only in making her jump, then keeping her attention studiously focused on the form she was filling out.

"I don't see Travis." He'd reached the counter and put down Boone's drawing paper.

"He's running an errand for me. I tried to tell you when you came in, but you were so busy laying down the law about Travis working every second I didn't have a chance to finish."

"Do you think that's a good idea? He's got a problem with responsibility, and you send him out running around on his own."

"He's never going to learn responsibility if he's not given some. Anyone who's never given any trust can't earn it."

As soon as she concluded that belligerent little speech, she picked up the telephone and punched in numbers. Then she deliberately turned her back and stared at the piece of old quilt she had in a frame behind the register.

Cully wandered to the magazines. None of the glossy periodicals on home, health or hunting held his interest.

He replaced one on business and looked out the front window.

Now, that caught his interest.

Across the street, four boys stood around a fifth boy, taller than the rest and clearly the leader. One of the four boys looking up to this fifth boy—literally and figuratively—was Travis. A frown tightened Cully's forehead as he watched the interplay among the youngsters.

He wasn't consciously aware of listening to Jessa's conversation, but as soon as she hung up the phone, he demanded, "Who's that?"

"Who's who?"

"That boy across the street with the others." He glanced around and saw her looking out the front door. Apparently she couldn't see the group from her angle, because she moved closer to where he stood.

"Which boy? Oh—" She frowned. "You're all bent out of shape because Travis stopped off to say hello to some boys? I don't think that's so bad. He's hardly had a chance to make friends, with working here and the way you've kept him so busy with chores out at the Westons. Besides, he's running the errand for me and still on my clock, so it matters what I think, not what you think."

He found her words interesting. Until the horseback riding lessons started, Travis had done virtually no work at the Westons and he still resisted Cully's efforts to introduce him to kids his age.

He found the way she looked up at him—eyes direct, head slightly tilted and hands on her hips—a lot more than *interesting*.

He wouldn't be sidetracked by any of that.

"Not Travis. The tall one."

"Oh."

She'd been all ready to battle over Travis. Stifling a grin, he tipped his head toward the boys. "The tall one?"

She looked at him an extra beat, then turned to the window. He didn't. Her hair caught the light here even more than it had when he'd first walked in. It glowed with a ruby shine. He remembered its softness against his cheek when they'd danced, under his hands when they'd kissed.

She's a fine-looking woman, and I surely appreciate fine-looking women. But that's all there is. Nothing more.

He'd lied. Sure as the sun rose to the east of the Blue Ridge Mountains and set to the west of the Rockies, he'd lied.

"That's Denny Sorenson. Why?"

When Jessa turned back to him, he gazed out the window, squinting at the boy across the street. Travis was talking; the boy named Denny wasn't paying much attention.

"I don't like the look of him."

"You don't even know him."

"Didn't say I did. I said, 'I don't like the look of him.'"

"So you're one of those cops who can tell by looking at a kid if he's good or a troublemaker? What gave you the special sight?"

"All I said is, 'I don't like the look of him.'"

"How could you have any idea what kind of kid he is?"

"Look, Jessa, like it or not, when somebody's worked as a cop he gets a feel for these things. It's based on observation and experience."

"What observations could you have possibly made about him in one look?"

"To start, he's hanging around. He's not helping his family, working or playing a sport like Pete and his friends do. So he's got time on his hands for getting into trouble.

"Next, he's surrounded by boys who look to be four, five years younger than him. He could be a Pied Piper type—but the Pied Piper wasn't leading those kids out of town for their own good. More likely it means he gets his jollies by showing off and bossing around a group of smaller, younger, less experienced kids.

"Third, he's got a knife in his pocket."

"How could you possibly know that?" she demanded skeptically.

"I can see the outline of it in his jeans."

"Lots of kids carry pocketknives. They need them for ranch work. Pete Weston, for one."

"This is no ranch kid. He'd be out helping his family this time of day. Besides, his hands are too soft, and he doesn't have the build. I've yet to see a ranch kid who doesn't have more upper body strength than that kid has." He turned to her. "Do you know him?"

"A little." She didn't return his look.

"Am I wrong?"

"He's not a ranch kid," she conceded. "But I wouldn't presume to judge anything else about him."

"Heard any stories?"

"Stories are not proof."

"True. But if you refuse to consider stories about stoves being hot, you're going to get burned a lot."

"He's a kid, not a stove. And if you can't see any difference, you shouldn't be—"

The bell over the front door stopped her words like a tape cut off.

Travis looked from Jessa to Cully and back. "I delivered that box to Mrs. Jergens. I guess I went the wrong way coming back. That's why it took me so long."

"That's okay." Jessa gave him her brightest smile. "Thank you for doing that. Did you have her sign the receipt?" Travis dug a rumpled paper from his pants pocket and handed it to her. She looked as if it were the Nobel Peace Prize. "Great. That's great. Thank you, Travis. And I'm sorry you ended up working late."

Cully snorted. Travis's mouth twisted.

"C'mon, Trav. It's time to go." Cully reached out to put his hand on his nephew's shoulder. The boy ducked the touch, pivoted and went back out the door.

The shop was absolutely silent for a moment. Cully stood where he'd stopped when Travis jerked away. It wasn't the first time the boy had made his feelings clear. It shouldn't have hurt so much.

"Cully…"

He heard the worry in Jessa's voice. It got him moving. Away from her. He picked up Boone's drawing paper and prepared to follow Travis.

"Boone said you'd put this on his tab. I guess he's good for it."

"Cully…"

He walked out with Jessa's voice trailing him.

"Travis, I heard you on the phone a while back, calling your mother."

It was a gamble. But a gamble was needed.

Travis Grainger had become perhaps even more difficult in the past week. She'd sent him on a fifteen-minute errand this morning, and he'd been gone an hour. When she'd asked about it, he'd been defiant.

On top of that rested her memory of Cully's worry and hurt.

None of this would get any better if she couldn't get Travis started talking. Holding everything inside was something she understood. In the aftermath of being stalked, Cambria had pushed her to talk to a counselor. It had been mind—and heart—opening. After initial reticence, feelings of anger, frustration, helplessness, distrust and anxiety had poured into words and out of her. Emotions she hadn't known she'd held, but whose weight she'd carried.

Perhaps it would work the same for Travis.

"So I used your phone. So what?"

He sat cross-legged on the floor in front of the "Presidents' Day" carton. She'd started him two hours ago doing inventory of her cartons for decorating the shop in keeping with holidays. Two hours and he'd completed a month and a half—not much progress.

"For starters, it's rude. You should never use something

that belongs to someone else without their permission.''
His eyes widened at her brisk tone. "But that isn't why I
brought it up. I heard you telling your mother you wanted
to leave here.''

She sat on the concrete floor, facing him.

"Is that a crime in Wyoming, hating the state?" A tinge
of sheepishness dulled the usual edge in his tone.

"What I wondered was if you're going to be leaving
soon.''

He looked so stricken she almost regretted her words.

"No," he mumbled. "She can't have me back right
now, that's all.''

"That's too bad.''

"It's hard on the widows of cops. Everybody comes
around before the funeral and stuff, and for a few days
after, but then it's like they don't exist anymore. Everybody forgets about the widow, and expects her to pick up
her life and get a job and run a house and take care of a
kid like she's Superwoman or something.''

Through the rush of words, one fact cut straight into
Jessa's heart.

Oh, God. Half prayer, half pain, she wanted to say the
words out loud. *His father—the father he'd said was
dead—had been a policeman.*

"It won't always be like that. She's gonna send for me
soon and it'll be like before…''

"Before your father died?" Jessa asked softly.

"Yeah.''

Had Travis's father been killed in the line of duty? Was
that the root of Travis's bitterness and despair? But
wouldn't Cully have talked about his brother's death in
that case?

Tread carefully, Jessa.

"My father was a cop, too," she said. "I know it can
be hard being the child of a cop. Hard with your friends,
proving you're one of them, and hard at home." So hard
at home.

"Yeah?" Travis sneered, his defensiveness snapping into place, "Did your daddy the cop off himself because he was a drunk, too?"

Jessa recoiled, both from his words and his anger. *How horrible. What a tragic burden for this boy.* The welling of sympathy and pain nearly impelled her to put her arms around his thin shoulders. She didn't.

He would close himself off from her if she did. She would be permanently relegated to the "them" he talked of with such derision. Instinct or insight, she knew that for a certainty.

"No, he didn't. My father isn't a drunk and he didn't kill himself." She swallowed, trying to keep her voice even. To bring everything out in the open, where it could heal. "Did yours?"

His head snapped back as if she'd slapped him. Almost as quickly, something else came into his eyes.

Honesty.

Stark, pained, confused, but still honesty.

Again the urge to take him into her arms was almost overpowering. Again she withstood it. Again, to her vast relief, it turned out to be the right reaction.

"Yeah." His voice trembled a little.

"When?"

"Three years ago."

She forced back words of condolence and sympathy. Travis had surely heard them all, and they'd done nothing to ease the pain.

"What happened, Travis?"

"I woke up early. I heard something. Mom wasn't up yet, and I couldn't find Dad. Not even in the basement. That's where he went to drink. Back then, I was just a kid and I thought he kept empty bottles there, but I figured that out—after."

Curling her hands around her knees to keep from touching him, Jessa asked, "What did you do when you couldn't find him?"

"I tried to get in the garage. The car was going. But I couldn't get the door from the kitchen to the garage open. I had to go outside. My feet got wet from the dew. I opened the garage door, and Dad was in the car. He looked funny. I didn't know what to do. There were towels stuffed under the door to the kitchen. I tore a couple pulling them out. Mom's good towels. I didn't want to wake up Mom, but... Then the ambulance came and the cop cars...."

Jessa couldn't say anything, not without tears that would surely drive him away.

Abruptly, he scooted around to face her.

"Maybe it wasn't really suicide. Maybe somebody snuck in and hit him over the head and stuck him in the car, and started it up and everything. Maybe they missed a clue or somethin'."

His hope—the hope that his father hadn't chosen to desert him, but had been taken away—was painful to watch.

"Cops usually investigate the death of another cop very, very carefully, Travis. They wouldn't have missed any clues."

He deflated instantly. "Yeah. I was just talking, that's all."

"But did you ever wonder about all those towels, Travis?"

"Whaddya mean?"

"Your father must have been very careful to push those towels around the door so tight you couldn't get through. He did that so the gas wouldn't get into the house and hurt you or your mother."

Travis shook his head. "He didn't want to lose the carbon monoxide. I read about it. If there's fresh air it doesn't kill you fast."

Jessa suppressed a shudder at the thought of Travis reading about his father's method of suicide. But perhaps it was natural, even healthy, for a child to want to understand as much as he could about something that, in the end, was incomprehensible.

"Were there towels under the big garage door?"

"No," he conceded. "But he probably knew he'd get enough gas without that. He didn't care. Now my mother's got a new guy. She doesn't want me around, either. That's okay. I don't need them. I don't need anybody."

"Your uncle—"

"Screw my uncle. He doesn't give a damn. Not about me. He barely showed up for my dad's funeral. He didn't even come to the house. Just stuck around long enough to see my dad put in the ground and then he was gone. He'd done his duty. He'd made his appearance."

The man he painted didn't fit Cully Grainger. She couldn't believe it. But was that because part of her didn't want to believe it? Travis's bitterness was strong and real.

"That's something you should talk to Cully about, Travis."

"I don't want to talk to him. I don't want to see him. Not ever. But I don't have any choice, do I? 'Cause I'm a kid."

"It's not only kids who sometimes get their choices taken away."

She'd allowed more to seep into her voice than she'd intended, but she couldn't regret it. Because, for the first time, Travis looked at her with genuine interest. Like someone really seeing the individual facing him.

She plunged ahead.

"It can be real hard, when you've had choices taken away, not to let yourself feel like a victim. Sometimes even harder for an adult than a kid because we're used to having choices. But if you let yourself feel like a victim, you give away all the choices you had left."

"Yeah? What do you know about it?"

It was a direct, raw challenge. He'd spotted the button and he pushed it for all he was worth.

"Have you heard of stalking, Travis?"

"Yeah."

"Do you know what it is?"

"Sure. It was on TV. Some guy was stalking Madonna. Following her all the time. Sending her stuff she didn't want. Stuff like that. So what?"

"Well, something similar happened to me."

"Why? You're not famous."

"It doesn't happen to only famous people, Travis. A man named Glenn Kaye stalked me when I lived back East. He came to my house and office. He called me all the time and sent things, and when I still wouldn't go out with him, he got angry. He threw my garbage all around and cut my car tires and broke a window in my house. He even tried to set fire to a shed where I stored things."

"What happened to him?"

"Eventually, he was arrested and put in jail."

"Is he still in jail?"

"No. They let him out on parole a few months ago. Do you know what parole is?"

"Sure. Aren't you afraid he'll come after you again?"

"No." Perhaps it wasn't the entire truth, but it wasn't a total lie. "He has people watching him back East. And I'm here in Wyoming. That's why I came here, for a fresh start. This could be a good place for you to make a fresh start, too," she added, rising from the floor and brushing the seat of her pants. "You might get back some of those choices."

He didn't say anything, but that was a big improvement over things he *could* have said, and had said in the past.

"Why don't you finish this box, then start on St. Patrick's Day after lunch."

"Okay."

Yes, a definite improvement.

All in all, talking to Travis had been worthwhile.

In fact, she'd suggest Cully try it.

His father's suicide had deeply wounded Travis. Who better to help him than his father's brother? But Cully couldn't help Travis unless he widened his perspective.

She couldn't turn her back on Travis, so she'd have to work on Cully's attitude.

If Cully did come to accept more "grays" and that helped him fit more comfortably in public police work, where Sheriff Milano and Boone and Cambria seemed to think his heart rested...well, that was a coincidence.

Chapter Six

Jessa surprised him again. Not only didn't she explode when more security devices arrived, she hung around while he installed them.

He wasn't used to surprises. Most of the ones he'd encountered in life hadn't been pleasant, so he preferred to avoid them. They made life...complicated.

Like he'd told Boone, he didn't need any more complications in his life.

Especially not ones smelling of jasmine.

A smell that seemed to linger faintly on the glass of iced tea she handed up to him where he perched atop the ladder, splicing electrical wires in the ceiling. It got so every sip seemed to taste the way jasmine smelled, and every swallow reminded him of her taste. Of kissing her. Of the feel of her skin under his lips.

"So what would you do in that case?" Jessa demanded.

"What case?" He looked down at her. She had her hands behind her, her head tilted back to look at him. Her dark hair showed off the pale length of her throat. He remembered kissing her throat. The warmth and pulse there.

"The one I've been telling you about, Cully."

She'd been posing another of her hypothetical questions, like the ones she'd peppered him with over the past two days while he installed the security devices. He didn't think much of hypotheticals, even as a training tool. As a student and eventually as a trainer, he'd preferred working with real-case scenarios, presented the way the real cops had had to deal with them. That was a hell of a lot better way to learn than pulling a story out of the air.

But he didn't tell Jessa that. She might leave.

He tried to remember the details of this hypothetical question he'd stopped listening to under the influence of jasmine. "The guy's got a kid who needs medicine the hospital has but won't give him because the father doesn't have insurance. And the father steals the medicine, right?"

"Right. And he's been caught and comes before you. You're the ruler and you have to decide what happens to this man. What would you do?"

"Depends on what the law is in this place I rule."

"There are no laws."

"Then I'd make laws."

"You *can't* make laws."

She looked exasperated, with that frown tucked between her eyebrows. He'd like to kiss her there, see if the frown would disappear under his lips. See if she tasted the way jasmine smelled there, too.

"If I'm the ruler, I can do anything I want, and I want to make laws."

"God, you're stubborn."

"I'm stubborn? You're the one who won't let me make laws, and I'm the ruler!"

"Okay, you just got demoted to vice ruler. I'm the ruler, and I say there will be no laws. But you still have to decide about this man."

"Then I'd get the hell out of your country. I don't want to live anywhere there are no laws, because without laws, it's chaos. It's confusion and frustration and never knowing what's going to get you in trouble and earn you a slap. It's screaming fights with no beginnings and no ends. It's—"

He broke off when he caught sight of her face. Head tilted back to look at him, lips parted, eyes wide with a blend of horror and sympathy.

If he'd been on the ground, he would have taken her in his arms and kissed away the look, the sympathy, the horror. He would have kissed her and touched her until she forgot his words and he forgot his past. He would have taken the simpler complication of desire over the one he saw brewing between them.

But he was stuck on top of a ladder, with a maze of wires still to unravel. And Jessa staring up at him.

"Jessa, I need a pair of needle-nose pliers if I'm going to finish today. Could you go to the hardware store and get them?"

At first, he thought she would refuse. Or ignore his request and demand an explanation for his earlier words.

In the end, she simply said, "Okay," and left.

He let out a stream of curses under his breath the wires had done nothing to deserve.

He was supposed to be keeping a barrier between himself and Jessa Tarrant, not yapping away about hypothetical questions. He should have kept his mouth shut. He should have sent her away. He should have ignored the jasmine.

And he should have told her to get something other than needle-nose pliers. Because it would be one more complication if Al at the hardware store happened to mention he'd bought needle-nose pliers yesterday.

The shop bell's usually sweet tinkling turned to a discordant clang by the force of the hand that pushed the door open. The hand belonged to Cully Grainger. His other hand was filled with the back of Travis's black T-shirt.

From her spot by the greeting card rack she had been straightening, Jessa saw Rita and Sally Randall pivot from discussing the relative merits of various arthritis creams, and Sally's daughter, June Reamer, crane her neck from the far aisle, where she'd gone after talcum powder.

"Jessa, I'd like to speak to you in private."

Cully's rumbling voice would have suited the Grim Reaper.

Rather than argue in front of an audience, Jessa nodded and headed toward the office in back.

As soon as she was through the doorway, however—behind Cully, still with Travis in tow—she said, "Cully, you're jumping to a conclusion here. I sent Travis on an errand. I don't care if you don't think he should be out running errands. It's my shop, and if I want to send him out to do something—"

"Did you send him out to drink?"

As much as his words, the smell of alcohol in the tiny office stopped her.

"Oh, Travis." His eyes were glassy, but still defiant. Dismay swept over her. With so many things she wanted to say, the first thing out of her mouth was, "You stink."

"Doesn't he? Like the cheapest falling-down drunk around."

"He was only gone a half hour at the most."

"It doesn't take long."

Cully was pale. Lines bracketed his mouth and more lines radiated beyond the edges of his sunglasses. There was anger in his tense jaw, but what struck Jessa so hard was the fear beneath the anger. And the pain.

She gripped the chair back to keep from touching him.

"Where'd you find him?"

"A call came into the sheriff's department that kids were using the empty movie theater building to drink in. I went along. They scattered, but I recognized this shirt—"

he lifted a little higher on the T-shirt's neck "—and went after him."

"It's not my fault," Travis said sullenly. His gaze drifted around the small area, never making contact with Jessa or his uncle. "I didn't do anything. It got spilled on me, that's all. It's not fair, Jessa. Can't you do something? He won't listen. He never listens."

She had no chance to answer.

"I could take you to the sheriff's department and test you for alcohol, Travis," Cully said. "'Course, then you'd be charged with underage drinking. You want that? Huh? I'm listening."

"I didn't buy the stuff. Why don't you go after those guys? You're such a big, tough cop. I know why, because they're too smart for you."

"I'm leaving that to the sheriff. But your faith in your friends is touching, considering how they rallied around you."

"They *are* my friends. They listen to what I say. They know I know stuff. Interesting stuff."

"So interesting that they get you drunk, then leave you on your own." Cully's mouth twisted into a bitter grimace as he told Jessa, "He got caught in the alley. His *buddies* could have helped him over the fence they could climb because apparently they weren't as drunk, but they left him. Was that Denny Sorenson I heard laughing as you hollered for help, Travis?"

Only silence answered that question. Travis wouldn't break the code against snitching. Why did kids in trouble follow that rule when they broke all others?

Cully switched hands on the back of Travis's T-shirt. The knuckles on his right hand stayed white even after the pressure eased.

"He can't be allowed off on his own anymore, Jessa. No more errands."

She released the chair, shaking her head. "Cully, I'm going to run my shop the way I think fit."

For a moment she expected Cully to walk out. Then the brackets around his mouth eased slightly.

"I can't tell you how to run your shop. But if he's overdue by more than five minutes, you call me. If you can't get me, you call the sheriff's department." He looked at his nephew, not waiting to hear if she agreed. "And we're going to have a few more rules around the cabin."

As they started out, Cully's fist still around the material of Travis's T-shirt, Jessa watched them go with a heavy heart.

After their talk the other day, Jessa understood Travis's anger and pain much more clearly. But she also saw how he angled for sympathy to get what he wanted. Cully was right about that. And it seemed any time Travis opened himself up to her, he counteracted that somehow. Was this episode a result of his talking to her about his father?

She fervently hoped not. Because, while she did not want the power over Cully to sway his actions or his opinions, neither did she want to cause him pain.

Travis had been quiet for the week since Cully had caught him drinking.

With Rita off today, Jessa was tied to the cash register, but there had been opportunities to talk earlier. He'd stayed away from her. Perhaps discomfort was natural after their emotional talk. Or perhaps he was roasting her with the same smoldering anger he displayed toward Cully.

Still, she was pleased—she'd sent him on a twenty-minute errand and he'd actually returned in twenty minutes. She had been almost light-headed with relief she hadn't had to face the consequences of calling Cully to tell him Travis was overdue, or of not calling him.

As far as she could tell, Travis also was seeing less of Denny Sorenson and his crowd.

At the moment, Travis was sweeping in the back aisle, and that was probably just as well, since she could see Sorenson and his youthful followers hanging out in front of the empty storefront next door. Across the street lingered three high school girls, one of whom she recognized as Theresa Wendlow, whose parents were among the most well-to-do in the county. Theresa seemed a genuinely nice girl and most times her wealth wasn't noticeable, since all the kids mostly wore equally faded jeans. But today she had on a flippy, short denim skirt and a pair of strappy sandals.

From her station at the cash register, Jessa idly watched the interplay of the three girls, punctuated with gestures and frequent glances toward the shop. She didn't fool herself that her stock or her dazzling window display provided the attraction.

It was the five teenaged boys by her magazine rack.

And if Jessa had been the age of Theresa and her friends, the one she'd have her sights set on was Will Randall. With sun-streaked brown hair and deep brown eyes, he looked a lot like his father, and no one could dispute Dax Randall was a most attractive man.

She half smiled. Of course Dax frustrated the women who wanted to do any more than notice how attractive he was, because he was not about to get involved. That was probably why they got along so well. She always felt comfortable with him. Not on edge the way she did around Cully.

With Cully, it was like when she'd been a kid and walked round in her socks in the winter and she'd touch something and—*zap!*—a charge went through her. It made every move, every touch a gamble.

She'd grown out of liking that kind of thrill a long time ago. She'd learned to always wear her shoes. And she'd learned to stay away from men like Cully Grainger.

Looking out the window, Will Randall dropped the magazine he'd held and half shouted, "Hey!"

At that moment, Jessa became aware of a girl's voice from outside, frightened yet belligerent, saying, "Leave me alone."

Theresa had crossed the street alone, only to be met by Denny Sorenson and his cronies outside Nearly Everything. They had encircled her, and Denny was lifting up her skirt with the tip of a stick.

Will charged for the door, followed by his friends, but Jessa was closer and reached the door first.

"Stop that! You stop that right now!"

Several of the younger boys who hung around Denny Sorenson appeared startled, and backed away. Denny simply leered at her.

"Or what'll you do?"

"For starters, call the sheriff."

"We aren't doing anything he could arrest us for," he said defensively.

"You ever hear of sexual harassment?"

"I was giving her what she wants."

"Giving her what—" Jessa spluttered.

"She wants it—look at the skirt she's wearing. It barely covers her—"

"What rock did you crawl out from under?"

Jessa knew she shouldn't have said it. Not with the disdain so clear in her tone. He was a kid, after all. Though for all her defense of him to Cully, she would admit he wasn't a nice kid. And she especially shouldn't have said it in front of his peers, whose giggling drove blotchy, harsh color up his neck and into his face. But his attitude made her so angry.

Still, it was clear she'd made an enemy.

"It's not like I'm dressed like Madonna or something," Theresa said.

"It shouldn't matter if you were. No matter how you or anyone else," Jessa added, trying to make this less of a direct attack on Denny Sorenson, "might judge her outfit, no woman is *asking for it* by the clothes she wears. A woman—or a man for that matter—has a right to walk down the street unmolested."

"I didn't molest her." Sorenson's sneer was salacious.

"You harassed her, and that's bad enough." She had lost patience with him. "Get out of here, Denny, before I call the sheriff."

"Who wants to be by this crappy little store, anyway?" Denny Sorenson had his sneer and his saunter back in place as he jerked his head for his entourage to follow.

As he passed Jessa, he crowded her, but she didn't move. He passed close enough that his under-the-breath-comment was perfectly audible.

"You'll be sorry for taking me on."

He gave a nasty chuckle and kept going.

Will Randall stepped ahead of the other boys who'd been in the shop. "What did he say, Jessa?"

Jessa stopped him from going after Sorenson with a hand on his arm. "Don't, Will. Just let it go. Let him go."

"He's a jerk, talking to you like that."

She nodded. "I'd have to agree with you there. He was an even bigger jerk for the way he talked to Theresa."

Will glanced at the girl, who had been staring at him until he looked at her. The girls flanking Theresa giggled, and Will turned on his heel and went back into the store. One boy followed, but three remained outside, shifting from foot to foot and looking at the girls.

With her gaze trailing Will, Theresa sighed. Then she turned to Jessa. "Thank you, Jessa. I'm glad you were here."

"I'm glad I was here, too. You should mention this to your parents when you get home, okay? And you girls stick together."

"Uh, we could, uh, walk, you know, walk with 'em," muttered Jerry Poolter.

"That's a good idea, Jerry."

Amid giggles and high color on cheeks male and female, the group started off. Theresa sent a final look over her shoulder to where Will was visible through the window.

Bittersweet memories of her first, desperate crushes were cut short by the sight of Travis, standing alone, by the shop door. The groups of kids had met, some had re-formed, and then they'd parted. Travis remained outside them, watching, not a part of any.

He needed security. He needed a champion. He needed Cully, if Cully would only see there was a better way to deal with him than listing rules and regulations as if he were in boot camp.

Travis became aware of her scrutiny, and jerked himself upright and into the shop.

Sighing, Jessa followed him. Sometimes growing up was hard, hard work.

"Well, now, you comfortable in that chair, son?"

Cully turned in the chair in question and looked around from the computer screen to the man standing across the desk from him. The man was Sheriff Milano, and the desk, computer and chair all belonged to him. Cully occupied the chair behind the desk for one reason and one reason only: it was also the chair in front of the computer.

"You look right at home there," Milano added with a glint in his eye.

"Just doing the job you asked me to, Sheriff." Cully started to rise.

Milano waved him back. "Sit down, sit down." He eased his bulk into the visitor's chair with a grunt. "Still foolin' with that gadget, huh? I told the county board they'd be better off giving us a trained search dog instead of these newfangled things."

Cully considered the older man. "Does anybody fall for that country-boy act of yours?"

"Oh, now and then they do. Now and then," the sheriff answered equably. "Seems to me you're not above slipping in a little down-home, yourself."

Cully ignored that. "I can't believe the people of Bardville fall for this con of yours."

"Con? That's a mighty harsh word. I'd be real hurt if I thought you meant it."

They both knew he didn't—not entirely. "What would you call someone presenting himself under false pretenses?"

"That would all depend on what sort of pretenses and what sort of man and what sort of reasons. And I 'xpect most folks 'round here would agree. They know things— and people—aren't always what they seem. So they aren't surprised much when it turns out that way."

That, too, Cully ignored. "I did some checking on you, Sheriff Milano. You were a real up-and-comer in Dallas. You got among the highest scores in their training."

"Now, that's supposed to be confidential," the sheriff complained.

"I've got friends."

The glint returned to the sheriff's eyes. "I imagine you do."

"So why have you buried yourself here?"

"I like the people."

"You could have had a career—"

"I've had a career. Better'n that, I've been mostly my own boss. I've made my own decisions—right or wrong. And I've had the opportunity to live with them. A man can't ask for much more. Best of all, I've had more than a career—I've had a life. Both have been real good here. Not sure I could've done that in Dallas. Least not the same way. Margie, bless her soul, and I decided to give this a try, and we never regretted it."

All right. Milano and his wife had made a choice based on quality of life. Cully could understand that. He could see the appeal. Especially being his own boss—as long as the voters kept putting him back in office. But one thing he didn't understand.

"Why didn't you let the people of Bardville know they got more than a small-town sheriff?"

"Because they didn't need a hotshot cop. A small-town sheriff's what they wanted and needed. No, what they really needed—and still do—is a man. A man who'd listen and get things talked through when he could."

"And who'd know things—and people—aren't always what they seem?"

Milano nodded and smiled as if Cully's words had carried no sarcasm. "That's right. Now you're learning, boy."

"You make it sound like Andy Taylor of Mayberry."

"Did you ever stop to think Andy Taylor must've been doing a pretty good job or Mayberry wouldn't have been such a peaceful place?"

"Hey, Jessa. How'd you like to come for supper and see the progress on the house?" Cambria asked over the telephone. "Boone and Cully have been working on the master bedroom all day, and Travis is off with Dad and Irene at one of Pete's baseball games, so it'll be the four of us."

The mention of Cully triggered Jessa's automatic response to say no. She overrode it. She could talk to him more about Travis. These past few days, he'd seemed more inclined to listen with an open mind.

"Aw, c'mon, Jessa," her friend urged. "It won't kill you to spend an evening with a guy who thinks you're hot."

"Cambria!"

"Well, he does. It's obvious. And that's good for any woman's ego. I'm not saying you have to take him up on the offer—though that wouldn't hurt you. But since you're not interested in Cully and you don't find him attractive..."

Jessa refused to be lured.

"At least you know it won't get out of hand. He doesn't bite, for heaven's sake." Cambria chuckled evilly. "Well, maybe he does, but not in public. And he'd never bite and tell."

"Cambria!"

"Oh, quit scolding me. I'm pregnant and my hormones are rampaging. I'm allowed to be a little spicy if I want. I'm also allowed to burst into tears if my best friend won't come to dinner."

Jessa laughed. "What was your excuse before you were pregnant? No, don't answer that. And don't burst into tears. I'll come."

"Good. I thought we'd have pizza—providing you pick it up from Maureen Elliston at the café."

She laughed again. "Nice invitation, Cambria—you can come for dinner if you'll bring it."

"That's about the size of it," her unrepentant friend agreed. "I'll call Maureen to have the pizza ready to go, and when you get here you won't have to do a thing. I'll even slice your pizza for you if you want, like the perfect little hostess."

Chapter Seven

"C'mon out and enjoy the view," Cambria invited as she preceded Jessa out of the house with a stack of paper napkins, a bottle of wine and a bottle of water. She placed them on the boards-and-sawhorse setup serving as a table in the area destined to become a patio.

Jessa sidestepped a lawn chair by the table and added the two pizza boxes. She looked up to the craggy wall of cliff that backed the house, and, to the right, to the slice of the valley glowing in the setting sun. "It is a great view."

"I thought you'd appreciate it." Cambria gave her a wicked grin. "Just remember," she added with a tip of her head toward a water tank by the bedroom wing under construction, "half of that view is mine."

Jessa followed the direction of Cambria's interest and spotted Cully and Boone, both stripped to the waist, washing off the grime of hard work.

Cully had his back to them. As he bent and splashed

water on his chest, then used a towel to wipe it dry, the
long, ropy muscles of his back flexed in rhythm. The muscles across his shoulders were more defined, but still suited
his long, lean looks.

Seven months ago, she'd let her hands explore and touch
his back and shoulders, feeling those muscles through the
fabric of his shirt, then flesh to flesh. Her palms almost
itched with the longing to touch him this instant.

In the act of pulling on a shirt, Boone looked up, caught
sight of her and Cambria and said something to Cully. He
turned his head, locking eyes with her. More slowly, he
turned the rest of the way.

Jessa was vaguely aware of Boone calling something to
Cambria, and of his heading toward them. Mostly she was
aware of the effort it took to keep breathing. She prayed
Cully couldn't read her mind.

Cully slowly dragged the towel across his chest one last
time, then snagged his shirt from atop a crate. He had it
halfway buttoned by the time he reached the level area.

"Hi, Jessa." He took a soft drink can from the cooler
by the table and offered it to her. She declined with a shake
of her head. "This is a surprise," he added with an eye-
brow-lifted look at Cambria.

"Didn't I mention Jessa was bringing the pizza?" Her
innocence fooled no one.

"No. You said I should stay for pizza, and it was being
delivered."

He sounded slightly annoyed. Wouldn't he have stayed
if he'd known she was coming? That possibility, combined
with Cambria's avid interest, broke Jessa free of memories
and desires.

"Tarrant Pizza Delivery service, that's me."

"And we appreciate it," Boone said.

Jessa wondered if Boone shared Cambria's belief that
Cully was attracted to her. If anyone knew, it would be
Boone. But he'd never given any sign.

"We certainly do." Cambria bit into her pizza. "Mmmm. This is delicious."

Boone rested his hand briefly on the top of his wife's head as he passed her chair on his way to the bottle of wine. "It's good to see you eating again."

"You must have blanked out the past six weeks if you haven't noticed me eating, Boone. It was just the first trimester that was the stomach killer."

Boone grimaced. "Yours and mine both."

"That's because you tried to take responsibility for my morning sickness—"

"I was responsible. At least fifty percent responsible."

"Well, yes, when you look at it that way. Come to think of it, you've got a lot to make up for, Boone Dorsey Smith."

Cully chuckled. "Now you're in for it."

"Jessa, will you help me avoid the moment of retribution by letting me pour you some wine?"

"Anything to help, Boone. Thanks."

He poured her a glass of red wine and one for himself, then returned to the chair beside Cambria.

"Hear you had a run-in with Denny Sorenson the other day, Jessa," Boone said.

From the corner of her eye, she caught movement as Cully, with a slice of pizza in one hand and the soft drink can in the other, turned toward her. She had the feeling Boone had meant him to hear.

"How'd you hear that?"

"From me," Cambria said. "Actually, I heard it from June Reamer, who'd heard it from Wanda Rupert at the library, who'd heard it from a library volunteer, whose sister cleans for Theresa Wendlow's mother."

"Ah, the joys of small-town living." Jessa smiled. "By the time it reached you guys, any resemblance to what really happened was entirely accidental, I'm sure."

"Then tell us what really happened," Cully invited.

"Nothing. It's not even worth talking about."

"That's not what I heard," Boone interposed. "And I had a more direct source than Cambria's chain letter. Dax Randall heard about it from Will, and Dax mentioned it to me."

"What happened?" This time Cully didn't invite, he demanded.

She fought off a glare, determined to keep a light tone. First because the subject didn't deserve more, and second, because she wanted Cully in a good mood when she talked to him about Travis. "It was nothing, really. He was bothering one of the high school girls, and I told him to quit."

"Did you call the sheriff?" Cully asked.

"No, I didn't call the sheriff. There was no need to bother him, for heaven's sake. It was nothing."

Boone shook his head. "I heard the Sorenson kid threatened you."

"What?" Cambria glared at Jessa, then her husband, then back at Jessa. "I didn't hear *that*."

"It wasn't a threat. He was a kid mouthing off. Trying to save face."

"What did he say?" Cully put down his pizza.

"The usual stuff, I suppose."

"What did he say?" he repeated implacably.

"I don't remember. It wasn't very memorable."

"It was memorable to Will," Boone said. Jessa frowned at him. He was deliberately stirring this up, and she wished he'd shut up. "He told his father Sorenson said he'd get you."

She shrugged. "I don't remember."

"The hell you don't. Tell Tom Milano."

She stared at Cully. She'd been a fool to think he could change. "That's ridiculous. I am not going to bother Sheriff Milano with this."

"Jessa, it's foolish to take a cha—"

"No." They'd returned to the impasse they'd faced over Travis, and they both knew it.

"Then I will."

"I'm sure he'll be thrilled to have you wasting his time. For heaven's sake, Denny Sorenson is a kid. He was acting up. I told him to stop. End of story. It's not a federal case."

"Maybe."

"There's no maybe about it. You have it in your head he's some adolescent gangster, the way you do with Travis, and that's ridiculous. And heartless."

He leaned back in his chair, studying her face. She wondered how much he could see in the quickly fading light. His face was impossible to read.

"We've had this discussion before, Jessa. I suppose we'd best agree to disagree. For now."

"Okay."

She didn't say it with much grace, but he didn't deserve any. He intended to go his own way on this, and she suspected he'd bend Tom Milano's ear. She couldn't stop him.

She took a swallow of wine, then another bite of pizza.

After a few moments of awkward silence, Boone started talking about the house, and the conversation settled into more natural rhythms.

By the time the pizza was gone and they'd switched to coffee, darkness had fallen completely and the talk was relaxed.

Perhaps darkness did that, Jessa thought.

Perhaps it made it easier to broach topics that could open the pain in a person's heart when you couldn't see his face. *His face.* Cully's face. She didn't want to see pain in his face.

Or perhaps she didn't want anyone to see her disappointment that they'd slid right back into the same old argument.

Either way, her cowardice didn't do Travis any good.

"Cully, I had a long talk with Travis the other day."

He turned his head toward her, but she couldn't see his eyes. Good.

"What's your definition of 'long'? Most I get is a sentence and a half."

"We talked for about a half hour." Instinctively, she reached across the gap between them and put her fingertips on his arm, seeking to soften the words about to come. A man who saw things coldly, who easily divided the world between right and wrong, shouldn't feel so warm. He shouldn't have a warmth that made her want to slide her hand over his arm, to experience the full contact of his skin against her palm. "He told me about his father's suicide."

A heavy silence fell on the group. Because she didn't take her eyes off Cully, Jessa sensed more than saw Boone's sharp look at his friend. It figured Boone knew the circumstances of the death of Cully's brother, since they were such close friends.

"It was hard on the kid." Cully sounded gruffer than usual.

"It's still hard on him. On you, too, I'd imagine. He also told me his father drank."

Cully cleared his throat and stood. Her hand dropped to her side.

"It's getting late," Cully said. "I better get going. I'm going to Billings in the morning to get computer supplies for the sheriff."

"What about Travis?" Jessa asked.

"He's going with me."

"That ought to be a fun day for him."

"He's not out here to—"

"Have fun," Jessa completed for him.

"Yeah, well... Good night. Thanks for supper, Cambria."

"If you have to leave, Cully, take the path around the side. It's faster than going through the house. But don't thank me for dinner—thank Jessa. She brought it," Cambria answered brightly.

"Thanks." Cully nodded dutifully toward Jessa. "Good night."

As soon as he'd rounded the corner, Cambria turned to Jessa. "Well? What are you waiting for? Go after him."

"Cambria, I've told you—"

Cambria slashed at the air with her hand. "Not that. Was that all you wanted to say to him about Travis?"

"No, but—"

"No *buts.* Go after him and say what you have to say."

"You're right. I will."

Jessa took one step to follow Cully, but Cambria gave her a shove toward the house. "Through the house. It's quicker. I lied."

"Cambria—"

Jessa heard Boone's protest, but she was already on her way.

Before her eyes could completely adjust to the lights of the house, she was out the door and plunged once more into blackness.

She sensed motion, rather than shape, then recognized it was Cully, standing between his car, parked nearer the house, and hers, just beyond. As her focus improved, she realized he'd turned toward the door when he heard her.

"Something wrong, Cully?"

"I thought I heard something…" He let his words trail off as he came around the back of his car and met her.

"Probably animals." She dismissed it. "Cully, I wasn't done saying what I had to say in there about Travis—"

"Jessa." He broke off, breathed out through his nose, then started again. "Look, this isn't your problem."

"I'm making it my problem—with an assist from you, since you're so adamant Travis work in my shop."

"You could make sure he puts in his hours of work and not do any more."

"No, I couldn't," she said, trying to curb her indignation. "He's a kid, and he's very unhappy. I can't clock him in and clock him out like a robot."

Cully transferred his car keys from one hand to the other, pushed his freed hand through his hair, then down to his neck, where he rubbed the back. The breeze ruffled his hair. "You keep saying he's a kid, but what he was up to in North Carolina is not just kid stuff. Stealing and vandalism and drinking—and not beer. The other day wasn't the first time."

At twelve years old? It surprised her enough that she hesitated—but not long. It was still possible these episodes were simply a youngster's fascination with the unknown, the fascination of a boy who remembered his father drinking. That didn't keep it from being troubling, but... "Lots of kids experiment with alcohol. He's young—"

"Not in my family he's not. His father—my brother Manny—started drinking at that age. He'd crawl in the backroom window smelling the same as our mother did when she passed out in the front room. I don't know when our mother started. I can't ever remember her not drinking. It's no experiment with the Graingers. It's a full-fledged addiction."

His pain and fear at finding Travis drinking made sense. She wished it didn't.

"But you—"

"I'm damned careful. All the time. Every time. It looks like the gene passed me by, but I'm not taking chances. I have never gotten drunk. Not once. Got a buzz in the army a time or two, and that was close enough."

She swallowed, trying to absorb this new understanding. "How about the rest of your family?"

"My sister, Ashe, pretends there's never been anything wrong with the family by pretending she doesn't have a family. She went out the door on a college scholarship nine years ago, and she hasn't been home but a half-dozen times since. Winston's addicted, too, but it's to running and success. He's strained, pulled and torn more body parts than I thought a human possessed, but he won't quit. Maybe it's a good thing, because it's the only time he quits working.'' He gave an aborted chuckle. ''A picture of emotional health, that's the Graingers.''

''Your father—''

''Oh, no, don't go looking to him for a role model. Jefferson Grainger's a fine match for his wife when it comes to that.''

''He's an alcoholic, too?''

''No. His particular talent is being absent. When he was younger, he ran around on Mom, with an occasional backhand across the mouth if she complained. Now he's just gone. I don't think even Mom knows where. She probably doesn't even know if she cares anymore.

''When I was a kid, though, that's what they'd fight about. Her drinking. His cheating. Round and round. Who knows where it started. There was never enough money. The house was always a wreck, and our clothes were cast-offs.

''I'd lie in bed listening to Mom and Dad fighting at night. Listening to the younger ones crying. Trying to hush them. Most times it was just words. Words and shouts and screams and curses. But one night it was worse. Mom was outside, screaming. Dad hit her with something. A piece of wood, I think. Somebody called the sheriff's department. And this deputy came out.''

Cully fell into a silence of remembering. Without his deep voice, the night was so quiet Jessa heard the soft *pat, pat* as Cully rhythmically tapped his key case against his palm.

''Harry DeWitt. I still remember his name. Deputy Harry DeWitt. He stepped out of his shiny car with the flashing lights, into taunts and shouts and crying. He made no accusations—he never got angry—he never got upset. He asked questions. Calm, rational questions. And when he was done, he'd sorted it out, sent Dad to a friend's to cool off, told Mom to sleep it off and took us kids to my great-aunt Philly's house.

''I sat in the front seat of his cruiser. I remember that

so clearly. The other three in back, and me in front because I was oldest. I asked how he knew what to do. I must have sounded pretty awed, because he said it wasn't anything magical. He said he followed the law, and as long as he did he couldn't go wrong.''

Cully slapped the key case more firmly into his other palm, then slid it into his jeans pocket. He put his hands in his front pockets and looked at his shoes.

"Sounds simplistic, I know. Especially to you. But to me, back then..."

"It must have seemed like a lifeline."

His head jerked up, and she saw he hadn't expected her to understand. Maybe in some small part of himself he hadn't *wanted* her to understand, because her understanding opened a door of his fortress, as his insights had breached some of her walls. He'd risked it, anyhow.

She swallowed hard and blinked at a burning behind her eyes. He couldn't have seen either betrayal of her vulnerability, because his gaze had returned to his shoes, with a faintly self-mocking smile touching his lips.

"Yeah, I guess it did. Well, it's gettin' late, and you don't want to be hearing any more of the personal life and times of Cully Grainger, or you're sure to fall asleep at the wheel going down this mountain."

For the first time she wondered if he wore sunglasses to keep other people out or himself in.

No, she didn't want to hear more, as he clearly didn't want to tell any more. Not because it was boring. Not because it revealed more of him than he was comfortable with. But because each word he said proved to her what she'd felt from the start.

Being a cop wasn't simply an occupation for Cully Grainger. She'd sensed that. Now she understood it had filled a great void in his life. It had given him structure and discipline and reason when his boyhood had lacked all three.

It made her want to reach out to him. To touch him. To console him.

And it made her realize she could do none of those things. He was, as she had suspected all along, a man who not only believed in rules and regulations and unbreakable lines between right and wrong, but who needed them.

The absolutely wrong kind of man for her.

As she drove down the corkscrew drive from Cambria and Boone's house, a glimpse of light to her left snagged Jessa's attention only for an instant. She might navigate this twisting drive with the ease of familiarity, but she gave it the respect it deserved, and that meant not letting herself be distracted.

Probably the gleam of an animal's eyes. Plenty of mule-eared deer around. A month ago she wouldn't have given it a second thought.

A month ago, she wasn't edgy all the time. A month ago she wasn't in an emotional tangle with a boy in pain and his uncle who might be in as much pain as the boy and certainly posed more of an emotional danger to her.

She had to set up some rules here. And follow them.

The first rule was, no touching Cully Grainger. If she hadn't touched him tonight...

But she had touched him. She had felt the heat of his body and the thrum of a pulse under his skin. It unsettled her.

Hell, be honest, Jessa Anne Tarrant, that's only part of what unsettled you.

The other part was the way that simple touch nudged up the heat and beat in her body. She hadn't felt that way since... since Cully had made her feel a good deal more on her living room couch on a certain night in October. Had made her feel enough more that she had guided him to the doorway of her bedroom. Had made her feel so much more that she had been out of her senses—no, she'd been *into* her senses, into feeling and touching and tasting and smelling—and almost forgot about caution and self-preservation.

Turning onto the winding, rutted road that eventually spilled into the paved highway to Bardville, Jessa shook her head.

She'd come a long way in recovering her trust since the stalking. In time she would ease back into dating. Perhaps sooner rather than later, with the double prodding of Cambria and her own hormones, which seemed to be rampaging lately. Whenever it was, it wasn't going to be Cully. She couldn't let a persuasive drawl, a pair of laser blue eyes and a shimmer of heat under her fingers change her mind about that.

The mind she was guarding against change abruptly registered that the steering wheel under her hands was tugging sharply and that the car had developed an odd, listing movement.

A tire probably going— *Thwump…thwump…thwump.* Flat. Very flat.

Automatically she applied the brake, then swore as the car lurched to the right.

"Stupid, Tarrant. Stupid," she muttered as she eased off the brake and let the car coast to a stop.

She didn't worry about pulling all the way to the side. First, a ditch bordered the road and she didn't want to spend her night there. Second, this road carried little traffic.

Very little.

A few locals used it as a back way between Sheridan and Bardville, but mostly during daylight.

With the car safely stopped, she considered her alternatives. It was a good two miles, all uphill, to Cambria and Boone's. The highway was closer, but also wasn't heavily traveled.

As she rolled down her window and turned off the engine, silence and dark gushed into the car. Then nature reasserted itself, the crickets' chirping and a rustling of vegetation filling the vacuum.

She hadn't changed a tire since driver's ed, but how hard could it be?

She dug the owner's manual from the glove compartment and wiped off a film of dust. For some reason, she hesitated. The dark beyond the familiar interior of her car circled her, ominous and strange.

Don't get dramatic. You just need a minute or two for your eyes to adjust.

Light suddenly blazed from the rearview mirror.

Blinking against momentary blindness, Jessa heard a car approaching.

It was close. Too close. She should have seen the headlights behind her a long time ago, unless...

She was scrambling out the passenger-side door before the possibilities even started forming. The interior light popped on, but she couldn't help that without unscrewing the bulb—too much time. Maybe the other driver wouldn't notice with his brights boring into her car.

The other driver. Who could have been following her with his lights off. Or been waiting by the side of the road when she passed. Or could have a perfectly reasonable explanation for suddenly appearing behind her.

Only, she wasn't going to wait to find out which alternative turned out right.

She skidded down the ditch, then up the other side among three cottonwood trees, finding the fence by the prick of a barb in her palm. She bit her lip to avoid crying out and burrowed into the tall grass on the road side of the fence.

The darkness was complete, with no moon and certainly no reflection of city lights. Only the muffled sound of a car engine reached her. It seemed to slow near where she guessed her car sat. She thought she caught another engine's noise then, but she couldn't be sure, as a bird disturbed by her presence set up a distressed racket.

After what seemed forever, the bird gave one more raucous protest and flew away to a quieter neighborhood with a disgusted flapping of wings.

Silence. Even the crickets seemed muted. Jessa slowly raised her head. She could make out the vague shape of her car as a deeper shadow than the others around it. She saw nothing else. She heard nothing else.

Wondering if she'd hidden away like a ninny from her only opportunity to get help with lug nuts and jack handles, she couldn't deny her heart was slowing and her nerves were settling. So, she'd change the tire alone. There were worse things. Lots worse.

Jessa stood slowly, loosening tension-taut muscles, and retraced her steps. The return trip up the side of the ditch was harder going, but she reached the top.

A hand circled her arm, strong and binding.

Her breath strangled into a gasp, then erupted as a scream at the same time she drove her elbow—hard—into the body behind her.

Chapter Eight

"Jessa, it's me. Cul— Oof."

She was scrambling away when the voice and words registered. She hesitated, poised to use the dark as cover once more.

"Cully?"

He grunted. "Yeah."

He slowly straightened from a doubled-over position of self-protection. When he didn't straighten all the way, her instincts switched from flight to concern.

"Are you okay?" She moved next to him, putting a tentative hand to his shoulder. He drew more erect.

"I'll live. What happened?"

"I...I had a flat tire. I was going to change it, but... Someone followed me... I saw—" Torn between relief and embarrassment, she blurted, "Oh, God, it was you! What an idiot—"

"Not me. Too far back."

"Oh... Maybe I imagined it, but..."

He touched her cheek, perhaps a simple reassurance.

Without thinking or planning, she stepped into his arms. They closed around her and she held on. She didn't cry. He didn't say anything. His chest was solid and warm under her cheek. His hand was steady and reliable as it stroked her back. That was what she needed.

She wasn't sure how long it was before he spoke. The adrenaline of fear had ebbed, but her heart rate showed no sign of slowing.

"You didn't imagine it, Jessa. When I came around the big curve I saw another car pulling up behind yours. I couldn't identify the car because of the brush, but it was angling to shine its lights along the side of the road, beyond the ditch. That's why I came looking for you there. When I came around the near curve, the other car took off."

His arms tightened around her a moment, then he released her.

"Okay?"

He stepped back half a stride, but didn't move away, as if to be sure she could stand.

She could, of course. She would have forced herself to stand at the moment if both her legs were broken.

"I'm fine, thank you."

"Good. Then I'll take a look at that tire."

"It felt like the right front, but I didn't check because..."

Because she'd been making a headlong dash into the weeds.

"That's okay. I want to look at all of them." He took a small, powerful flashlight from his back jeans pocket, flicked it on and started a circuit of her car.

She adjusted her sweater, turned askew at some point in the past few minutes, and brushed grass and leaves from her side.

Allowing herself to be embraced had been a natural reaction to relief. The coolness she felt now was an equally natural response to hearing his account and realizing the episode was not the result of an overactive imagination.

Cully squatted by the right front tire, slowly moving the flashlight beam over the surface.

"Your tire's been cut."

She froze, one hand to her throat. "These are rough roads. I probably drove over something."

"Not unless you've been driving over knives. See this?"

She moved closer and looked at where his left hand pointed to a gash spotlighted by the flashlight's beam.

"A smooth, even cut. Clean entrance, no ragged edges. I'm no expert, but I'd wager an expert would tell you a sharp knife did it." He shifted the flashlight to another point on the tire. "Here's another one. Only, this one hasn't broken all the way through. And here's another. A couple hundred yards more and that one would've popped."

"But..." Questions rushed through her mind, then jammed up before she could decide which to ask first.

Cully twisted around to look up at her. Even in the harsh shadows and stark light thrown by the flashlight he looked particularly grim. "Seems like somebody wanted you to get down the road some before the cut broke through and you had a flat."

"It must have happened in town this afternoon. The car was in the alley behind the shop."

He shook his head. "I don't think so. These cuts were deep enough that you wouldn't have gotten halfway up the road to Boone and Cambria's house if your tire had been cut in Bardville."

"But that means... How could somebody have gotten to the car at the house?"

"It wouldn't have been hard. Your car was farthest from the house and this side wouldn't have been visible even if we'd been looking right at it, as long as somebody stayed low. All they had to do was park away from the house, come up quiet, cut the tire, then slip back and wait for you to go past. Give you a little head start, then come down after you, knowing you'd be pulled over somewhere along here with a flat. Most likely well before you reached the highway.''

Her lips felt numb, her throat tight. ''Who would do that? *Why* would anyone do that?''

Cully rose slowly, brushed his hand off on the side of his jeans and turned off the flashlight before he answered.

''You'd know the answers better than anybody else, Jessa.''

While he changed the tire, followed her home and insisted on checking through her house before she entered, she came up with no real answers. Only fears.

Cully pulled up by the cabin he and Travis shared and turned off the ignition. He sat there, letting the silence flood in to replace the engine's drone. Then listening as the silence dissolved into individual sounds of the night.

Finally, stifling a sigh, he got out. He rubbed at the back of his neck and rolled his shoulders. He was weary. Not tired, not muscle aching. But weary from the inside.

The cabin was dark. He'd always had good night vision and he made his way across the living room to the sofa bed where his nephew slept with no trouble.

Aunt Philly had said his peculiar eyes gave him the ability to maneuver in the dark. More likely it came from prowling around the old ramshackle house he'd grown up in. Usually he'd been checking on his mother. If she was passed out, he could have set the place on fire and she wouldn't have cared, but if she wasn't that far gone and he turned on even the smallest light, she'd scream and curse him. He wouldn't have minded so much, but it woke the others. Manny, especially, was hard to settle down again.

Once in a while his night prowling had been to let his father into the house without rousing his mother, so there'd be one fewer fight—dodging a raindrop in the middle of a flood.

Travis was asleep, his breathing regular and deep, his face relaxed. Without the sneer that usually guarded it he looked very young. He looked very much like Manny. Cully could almost make himself believe it was Manny he was watching over. Manny before he grew up. Manny before he battled the bottle. Manny before he gave up the battle.

But it wasn't Manny. Manny was dead.

For an instant, the pain was so fresh, Cully almost cried out with it.

He tipped back his head, closed his eyes and reminded himself what he had to do. He drew a slow, even breath, then reached for the pack Travis often carried.

He sat on the sturdy coffee table and searched his nephew's pack methodically and silently. Travis never stirred.

In the bottom of a deep interior pocket, he found what he'd feared.

A four-inch-long red-encased pocketknife, with gadgets and tools galore. And with a sharp blade long enough to have made the cuts in Jessa's tire.

He glanced at Travis's sleeping face, then away.

It didn't matter that Travis looked innocent lying there. Cully had seen a double murderer who could have passed for a choirboy.

If Travis did the tire cutting, he couldn't have done it alone. He'd have needed transportation. He'd have needed an accomplice. Someone old enough to drive, and someone who knew the area. Denny Sorenson.

Cully had waited for Jessa to bring Travis or Sorenson up as a possible culprit. She hadn't. Lord, the woman was stubborn. She was determined to see only good—not only in Travis, but in this Sorenson kid, who seemed well on his way to becoming a thug. It was foolhardy, possibly dangerous...and maybe he was jealous because she didn't show much inclination to see the good in him.

Holding her had felt so right. And so frustrating. When he found himself wishing they could stand like that for a couple of days, it was time to let go.

It was hard. Nearly as hard as leaving her in her small house, with her careful composure.

The ache in his right forearm brought Cully back to the moment. He'd clenched a hand around the pocketknife so tightly his muscles were complaining. How long had he been sitting here, letting his mind wander?

He silently slipped the knife back into Travis's pack and went to bed.

All it took to break Jessa's concentration was the shop's front bell filtering to the office. The bell hadn't been quiet all morning—good for business, bad for Jessa's productivity.

Every time the bell sounded, she tensed, waiting to hear who it was.

"Hello, Cambria. How're you doing today?" At Rita's greeting to the new arrival, Jessa's muscles eased and she focused on the tax forms she should have finished this morning. *Would* have finished if her mind hadn't ricocheted like a demented Ping-Pong ball from a Southern-slow drawl to a pair of piercing blue-green eyes.

How could he irritate her so much, as he had with his assumptions about Denny Sorenson? Then make her feel so connected to him, as he had when he'd spoken of his past. And then make her feel so protected, as he had holding her by the side of the road.

She shook her head and picked up her pen. This was not the time to be thinking of that. She'd ticked off only two items, when the door from the shop creaked a warning and Cambria appeared.

"Busy?"

"Moderately. But come in."

"I came into town with Cully and thought we'd have lunch."

"'We'?"

"You and me. Don't get so prickly. Cully only came in here to get new sunglasses because his others broke."

She had cause for being prickly. She didn't want to think about Cully. She didn't want to wonder about him. She sure didn't want to go to lunch with him. She just couldn't say that to Cambria, not without a discussion she didn't want to get into. She was feeling cranky about the whole situation.

"He'd need solid steel to hide those eyes." *Or at least to protect me from feeling they see too deeply and feel too much.*

Too late, Jessa realized that first, Cambria's words meant she hadn't come in alone, and second, the shadow behind Cambria was long and lanky. Blue-green eyes pinned her to her chair, while heat flashed across her cheeks.

"Didn't see any steel models on your rack," he drawled. "Hope polarized will do."

He slid on darkly tinted aviator glasses. It didn't help.

"I'm sorry. I didn't mean—"

"No need to be polite." He took off the sunglasses and tapped them rhythmically against his thigh. "I told you that."

All the more reason she intended to keep a curtain of politeness between them. That and the sudden urge to slide her hand along the denim-covered length of his thigh.

"I thought you were going to Billings."

He quirked a brow at her. "Had a late night last night, so I decided to do it another morning."

Turning from him to Cambria, who watched the exchange with avid interest, Jessa blatantly brought the conversation back to its original topic. "Sorry, I can't join you. I got a late start and I've got a lot to do. Have a nice lunch, Cambria."

"A late start?" Cambria looked significantly from Jessa to Cully.

He returned the look blandly. "I expect Jessa was getting her tire seen to this morning."

Cambria's look of bright expectation dimmed. "What's the matter with your tire, Jessa?"

"I had a flat last night on the way home, that's all. Cully came by and—"

"A flat?" Cambria demanded as if she didn't quite believe it.

"Helped me fix it. And Cully's right," she added, hoping to stem more questions. "I stopped off first thing to deal with the tire. I didn't want to be driving without a spare."

"Good. After I leave here, I've got work to do for the sheriff, and I'm going to tell him about last night."

"There's no need—"

She didn't have a chance to get out more than that before Cambria weighed in.

"The sheriff? Why would he be interested in a flat tire?"

"Because the reason it was flat was it had been cut."

"What?" Cambria's head whipped around from Cully to Jessa. "And you didn't tell me? You didn't tell anybody?"

"A flat tire is not worth going to the sheriff about."

"Even if it was meant as a prank," Cully responded, "you could have been hurt. A tire suddenly going flat could have pitched your car into the ditch. Or it could've blown."

"It didn't, so there's no reason—"

"Your tire was *cut*, Jessa. That's plenty of reason," argued Cambria.

"That's Cully's theory. There's no proof—"

"He's a professional, Jessa. He knows about these things." She turned back to him. "Cully?"

"It was cut. Deliberately. Whoever you took the tire to will tell you the same thing, Jessa."

"I took it to the dump and bought a new one."

He tapped the folded sunglasses against his thigh. "That's not going to stop the guy who followed you last night. He'll be back."

"What guy?" Cambria was in full outrage. "A guy followed you? Who? What the hell went on last night?"

Cully gave a succinct account of the incident the night before. One thing about cops, Jessa thought gratefully, they didn't indulge in highly emotional accounts designed to inflame the anxiety of overprotective friends.

It didn't matter. Cambria's anxiety was already fully inflamed.

"I'm calling Boone. He's got connections. He'll get you twenty-four-hour protection—"

"No!" Jessa had seen Cully's eyebrows climb, and it made her answer sharp. There was no reason to tell him the unpleasant details of her past. But if Cambria kept going that's exactly what would happen. She put a full load of warning into her next words. "We'll talk about this later, Cambria."

"We'll do more than talk. We'll—"

"I better be going," Cully interrupted. He straightened away from the shelving unit he'd used for support. Jessa didn't know whether to be thankful for his willingness to leave or suspicious. "Turns out I've got an extra errand before I go see Tom Milano."

"Errand?" Cambria demanded.

"Yep. Gotta stop by the dump and pick up a tire."

"Cully—"

"Good!"

With her protest cut off by Cambria's approval, Jessa gave up. She suspected the only way to stop Cully would be to try to outwrestle him for the wretched tire, and there wasn't much chance she'd win.

"I'll be seeing you, ladies."

He was barely out of the office area, when Cambria demanded, "Well? What are you going to do about this? It's got to be that maniac, Glenn Kaye."

Jessa waited for the sound of the door to the main shop closing before answering. "It's not Glenn Kaye. I called the prosecutor in Maryland this morning. He looked into it and called me right back. Kaye has checked in with his parole officer the way he's supposed to. He hasn't missed an appointment, and he has a job."

"So? He could fly to Billings and drive here any day of the week, and they wouldn't know."

"He could," Jessa agreed with a calm she didn't entirely feel. "But the prosecutor and parole officer are sure he hasn't. And they don't think he will."

"That's enough for you?"

"It's going to have to be. I'm not going to hide, Cambria. And I'm not going to move again."

"Boone could make some calls—"

"No."

"Jessa—"

"No."

Cambria stared at her for a long moment, then abruptly sighed. "At least tell Tom Milano—and Cully."

"Cully? Why would I tell him?" *Other than because he'd held her last night when she'd felt as if she might splinter. Held her until she put herself back together. Then let her go without asking for explanations and answers.*

"Because he knows this stuff from being a cop, and he might be able to help you. And I'm damned sure he wants to help you."

Jessa didn't have the energy to fight that fight again. She held off Cambria's continued arguments with a palm out. She loved Cambria dearly, but her friend was stubborn enough to wear down the Rock of Gibraltar.

"I promise you I'll tell Sheriff Milano the whole situation. Is that good enough?"

"No. But I suppose it'll do—for now. As long as you go over there now." Jessa opened her mouth to protest, but Cambria hadn't finished. "Don't give me any excuses. The real reason you don't want to go over there is Cully.

But he's not there, remember? He's making a detour to the dump, so you've got plenty of time."

Halfway through telling Sheriff Milano of the previous night's incident, Cully was certain Milano knew more than he did.

It wasn't anything he said. Because, in fact, he didn't say anything, just settled in his big chair, listening. It was the *way* he didn't say anything.

Cully finished by offering, "I've got the tire if you want to see it."

"No sense. You know a good sight more about it than I do."

The sheriff seemed inclined to leave it at that. Cully was not. "What are you going to do, Sheriff?"

"Better question might be what you're thinking you'd like to be doing if you could."

"Me? What does that have to do with anything?"

"Humor an old man. What do you want out of all this?"

"To do what's right." The words sounded stiff, awkward. "To make sure no harm comes to Jessa or—"

"Well, now," the sheriff interrupted with gusto, as if Cully had said the very thing he'd hoped for, "that's not so simple, figuring out what's right."

"It used to be. It used to be clear-cut." Cully knew the thoughts were his, but was uneasy they came out so harsh.

Sheriff Milano scratched his ear, and tipped back his chair. "Now, I've given that a deal of thought, and I don't believe that's so, Cully. It wasn't so all-fired clear-cut any time I remember. It's only looking back things seem simple. It's like being in battle. It's not till history books start writing about it that it's all strategy and counterstrategy and such, with lines moving here and flanks there. When you're in the middle of it, it's smoke and smell and confusion and fear. You're trying to move forward a foot without getting shot dead. That's what life's like. It's not till you get a ways down the road you can look back and see where you've come from. Can see where you took a wrong path, too.''

"Sheriff, I appreciate the philosophy, but I'd think you'd be more interested in a citizen's safety. Somebody wanted her to have a flat tire on a deserted road at night. I'd put money on Sorenson—'' Milano hadn't been unduly surprised by Cully's account of that incident, either. The grapevine was working overtime. "But whether it was him or somebody else, I don't like it.''

"Don't imagine you do.''

The old fox thought he had a hold of something. Cully kept words and tone neutral. "People like that give me a bad feeling trouble's coming.''

"Any time you have people, you've got potential for trouble,'' Milano observed. "Folks have been looking to start Utopia for as long as they've walked and haven't succeeded yet.''

Exasperated, Cully stood. "Fine. I'll check into it myself.''

"It's my county, son.'' Even with his genial expression intact, it was clear the sheriff meant business.

"You're not going to do anything, but you're warning me off?''

Tom Milano steepled his fingers over his rounded middle. "You like baseball, Cully?''

"What?''

"Baseball. Pitcher, batter, World Series, hot dogs, home runs. You like it?''

The sheriff clearly intended to take this road. The only choice was to follow and see where it led.

"I like it well enough.''

"Yeah? Me, too. Like to watch the kids play. Pete Weston, he's a fine player. Don't get to see much pro ball, 'cept on TV. But I did one summer when I was in your neck of the woods. Training course near Washington, D.C., at a place called Quantico.''

Cully had parted his lips to tell this Wyoming sheriff

that hundreds of miles in distance and light-years in attitude separated his North Carolina home from D.C. The final word stopped him.

"*Quantico?*" The FBI Academy, where they trained agents and offered a special course for law enforcement officers from around the world, was in Quantico. Competition to get in was fierce.

Milano linked hands behind his head and grinned. "Learned some real important lessons there. Sorta like the one you're learning right now."

"What lesson is that?"

"Sometimes things ain't what they seem." Milano looked at him from beneath lowered eyelids. "Same thing for people."

Cully said nothing. He'd heard this refrain before.

"Though, I'd have thought a smart guy like you would've caught on sooner," Milano mused. "Still, some folks have a blind spot. Now, like I was saying, that spring at Quantico, some of the boys and me got ourselves up to Baltimore a couple times to see the Orioles play. I followed them regular after that."

Milano rocked forward and back, his chair creaking in protest.

Cully waited.

"The year they won the World Series I was reading near everything about 'em. That's how I came across this quote." He stopped rocking. "Least I think it was in the series. Could've been the play-offs."

"Does it matter?"

Milano lifted a hand. "You got me there, because it doesn't. Not a bit. Play-offs or World Series, the paper had an article after a game talking to this Orioles pitcher, name of Mike Boddicker, and he said something real interesting. Don't know if I remember it exact, but it was something like 'All I can do is do the best I can do. I can't do anything else. It's really very simple.'" Milano nodded. "That's what he said, 'It's really very simple.'"

They weren't talking about baseball anymore. Maybe not law enforcement, either.

"What if your best isn't enough?" Cully asked with detached curiosity.

"Then you gotta let it go," Milano said. "You can't do anybody else's best for them. You're not the whole team. You're one part. It's not all your glory if you win. It's not all your shame if you lose. You can only do *your* best."

Cully stood. "Thanks for the fable, Sheriff. But I don't see anything easy about that."

"Didn't say it was easy. Said it was simple. Some of the simplest things aren't easy at all. Like living a good life. Being a good friend. Loving a good woman."

Cully had no answer. He turned the doorknob and opened the worn wooden door with its hazy glass.

"Interesting thing is—" Milano's voice came from behind him "—I can't remember which game it was he was talking about. Coulda been one he won. Coulda been one he lost."

Maybe he was being a sap.

The possibility didn't bother Cully much, but the potential results did.

There was the knife in Travis's bag. The cuts in Jessa's tire. Transportation by way of Denny Sorenson, who'd threatened her. And, no matter how much she thought the boy was opening up to her, Travis's attitude toward working for Jessa.

He had more than enough to tackle Travis with.

Jessa thought he'd been rough on the boy? She didn't know what rough was. If it was a choice of Travis's sensibilities or Jessa's safety, Cully had full confidence in scaring the boy enough to end any shenanigans.

What stopped him was this feeling that more was going on than he knew.

There was Cambria's reaction to Jessa's cut tire. She

wasn't thinking of Denny Sorenson when she'd talked about getting protection for Jessa.

There was Milano's knowing-more-than-I'm-saying attitude.

There was even Boone, with his sidestepping of questions about Jessa's attitude on cops.

And, of course, there was Jessa.

He made a decision.

He'd hold off tackling Travis until he'd tackled her.

He headed for Irene Weston's kitchen, looking for an ally.

Chapter Nine

A metallic knock jerked Jessa around.

Cully stood in the doorway, propping a shoulder against one side, with a hip cocked insolently out, sunglasses in place and a hint of a grin on his wide mouth.

Jessa's heart thundered and her throat closed. A reaction to the scare he'd given her. *That's all.*

"Sorry I startled you. I came in the front door this time. Rita said to come on back."

"If you'd come in the back door, you would have set off so many alarms the county would think we're under attack. And you didn't startle me," Jessa lied. "I'm doing paperwork."

"They're mostly silent alarms. There's only one loud one—that's to scare the real amateurs and make the semi-pros think they've taken care of any alarms."

"I see. Did you come to explain all this?"

"No. Irene Weston asked me to drop by these jellies." He straightened and she noticed a bag at his feet.

"Thank you." The jellies, jams and preserves Cambria's stepmother produced could brighten a whole winter of breakfasts.

"You're welcome. Irene said she expected you to come for supper last night."

"I called and told her I couldn't come." Jessa guessed he thought she'd skipped dinner with the Westons because he was there, and he was partly right.

After the past few days, especially the way she'd tumbled into his arms at the roadside the other night, she'd thought it better to stay away from him. He'd said she didn't know what he was thinking—he was right; she didn't have a clue what he was thinking. Worse, she didn't have a clue what *she* was *feeling*.

There'd also been the unpleasant and reminiscent matter last night when she got home from work and found her garbage strewn across her yard. Two of her neighbors were picking it up when she pulled in. An animal, Mrs. Griler had speculated, probably a raccoon, and Red Colback had concurred.

Jessa wasn't so sure. It was safer not to expose her uneasiness to Cambria's and Irene's sharp eyes, even without Cully being there.

Cully nodded toward the papers covering her desk. "Need help?"

"Not anything anybody can help with."

"Hey, cops are paperwork experts. And I got my paperwork training at the only place on earth that's worse—the army."

She smiled slightly. "I hear it's pretty bad."

"Pretty bad? You have to requisition toilet paper—it can't get much worse."

That surprised a chuckle out of her. "You're right. That's bad. So, why'd you stay in the army so long? You could have gotten out after a short hitch like Boone."

He shrugged. "I didn't mind short hair as much as Boone."

She considered him. He had the kind of face, with its strong planes and pronounced bones, that would look good with a military haircut. An image of Cully's rangy body in a uniform burst into her head without the least warning.

"There must have been more than not minding haircuts to keep you in the army."

His face was serious, his eyes intent. "I liked it."

"Having someone telling you what to do and when to do it and how to do it?"

"Having rules and discipline doesn't mean you don't think."

"What about all the horror stories about getting up early and drill sergeants and regulations?"

"All true. But they have a purpose. And some people like the rules and the discipline." He paused barely a second. "And the security."

Rules and discipline. Regulations and standards. She'd had her fill. But not Cully Grainger. He thrived on them. Could there be two people further apart in their thinking?

"Something wrong, Jessa?"

"What?" His quiet question made her aware of a tightness in her forehead and around her mouth, the kind that went with scowling. "No, nothing's wrong." She smiled brightly. "Rita says you're getting Tom to trust the computer. That makes you something on the order of a miracle worker. Between that and working with Boone you must keep busy. Do you do design work, too?"

Cully didn't answer right away. She glanced up and found him studying her. It didn't take military spies to figure out he was trying to assess her change of subject.

"Nope. I tote beams and hammer nails straight and hold something where I'm told, when I'm told. Learned in the army. I contribute brawn and no brains on this project."

"Must be kind of boring for you." For all that he presented himself as a slow-going, slow-talking good ol' boy, Cully was not slow thinking.

A lift of his mouth indicated he'd recognized her assumption. "I keep my brain occupied the times Boone's got no use for my brawn. Besides getting the sheriff's computer organized, Boone's got a nice computer setup I use. And there's always reading."

"What kind of reading?"

He levered himself away from the shelf with slow grace and took two steps toward the desk. She got up and filed the single sheet she'd finished, restoring the gap between them.

"Mostly professional journals. A cop's gotta keep up on the law, what the legislature's passed and how the courts interpret it, in order to enforce it."

"You aren't with a police department anymore." Instantly, she wanted to recall the words. A tightening of the skin over his jaw hinted it was a sore subject.

"Even private investigators or bodyguards or whatever have to know the law. It's interesting how laws keep changing. Laws have changed a good bit since I started. For cops around longer, it's like learning the job all over every few years."

Jessa turned away, reaching for a blank label and a marking pen to address a box she'd sealed before lunch.

She didn't want to have this conversation. Given a choice of conversational topics, the demands of law enforcement ranked near the bottom of her list, just above gall bladder operations.

She also didn't want to reveal how much she didn't want to have it.

"I suppose that's true."

"Take domestic violence. They used to just hush up the noise. Now there're all sorts of things they can do—intervention, counseling, arrest." Cully slid his narrow rear end onto her desk. "Some old-timers aren't as up on that as they should be—some younger cops, too. Comes back to reading and having an open mind."

He had one big, athletic-shoe-encased foot on the chair

seat and the other long leg extended. His whole pose proclaimed assured male.

"How fascinating. Now, if you'll excuse me." She stepped toward the desk.

He acted as if he didn't know what she wanted.

"Excuse me. I need something from the box behind you so I can get back to work."

He made a movement, and she thought he would get up. Instead he shifted to one side. "There you go."

She could reach the paper with the shipping information—if she stepped into the vee formed by his legs.

Swallowing, she parted her lips to ask him to get up, but nothing came out.

A lift of his eyebrows seemed to ask: *Are you going to get the paper?* After a slight shrug, he twisted around and pushed the box forward. One large hand gestured to it.

It was a dare. It was also a test. Not so much him testing her, as her testing herself.

"Thank you."

Head erect, back straight, she stepped closer. She still had to lean across the angled top of his outstretched leg, still had to face the awareness of his other thigh beside her hip, hemming her in. Still had to ignore the width of his shoulders and chest. Still had to cut through the heat and faintly earthy scent that swam off his body like the haze of a North Carolina scorcher. She clutched the top paper from the in box, grateful down to her curling toes that she didn't have to paw through the file for what she needed. Straightening, she had yet one more obstacle to overcome—the glint of his eyes through sunglasses, as they followed her every move.

"Thank you." A step free, and she drew in a gallon of air not tinged with his presence. His gaze followed that, too, and she realized his eyes caught not only her every move, but her every breath. She became excruciatingly aware of her breasts moving with each breath, of the slightest friction of them against the encircling fabric of her bra, like the lightest touch of a lover.

"You said that."

"What?"

"Thank you. You said it twice. You always so polite when you don't want to be?"

She raised her chin. "I was taught good manners are a requirement, not an option."

"Yes'm," he said in mock humbleness. "But I'd just as soon you didn't polish your good manners on me."

That surprised an unguarded "Why not?" out of her.

"I figure you've got being polite to a man all tangled up in your head with the way that man hurt you."

"What man?"

"Whatever man hurt you so bad that you're steering clear now. I figure he was either a cop, or a cop let you down when it came to dealing with the bastard."

"I don't—" She didn't know how she would have ended the protest, because he wasn't right, but he wasn't far off, either. He gave her no chance to finish.

"I figure being so polite's one way you keep distance from any man who tries to come too close. But—" He narrowed his eyes to a blue probe. "I don't want you confusing me with any other man."

Cully saw her face close off the instant before she dropped her head in apparent total fascination with the roll of tape she held. She retreated without moving a step.

He couldn't blame her.

He'd been pushing her since he walked in. Maybe pushing himself, too. Challenging her to step so close he could practically taste the jasmine at the same time he could feel her warmth on the inside of his legs. That hadn't been smart.

But the last few words were worse.

What was he doing telling Jessa something like that? It was practically a declaration. And he couldn't do anything with a declaration except take it back.

"Jessa, I'm sorry." He stood. "I shouldn't give you a hard time. It's none of my business what happened to you—if anything happened. I probably got it all wrong. When you go 'round thinking you can figure other people out—"

"No."

She said it so softly he wasn't sure he'd heard it. "No?"

"No." This time it was clear.

"No what?"

"No, it's none of your business. And no—" she drew in a quick breath "—you didn't get it all wrong."

He eased back onto the desk. She was going to open those secrets she'd been holding so tight.

Suddenly he wasn't sure he wanted to hear.

Complications.

"You don't owe me any explanations," he said gruffly.

"No, I don't. But after you helped me the other night... It's not a big secret or anything, I just..." She put down the roll of tape with a *thunk.* "I was stalked. That's it. No great mystery. A man who asked me out in Washington couldn't take no for an answer. That's all."

"That's all?" he repeated softly. "What happened?"

"This man came into the PR firm where I worked to fix our computer system. He asked me out to dinner the third day he was there. I said no thank you. I thought that was the end of it."

"Instead, he what? Called you all the time—home and work—followed you, sent letters and packages?"

"Yes."

"Worse?"

"Yes."

"Cut your tires?"

"Yes."

He released a stream of air. "Most stalkings start as domestic cases—estranged husband, rejected lover—"

"I never went out with him. I... Maybe I shouldn't have been polite when I turned him down." She looked at him—to gauge if he'd caught that chink of self-doubt in her armor of calm, he figured. He had, and she immediately looked away. "I was pleasant, no more. I didn't encourage him. I did nothing wrong."

"Didn't say you did." But he sure as hell wondered who *had* said that to her.

She opened her mouth, then shut it with a snap. He suspected she had a right to be defensive, and he pushed down a wave of anger at unknown strangers who had given her that right. She'd probably been asked, sometimes obliquely, sometimes point-blank, what she'd done to bring this on herself.

Cully knew the attitude Jessa had faced, had seen it in action, could understand her wariness. But he'd be damned if he'd let her paint him with the same brush.

"Look, anybody who's had a crime committed against them gets to feeling they're alone, hip deep in alligators, and I suppose that's especially true for a stalking victim—"

"I am not a victim." The intensity of her words seemed to vibrate in the small area. She turned partly away, fussing with a stack of boxes on the shelves. "Someone stalked me—I can't change that, but it's up to me if I become a victim because of it. If I let it rule my life, then I'm truly a victim."

"I can understand that." He could admire it, too. "I know how you feel, but—"

She spun back to face him. "You know how I feel? You have no idea how I feel. No idea. You know what the police called it? Harassment. Doesn't sound so bad, does it? A misdemeanor. A trifling matter, really. Unless it's your life."

"Jessa..."

"Have you ever had a burglar alarm that couldn't be cut off—one of those blaring car alarms? It's like that. On and on. Never quitting. Only, this alarm follows you everywhere. You can never get away from it. Sometimes it slips into the background, almost fades. Then bam, it starts again. Shrieking, so you hear it in your head even when it's quiet.''

"That's why you moved here?''

She looked up, her eyes midnight dark, then away. "Yes. They put him in jail eventually, but...I wanted a fresh start. Cambria's family needed her help with the bed-and-breakfast. The shop was available. It seemed like a good move. It *was* a good move.''

"Is he still in prison back East?''

"No. That's why Cambria was so wound up when you said my tire was cut.'' She held up a hand to hold off his words. "I checked with the assistant DA who prosecuted him, and Glenn Kaye has been a model parolee. There's absolutely nothing to indicate he's been anywhere near Bardville.''

"I'm glad you checked. I hope you don't mind if I check.''

"I do mind. There's no reason—''

"There's every reason.''

"Cully—''

"It's like I told you with the alarms—I've got my nephew to think of. I told you I've been reading, and stalking's a hot topic. One thing I've learned is most stalkers are the domestic type I mentioned. The ones who go after a stranger are even more likely to turn out to be nutcases.''

Another thing he'd read occurred to him: women who'd been stalked had a hard time trusting men. Any man who tried to get close to them they tested and tested again. It might not be fun for the man in question, but it made a lot of sense.

"You're trying to scare me,'' she said indignantly.

He sure was. It might make her more cautious, and, hopefully, it would persuade her to cooperate.

"Just telling you what I read,'' he said blandly. "But that's why I'd like to do some checking. His name's Glenn

Kaye? What jurisdiction was he prosecuted in, and who's the assistant DA?''

She looked startled he knew the stalker's name. He saw the moment she realized she'd told it to him, and there might have been a glint of respect in her eyes that he'd caught it and remembered it.

When she still hesitated, he added, "I could find out other ways, Jessa."

"The cops' good ol' boy network?" she said with an edge.

She really didn't like cops, did she? He added another name to his list to contact: the officer in charge of her case. But he wouldn't tempt this truce by asking her for that. "Actually, a computer network, but it boils down to the same thing."

After another moment of hesitation, she gave him the information. He thanked her, then stood to leave.

"One more thing." He didn't know he was going to go through with this until he stopped in the doorway. Not many minutes ago, he'd been wishing he could take back some words. Was history about to repeat itself?

"What?"

"Irene says you're to come to supper tonight. No excuses. She says if you don't come, she'll want the reason."

"Cully..."

It was as clear a warning as a yellow light. Like most drivers, he sped right through.

"Are you willing to tell Irene it's because you're afraid of me?"

"Travis, hold on there."

Cully snagged his nephew with a hand on his arm as he dashed for the cabin door.

"What? I gotta help Cambria feed the horses."

A spurt of pride warmed Cully. His prediction was coming true: Travis was becoming a fine horseman. And he

was proving reliable in his duties helping Cambria care for
the horses. He'd nearly taken over Pete's share.

The boy practically hummed with impatience, so Cully
cut to the point.

"Has Jessa ever told you anything about her past?"

Travis looked at him, then away. Cully awaited the eva-
sion.

"You mean like where she grew up and stuff?"

"Like why she came to Wyoming."

"Oh. She came here for a fresh start."

Travis's willingness to answer threw him off stride.
"Yeah? Why'd she want a fresh start, you think?"

"Some guy in Washington stalked her. A real jerk. He
messed up her garbage, broke windows and cut her tires,
and there was a fire or something. They put him in jail."
Travis looked out the screen door toward the barn. "Can
I go?"

"Yeah. Okay."

The words had barely left his mouth, before the boy was
gone, sprinting along the path toward the barn.

Cully stood watching him.

Well, now, that was real interesting. Travis knew Jessa
had been stalked. And he knew she'd had her tires cut and
some other specifics.

That should keep Travis right up there as a possibility
for having cut Jessa's tires last week.

Although his very willingness to admit his knowledge
so readily would argue against Travis's being the culprit.

But Cully kept finding himself wondering what else it
was the boy had been so relieved Cully *hadn't* asked about
that he'd talked so willingly about the stalking.

Being blackmailed into attending a dinner was not the
most comfortable sensation. Sharing the porch with one of
the coblackmailers as your sole company wasn't conducive
to small talk, either.

"Nice day," Cully said, taking a sip from his coffee cup.

"Yes, it has been." Jessa wished she hadn't come. She wished Irene hadn't shooed her out of the kitchen. She wished she hadn't encountered Cully alone on the porch.

As long as she was wishing, she wished her nerve endings wouldn't shimmer every time she was around this man.

"Good strong sun, but with enough of a breeze to keep it from being too hot."

He could at least have the decency to seem as uncomfortable with her as she so often felt with him. But there he stood, propped against the support pole, pronouncing meaningless observations like the best stereotype of a laconic countryman, totally at ease.

"Yes."

"Wind's moving those clouds along real well now."

She gritted her teeth. "Yes."

"Shaping up to be a fine sunset."

"And after that, it'll be a fine moon and a fine sunrise and another fine day. All right? Have we covered the weather?"

He had the gall to chuckle.

From the other end of the porch, the screen door to the kitchen squawked open.

"You'd think nobody in this crew was hungry." Irene stood at the door, hands on her aproned hips. "Where is everybody? Supper's ready."

"Travis and Cambria are down at the barn. Or maybe at the corral with Midnight," Jessa said, grateful for the interruption, even from the other half of the blackmailing team. "I don't know where Boone and Ted went."

"They're down at the creek," Cully supplied. "Cambria is with them. In fact," he went on, straightening slowly, "there she is."

They saw Cambria coming toward them, with the fig-

ures of her father and husband still some distance behind
her.

"Then where's Travis?"

Jessa's question had its answer in a terrified shout,
nearly drowned by the shrill scream of a horse.

In the fading light, the rearing horse with a small form
clinging to its back stood out for a frozen second as an
outline. Then the horse plunged and the sounds blurred
into a shriek of terror and fury.

Cully carried his coffee cup with him the first two
strides of his all-out sprint, then simply dropped it. Jessa,
close behind him, dodged to one side to avoid the splin-
tering pottery.

But Cambria was closest.

They saw her clamber over the fence and drop into the
corral before they were halfway there. It happened in an
instant—an instant that expanded into an eternity. Jessa
could see each frame of it, separate, individual, chilling.

Cambria, with her middle thickening with the child she
carried, moving in toward the horse. Picking up the trailing
reins. Talking softly, firmly. The shuddering horse, wild
eyed, but with all four feet on the ground. The flare of
hope. Then a movement from the saddle, and the powerful
animal rearing back, throwing the boy from the saddle,
dragging the woman who held his reins close.

So close she couldn't avoid the front hooves of the fren-
zied animal.

Cambria crumbled to the churned dirt of the corral.

Midnight jerked the reins from her slack fingers and
retreated from the shouting humans converging on the corral from the house and the creek. Travis stumbled to his
feet, went down to one knee, then stood.

Cambria didn't move.

Chapter Ten

Cully reached Cambria first. "Are you okay, Travis?" he shot over his shoulder, even as his hands went to pulse points at Cambria's throat and wrist.

"I'm okay."

The boy stumbled over the words and a sob, but once she heard the words and saw the truth of them Jessa paid no more heed to Travis. Travis was okay. Cambria wasn't.

She dropped to her knees by her friend. Cambria's eyes were closed. Dirt streaked a swath across her pale face and into her hair. Red bled through her blouse by her right shoulder.

"Is she...?"

"Strong, steady pulse. Breathing's good." Cully was stripping off his shirt as he spoke in terse bursts. He folded his cotton shirt into a rough pad. He slipped open two buttons on Cambria's blouse and slid the pad underneath it to her shoulder. "Hold that. Keep steady pressure, not tight."

He ran his hands along Cambria's arms, turning them gently, watching the reaction. Jessa wasn't surprised he knew what he was doing. He'd clearly had training, both in the military and as a civilian. Even if he'd had no training, she would have bet he would never panic in an emergency.

He'd started checking Cambria's legs, when they heard Boone coming over the fence, followed by Ted.

"Cambria!" Boone's hoarse shout drew Jessa's head around. Keeping her hold on the impromptu bandage, she moved above Cambria's head to give Boone the spot at his wife's side.

"Cambria," he whispered as he dropped to his knees in the dirt and took her hand.

Her eyelashes fluttered, then opened. "Hi, Boone."

It sounded so like Cambria's everyday voice Jessa strangled a laugh of sheer release, and Boone gave a half-choked chuckle.

"Hi, yourself."

Cambria started to shift, as if in preparation to sit up, and three sets of hands immediately stilled her.

"You stay right where you are," Boone ordered.

"Tyrant," she muttered, but she didn't try to move again. "I got thrown and I wasn't even riding," she grumbled. "Midnight?"

"He's fine. I'll take care of him," said Ted, without moving from where he now looked down at her, worry and love etched in his weathered face.

"Thanks, Dad."

"What do you think, Cully?" Boone asked.

"Nothing seems to be broken. I don't know about concussion, though her coming 'round so fast's a good sign. Looks like a hoof slashed her shoulder, and that'll need cleaning and stitches." His voice stayed even, reasonable and assured. It wouldn't be possible to panic when you listened to that voice.

Cambria's hands covered her abdomen protectively. "The baby?"

"You probably know best right now," Cully said. "How do you feel?"

"I hurt."

"Where?"

"Everywhere." She tried to smile. And failed. She grimaced. "I... I think I'm cramping." The movement of her throat showed she swallowed twice, as if the words were hard to force out. "I better see a doctor."

"You shouldn't move," Boone protested.

"It's okay, Boone." Jessa saw Cambria squeeze Boone's hand, and saw their eyes lock.

"But—"

"I'm sure everything's okay. I just want to see the doctor as a precaution." Jessa didn't believe her friend was nearly as certain as she tried to sound. "Besides, I'm not going to lie here in the dirt all night, waiting for the doctor."

The barest ghost of a smile eased the lines around Boone's mouth. "Okay. You're the boss."

"Glad to hear you admit it."

She started to make a move to stand, but Cully pressed her good shoulder back. "Oh, no, you don't. Ted? Do you have a board or something we can put her on? Wide enough to hold her, but that'll fit in the back of the station wagon."

"You think—" Boone began anxiously.

"I don't think anything," Cully interrupted. "But we're going to play it safe."

"I've got an old door in the barn. I'll get it." Ted started off.

"Good. You better get Midnight in there, too. Irene—" Cully turned to the woman who'd knelt in the dirt to hold her stepdaughter's hand, taking Cully's place. "Can you gather whatever Cambria might need to take along—purse, jacket, whatever—and some blankets and stuff? Make sure you get her doctor's number so you can call her once they're on the road.''

"Mama," Cambria murmured as the older woman levered herself to her feet.

"Don't you worry, Cammy. I'm going with you. I'll be there every step. I'm going to do what Cully said because it makes sense, but I'm leaving the doctor's number for *him* to call after we leave."

"Yes, ma'am," Cully agreed humbly as Irene moved past him toward the house to fulfill her duties.

Ted came from the barn at a jog made awkward by the burden of the door.

"I'll get the station wagon and back it up close to the gate," Jessa said.

"Good." For an instant her gaze met Cully's, and she saw such calm and strength there that she felt her own returning. Then she sprinted for the house and the car keys.

The three men carefully moved Cambria onto the door, then loaded it into the old station wagon. The movement started her shoulder bleeding again. Cully made a new bandage from the supplies in the first aid kit Irene had brought along with a bundle of blankets that they had tucked around Cambria.

Before Jessa would have thought possible, it was sorted out that Ted would drive, Boone would sit in back with Cambria and Irene up front beside her husband.

"Oh, gracious, I left the potatoes on the stove—"

"Irene, don't worry about a thing. I'll take care of it," Jessa promised.

"We'll take care of everything here," Cully amended, broadening her promise and sharing the responsibility.

Only when the station wagon disappeared from sight, smothered by its own dust plume, did Jessa turn and find Travis standing in the same spot in the corral, his face tight with fear.

She wanted to reassure him, to tell him everything would be okay, that it wasn't his fault. But it was. And she didn't know if everything would be okay. She could think of nothing to say to him. She could think of nothing but Cambria's pale face and pain-laced voice.

"C'mon," Cully said from behind her. "We better see about getting cleaned up, and then some supper. After that, you and I have chores to do, Travis."

Prosaic words, but Jessa felt as if they'd liberated her. Details of potatoes left on a stove, of cooking to finish and a kitchen to clean, flooded into her mind, pushing back ever so slightly the helplessness and worry.

"You're right. We have work to do."

She threw Cully a grateful look as she passed him. For an instant, she caught a glimmer of fear and worry behind his determination. On instinct, she placed her hand on his forearm. He covered it with his large, warm palm, and she knew the gratitude was not a one-way street.

Cully heard their voices as he moved quietly down the darkened hall of the main house. He'd put on a fresh shirt before supper. But feeding the animals had been a messier business than he'd expected. They sure as hell ate more than the three humans had put away in a tense, silent supper at the Westons' kitchen table.

The empty places at the large table had seemed a reproach.

After sending Travis to bed in the Westons' guest room for the night, he'd finished up in the barn, then taken time to shower and change. There was no remedy for this being a long, tense night, but he didn't have to smell like a horse barn.

Returning to the main house, he'd found the kitchen and the den empty, so he started down the hallway to the bedrooms. He stayed where he was, listening.

"Time to go to sleep now, Travis."

That was Jessa. She stood in the guest room doorway, looking inside, caught between the light streaming from the room and the shadows of the hallway.

"It wasn't my fault." Travis sounded as if he was in bed. He also sounded defensive.

Jessa said nothing.

"I didn't mean for anything to happen." This protest carried less defensiveness, more sorrow.

"I'm sure you didn't."

"I was sure I could ride Midnight."

"Cambria told you not to try."

"I thought I could ride him." Cully heard the plaintiveness in that, and even with a knot of anger and worry still tied deep in his gut, he felt regret for the kid's pain.

Apparently Jessa heard it, too. She took a couple of steps into the room, until he could no longer see her. When she spoke again, he guessed she was sitting on the edge of the bed, next to Travis.

"Cambria knows a lot more about horses than you do. But even if she didn't, Midnight is her horse. She makes the decisions about who can ride him and when. And everyone else has to honor her decisions."

"I didn't mean for Cambria to get hurt. Or the baby. I didn't mean for anything bad to happen."

"I know you didn't, Travis. I know you would never hurt them purposely. But not meaning for something bad to happen isn't enough. Your actions have consequences. Everybody's actions have consequences. Like Cully says."

Cully caught the muffled sound of a boy trying to pretend he wasn't crying. Then the sounds of Jessa moving to the door.

"I'm going to let you get some sleep now, and think about what we said." Neither her words nor tone gave any hint she was aware of Travis's tears. She was letting the boy preserve that bit of pride. "We'll talk more in the morning."

Cully stepped back, around the corner into the deeper shadows.

Jessa had been in the den about ten minutes when Cully came in. He looked from the magazine she was flipping through without attention to the TV turned on with the sound so low no human could hear it.

"Travis?" he asked.

"He's in bed."

"Thanks. I needed a shower, but I shouldn't have left Travis to you."

He sounded gruff, almost gravelly. He wore fresh clothes; his hair was nearly dry.

"It's okay. He talked a little. I think that's good for him."

Cully grunted as he sat in the overstuffed chair at right angles to the corner of the couch where she sat. Between the couch and chair was a square end table, where the telephone rested. It was within easy reach for both of them.

"And he probably wouldn't have talked to me."

"I'm not saying that, but..."

Jessa had been about to say Travis didn't need to hear Cully's same old lecture, when she realized that this time *she'd* delivered Cully's sermon. She'd wanted to comfort Travis, but she'd never considered telling him it wasn't his fault, that he didn't bear responsibility for his actions. And wasn't that what Cully had been saying all along?

"But?"

She'd have to think about this more. Later. "But it doesn't really matter, does it?"

"No, I guess not." He stretched his legs out and rested his head on the top of the chair's back. Despite the relaxed pose, she was aware of tension in him. In the tightness of his arms crossed over his chest, in the set of his shoulders. "We're not going to hear anything anytime soon. Maybe not at all. Why don't you go home and get some sleep? I'll call if there's news."

"Yeah, right. I'll drop right off to sleep like nothing's happened."

A ghost of a grin touched his lips.

"Okay. If you're going to stick it out here, why don't

you get comfortable? Take a shower, change into some of
those clothes Cambria has in the back closet down at the
cabin. I'll stay here by the phone.''

He had a point. A shower and fresh clothes would feel
awfully good. And there was no point being touchy about
using the shower in the cabin with Cully here in the main
house, waiting by the phone.

At least, that's what she thought until the moment she
caught a glimpse of herself stepping naked out of the
shower, framed in the steamy mirror by the jeans and shirt
Cully had worn earlier, which now hung from a hook on
the wall, and the can of shaving cream and razor he used
every day. It seemed oddly, joltingly intimate.

Hastily, she wrapped a towel around herself. But then
she stood there, dripping onto the bath mat, looking at the
accoutrements of Cully's daily life. Shampoo. Toothbrush.
Comb. Nail clipper.

A towel hung from one rack, still damp from the shower
he'd taken. A short time ago, he had stood where she did
now. Naked, as she was now.

A faint shiver trembled along her bare arms. She rubbed
her hands over flesh that should have felt chilled. It was
warm.

She dried herself with sudden urgency and jerked on
Cambria's clothes as if she were in a race. Only when
she'd closed the cabin door behind her and started toward
the main house did she slow.

What was she doing? Her best friend was in the hospital,
condition uncertain, and she was indulging in lustful
thoughts about a man she couldn't afford to want. Not if
she hoped to keep her emotional health intact.

Instead of going directly to the den, she went to the
kitchen, where she wiped counters already clean and
checked appliances already turned off.

When she went into the den, Cully was loading a tape
of *The Sting* into the VCR. It was perfect. Complicated
enough to require some attention, familiar enough that

when her mind inevitably slipped to Cambria, she didn't get lost in the twists.

With the credits rolling, Cully asked, "Anything you want to see next?"

Before she could answer, the phone rang. Jessa jolted. She reached for the phone, but Cully's hand was already on the receiver, and her hand covered his. His eyes met hers. Before the phone rang a second time, he released the receiver and slipped his hand from under hers, letting her answer.

"Hello?"

Cully grabbed the TV remote. He punched two buttons, and the tape stopped and the TV fell silent. Then he turned to her, clearly trying to read the news she was hearing from her face.

"Jessa? It's Ted. Everything's okay."

Jessa squeezed her eyes closed against tears of relief and gratitude.

"Thank God," she said. *And bless Ted for coming right to the point.* She opened her eyes and repeated for Cully, "Everything's okay."

She held the phone partly away from her ear and gestured for him to listen, too.

Cully moved beside her on the couch. Their heads nearly touched.

"Ted, Cully's on, too."

"Good. The doctors are going to keep Cammy through tomorrow night as a precaution, but they say things are okay." He chuckled quietly. "She told one doctor she wished he'd quit saying she was fine, when half her body ached. He said that's what she got for trying to wrestle a horse."

Ted went on to tell them the tests and procedures Cambria went through. Jessa swallowed. It hadn't been an easy night for her friend while doctors poked and probed in order to tell her she could still expect a healthy baby come October.

"We're all going to stay here until they release Cammy, if you two will keep an eye on things. If that's a prob—"

"We'll take care of things," Cully interrupted.

"Of course," Jessa agreed.

"Thanks. Jessa, Irene says if you'll look at the calendar in the kitchen, you'll see a phone number for the church committee she was supposed to go to tomorrow night. Could you call them in the morning?"

"Of course. Tell her not to worry about a thing."

"Good. Thank you. She fretted about the stove being left on, but I knew you'd take care of it. Cully, I'll give Dax Randall a call tomorrow and postpone his coming to shoe the horses. Other than that, if you'd feed the stock in the barn... Pete won't be back until tomorrow night from his baseball trip, but Travis knows how much feed the horses get." Cambria's father hesitated a moment. "How is the boy?"

"He's fine," Cully said.

"Good, good. Well, I guess that's all..."

"Ted?" Cully put his hand over Jessa's to hold the receiver steady. "You think Cambria would be up to a visit tomorrow? From Travis, too."

"She's got a lot of bruising, Cully."

"If you don't think it's a good idea for Cambria, say the word, Ted. But if it's Travis you're thinking of, he ought to see what Cambria's going through."

The line carried only silence for a moment.

"I'm sure Cambria would tell you all to come ahead," Ted said at last.

"Okay. Thanks. We'll see you tomorrow, then."

"Good night, Ted," Jessa added. "Thanks for calling."

She heard the other end go dead before Cully released his hold from atop her hand. Even as she replaced the receiver, she felt hot tears held back for so many hours begin sliding down her cheeks.

When she turned back to Cully, sitting solid and warm beside her, with understanding for their shared fear and relief in his eyes, it seemed the most natural thing in the world to move into the comfort of his arms as she had the dark night she'd had the flat tire. This time, also, to let the tears flow faster against the clean, crisp cotton of his shirt.

She felt his lips against her forehead, then in her hair, before the weight of his jaw capped the top of her head, tucking her firmly into his body. She held on as the tears eased.

Cambria was okay. Her baby would be okay. Everything was okay. And the man who held her and whom she held understood what that meant to her, because it meant the same to him—the safety and happiness of a dear, dear friend.

She pushed back from him slightly, and his hold on her immediately loosened. But he didn't let go, and she was glad.

"It's going to be okay, Jessa."

"I know." She smiled, while another tear slipped loose.

"Ah, Jessa."

He barely breathed the words. Then he leaned forward and touched his lips to her damp cheek. A second soft kiss touched below her eye, catching the teardrop. A third kiss closed her eyelids.

His mouth brushed against hers, and she sighed.

But that touch was not followed by others. She opened her eyes and found Cully watching her, his face intent, yet wary.

He'd given her solace. He would take nothing in return.

But she could give.

Without thinking any more than that, she closed the space between them and pressed her lips to his. She put her fingertips to the stubble-roughened line of his jaw and kissed him again and again.

It seemed to her later that they kissed for hours. Long, slow, deep kisses. Kissing mouths and faces and throats. Holding on to each other, touching each other's faces. Then kissing again. Always with an intensity less fiery than passion. Knowing the passion was there if they chose to let it loose. Choosing—maybe needing—to hold it in check.

It was the kind of kissing she had seldom known. The kind of kissing that was not a preliminary to anything else, but an end in itself. It satisfied. It sated.

Finally, the kisses slowed; the periods of simply holding each other lengthened. It seemed she had never been anywhere other than on this couch, in this man's arms.

She awoke knowing dawn would not come for still a couple more hours, and with no question of where she was. She was in the Westons' den. Stretched out on the couch. Wedged between the couch's back cushions and the long, tough body of Cully Grainger. With his arms wrapped securely around her and his shoulder and chest pillowing her head and shoulders.

He'd pulled an afghan over them at some point. But his body had provided not only pillow but blanket.

She started to ease up, thinking she'd crawl over his sleeping body and find a safer haven in the chair.

His right arm, the one that circled her back and ended in a hand resting on the side of her breast, tightened. He drew her back against him. Through the layers of fabric, his extended fingers brushed against her nipple, sending a jolt through her veins. Her leg jerked at the sensation, brushing against his groin and encountering a bulge that pulsed with heat even through the denim of his jeans.

Still he held her gently against his chest, urging her back to the haven she'd enjoyed.

"Relax." His voice was a rumbling rasp. "Go back to sleep, honey."

To her astonishment, she did.

How much tension could fit in the cab of a pickup truck? It sounded like one of those riddles that leads to a punch line, only Jessa couldn't think of a thing funny about the situation.

Driving to visit Cambria in the hospital took two of the longest hours in her life. Travis, in the center of the truck's seat, practically vibrated with nerves and discomfort.

Cully and Travis had gone off to the barn this morning to tend to the animals. She didn't know what Cully might have said, but there'd been no dissent from Travis about going to the hospital.

Cully, as usual, presented a facade of calm reasonableness, of a man as in control of his emotions and the situation as he was of the truck he guided along the straight stretch of Interstate 90.

But Jessa was coming to believe that's what it was—a facade. He kept his hold on the steering wheel easy and steady, but Jessa noticed not long after they'd started out that the truck's speed would pick up under Cully's heavy foot the way it might when a driver had other matters on his mind. Then the speed would abruptly be curtailed, as Cully apparently noticed the dial on the dashboard had spun way to the right. Then the process would repeat.

As for herself, Jessa wished this were all over so she could crawl off alone and pretend last night had never happened.

When she had awakened a second time, shortly after dawn, she was alone on the couch, with the afghan tucked securely around her. So far, so good. When she faced her reflection in the bathroom mirror, she realized it wasn't going to be easy to pretend last night hadn't happened.

Her lips remained slightly swollen from the many kisses. Her skin showed faint irritation, especially around her mouth and down her throat, from being rubbed by stubble. Maybe no one else would notice, but she did. And she couldn't imagine Cully would miss the signs.

What had she been thinking?

To make the mistake once, the way she had last fall, was foolish. To make it a second time was downright stupid. It was also totally unfair to Cully.

In her admittedly few brushes with a relationship since

being stalked, she'd been excruciatingly careful to be straightforward about her feelings and expectations.

As the three of them silently climbed out of the truck at the hospital parking lot, she vowed that when they got back to the ranch she would set things straight with Cully.

Cambria's shoulder was swathed in white and a Technicolor bruise streaked one side of her face. But her eyes were bright, she was sitting up, and she was as bossy as ever.

"Come in, you guys. C'mon in," she invited when she saw them through the partially opened door. Ted and Irene sat in chairs on the other side of the bed.

"You go in, Jessa," Cully said. "Travis and I'll wait."

"All of you come in," Cambria said.

"You're not supposed to have more than three visitors at a time, Cambria. They told us downstairs."

Cambria snorted. "What do they know? I know what'll make me feel better, and it's having all you guys around me."

Irene stood. "Ted and I'll go get a bite to eat while you're here to sit with Cambria, and that'll keep the number at three."

Cully put a hand on Travis's shoulder to steer him into the room.

"You're going to eat lunch out?" Cambria sounded inordinately dismayed.

"We'll bring you something back," Irene said. She kissed Cambria's cheek, then patted Cully's arm as she passed him on her way to the door. Jessa wondered if the gesture was meant to reassure or calm. Either way, she thought Travis probably needed the support more at the moment. His face had gone decidedly paler than Cambria's, and the hands holding his skull and crossbones baseball cap in front of him had a death grip sure to leave permanent wrinkles.

"Promise, Mama?" Cambria asked.

"Promise. But no pizza."

"She's been trying to get us to order in pizza." Ted wore a big grin. "She doesn't think much of the cooking here."

"It's not food—it's torture."

With farewells said to Ted and Irene, Jessa took a chair. Travis remained standing at the corner of the bed, with Cully still beside him, still with his hand on his nephew's shoulder. Cambria smiled, but Travis couldn't have seen it, not with his gaze trained on his toes.

Cambria turned to her. "How'd it go last night at the ranch?"

Jessa felt a flush burning her skin. "Fine." She hurriedly added, "I borrowed some clean clothes of yours. I hope you don't mind."

"Of course not." Cambria's gaze turned speculative, and her gaze seemed to linger on Jessa's throat. "I never liked that high-necked blouse much. It was in the back closet, wasn't it?"

"Yes, but..."

"Travis slept in the guest room and Jessa and I sat up in the den by the phone, waiting for Ted's call." Cully's interruption was level and emotionless.

Jessa was torn between relief he'd cut through the cat-toying-with-a-mouse tension and embarrassment at the acknowledgment of the direction of Cambria's questions.

"Ah." Cambria's tone was too knowing by half.

"Where's Boone?" Jessa asked, partly to fill the silence, mostly to change the subject.

"Went to find a pay phone. He was driving me and the doctors nuts, so I reminded him it had been a couple days since he called his office, and suggested he check in."

"That's dirty."

"Hey, they're paid to deal with his instinct to take on the troubles of the world."

"I thought you'd reformed him, Cambria."

"He's relapsed the past twenty-four hours. It's their turn to handle his General Manager of the Universe act. Besides, they're a thousand miles away and they're not stuck in the hospital.''

"No, they're not stuck in the hospital." Cully's grim tone put an abrupt end to the lighter mood in the room.

Cully's hand tightened slightly on Travis's shoulder, and the boy took a half step forward.

"I...uh." He swung his head around, as if looking to Cully for help.

Cully returned his look steadily.

Travis gulped, and Jessa thought he might be on the verge of tears. But he faced Cambria again. "I don't see any, you know, machines hooked up. Like you see on TV." The words came out in fits and starts, with full stops between them.

"Not anymore. They had me hooked up to a fetal monitor last night.''

"Oh." It was strangled with panic.

"But everything's okay," Cambria said hurriedly. "That's why it's not on anymore."

"Oh." This time the syllable released a ton of anxiety and drew in relief.

"The baby's doing just fine," Cambria added, still focusing on Travis. "We talked to Pete on the phone this morning and he says it's a sure sign the baby'll be a cowboy, because it already knows how to take a fall.''

Travis's mouth moved, but nobody would call it a smile. He glanced up for the first time, then immediately down, as if Cambria were the sun and the glare hurt his eyes. He looked over his left shoulder to his uncle once more. Jessa could read nothing in Cully's face, but perhaps Travis took some comfort or some strength from it, because when he turned back to face Cambria, he issued a spate of words.

"I'm sorry. I'm real sorry you got hurt, Cambria. And the baby... I'm glad it's okay. I didn't mean—" He gulped and clutched the hat tighter. "But I shouldn't have taken him out—Midnight. Not after you told me not to. See, I thought… I was doing so good, and I thought… But I couldn't. I shouldn't have taken him out."

"No, you shouldn't have," Cambria said evenly. "It was very dangerous. That's why I told you you couldn't ride Midnight."

"I know. You could've been hurt real bad—I mean, even worse. And the baby."

"That's right. You could've been hurt, too."

Travis shrugged. Jessa wondered if he didn't believe it or didn't care.

"And Midnight could have been hurt. We might have had to destroy him."

Pulled out of his self-absorbed discomfort, Travis looked straight at Cambria for the first time. "You mean like if he broke a leg or something? Like they do with racehorses?"

"That could have happened." She nodded. "Also, with a horse like Midnight, you worry about his being ruined in other ways. You see, the man who owned him first didn't know about training horses, only about breaking them. Midnight wouldn't be broken and the man got rougher and rougher. When I got him last summer, Midnight didn't like people and he sure didn't trust people.

"It took almost two months before he got used to me being around. After I was away for the winter, it took another month this spring to get back to where we were last fall."

"What'll this do to him?" Travis asked in a small voice.

Cambria shook her head. "I don't know."

Travis considered the hat in his hands. Jessa and Cambria exchanged a look, a mutual wondering of how much of this lesson Travis was absorbing, then Cambria's gaze went to Cully. He was watching the boy.

"He was scared," Travis mumbled.

Cambria frowned. "What?"

"He was scared—Midnight. When I was saddling him and then when I was on him. He was trembling like, and making that blowing noise. And a high sound like a...a—I don't know what to call it.''

"A scream," Cambria supplied.

"Yeah. Like a scream. I think Midnight was scared."

"You're probably right."

"If I let him get used to me, if I show him there's nothing to be afraid of... I could go to his stall, let him get used to me and—"

"Oh, no. We'll stick with Snakebit and Jezebel for your lessons for a while," Cambria said. "I don't know about you, Travis, but I don't think my rear end can take another close encounter with that corral ground anytime soon. That dirt's *hard*."

"You don't go near that horse," Cully said in something close to a growl, "unless Cambria tells you it's okay, I tell you it's okay and you're with Cambria or Ted. Or you'll have a close encounter with something else hard."

To Jessa's amazement, Travis merely ducked his head and muttered, "Okay."

Chapter Eleven

On the drive back, Cully started talking.

First he told a story about his first time visiting a hospital. His great-aunt Philly took him and his two younger brothers to pick up their mother and new baby sister.

"For years," Cully said, "I thought if you wanted a baby boy you had the birth at home, because that's what my mother did with the first three kids and we were all boys. If you wanted a girl, you went to the hospital."

The anecdote held no great drama, but Jessa's heart pounded harder. Cully was trying to reach out to Travis. And she knew, both from the quality of his listening and his sidelong glances toward his uncle, that Travis was interested.

He probably hadn't heard family stories like these. From things Travis had let drop, she'd realized his mother had discouraged contact with his Grainger relatives—until she needed Cully's help—so it was unlikely she would have told their family stories.

Travis's craving was apparent when he actually asked a question.

"I guess my dad was always a perfect kid, huh?"

A perfect kid. So unlike him. A father, now dead, whom he could never live up to. Jessa held her breath, praying Cully didn't add to that burden for the boy.

Cully snorted. "Don't believe I've ever seen a perfect kid. Manny sure wasn't it. I guess I wasn't, either."

Relief and something like joy stung her eyes.

She listened with pleasure as Cully told stories about his siblings' childhood pranks, centering on Manny. Jessa doubted Travis noticed the absence of his grandparents from these stories. She did. By listening carefully, she could tell Cully had shouldered most of the responsibility and everyday care of his siblings.

It took less careful listening to realize how Cully pointed out how Manny had tried to be better as he grew older. Stories of pranks mixed in with stories of striving.

"How...how'd my dad, you know, uh, get along with his dad?"

The truck cab was silent a full minute.

"Our dad wasn't around a lot of the time, Travis."

"Did he drink, too?"

Cully cut his eyes to his nephew, then over his head to Jessa.

This was hard for him.

She remembered telling him to talk to Travis about the things they had in common. God, she hadn't thought it would be something like this. Still, she was more convinced than ever that having Cully talk to him would help Travis—especially about this.

She'd felt the echo of her own isolation in Travis; she'd seen the signs. He felt no one understood how he felt. Who better to let him know someone did understand than a man who had shared childhood with his father? But how would it affect Cully?

"Some. Mostly he was just gone. It was our mother who drank."

Travis digested that in silence. "My teacher in school said drinking is like a disease a family gets. Is that how come Dad drank, because his mom drank?"

Cully's voice sounded tight. "I 'xpect it had something to do with it."

"It's something you can't help, I guess."

"It's hard—no disputing that—but people can lick it."

"Did you?"

"I haven't had to lick it, not like your daddy. But he did it once." Cully glanced at his nephew. "Did you know that?"

"No."

"Your dad started drinking when he wasn't much older than you. He said he didn't like it, but he couldn't shake it, not for a long time. Then he found out your mom was pregnant with you. That's when he quit. He said he wouldn't have his child brought up by a drunk."

There was so much pain in this for Cully. Memories of his own difficult childhood, and the fresher loss of his brother. The stories he'd told Travis had told Jessa something more—how deep his bond with Manny had been. He must have felt as betrayed as Travis did by Manny's suicide.

But Cully hadn't allowed himself to show it.

He'd had to be strong. First for his brothers and sister, now for Travis.

He blinked hard and addressed his nephew. "He quit drinking for you."

"But..."

Cully nodded. "I know. He started drinking again. I can't tell you why. He was real upset about it. He tried to kick it. He tried a couple times."

"I remember..." Travis mumbled.

"He didn't want you growing up the way we did, Travis. He wanted better for you. He couldn't face..."

When Cully broke off, he turned his head as if checking traffic coming up in the left lane. But there wasn't any traffic.

Tears for a man she'd never known welled up in Jessa's eyes. Tears that Manny Grainger hadn't believed he could conquer his demon. Tears that he had believed the only way to protect his son was to kill himself. She fought them back for the sakes of the boy and man beside her.

"Is suicide a sin?" Travis asked abruptly.

"What?"

"Is it a sin? Does it mean my dad can't go to heaven? That's what Mrs. Jensen across the street said. That anyone who kills himself is an abomination in the eyes of the Lord."

"Mrs. Jensen should—"

"Cully." Jessa's only contribution to the conversation stopped his hot words, but his scowl didn't lift.

"I don't know about that, Travis. I don't know that anybody down here knows all the ins and outs of who gets into heaven. But I do know suicide's wrong."

His flat statement sparked familiar heat in Jessa. Why did he have to divide everything into right and wrong? But the anger died as quickly. After the past half hour she understood that dividing everything into right and wrong had helped Cully survive a childhood where nothing was right and too much was wrong.

"But if the only people who get into heaven," Cully was going on, "are the ones who don't do anything wrong their whole lives, then it's going to be damned empty. I'd think God would want more company than that."

Surprised, Jessa looked over Travis's head to the intent profile of the man driving the truck.

The strength she'd always sensed in him remained, built into his bones and soul. But she also saw beyond the obvious strength. She saw the concern and vulnerability and even tenderness.

Oh, God, she was very close to falling for him.

* * *

Cully stood beside her on the porch, not touching her. She was fully aware that he studied her profile a moment before joining her in staring out to the western horizon, where the blazing ball of the sun set fire to a river of red in the clouds over the Bighorns' peaks.

He seemed in no mood to discuss the sunset the way they had twenty-four hours ago.

"I'm getting mixed signals, Jessa. Sometimes hot, sometimes cold. That's how I'm receiving them. Could be my fault—"

"No. No, it's my fault." She flicked a look at him. After a long, deep breath she turned to him. He shifted, propping one hip against the railing and met her face-to-face. "I'm sorry. I haven't meant to mislead you. That—"

"Is that what you've done? Mislead me?"

"Yes, I'm afraid I have. And whether I meant to or not doesn't matter. I apologize for letting you think there might be something between us when there's not."

Silence. Enough silence that the distant sounds of birds and the flutter of cottonwood leaves in the breeze seeped in. So much silence she wished he'd say something, anything.

Well, almost anything.

"There's not?"

His deep, soft question sent a shiver down her back and up her neck to tingle in her scalp. As if his voice alone was plunging her back into the madness of last night.

"There's not," she snapped.

"I could've sworn there was something between us." His drawl headed deep south. "Wouldn't you say Travis was something between us? And Boone and Cambria. They're all connections between us, wouldn't you say?"

"You know what I mean."

"Ah, maybe you mean something—" He was closer, looking down at her. His shoulders were ready to be held on to by a woman who might need something to hold on to if she happened to be kissed by a knee-weakening expert. "Something physical. Something sexual."

She retreated a step, to firmer ground, though no firmer knees. "Cully—"

"Is that how you're thinking of last night? Something entirely physical? I've got news for you, Jessa. There's a lot more to physical than that. Like there's a lot more than physical to what happened last night."

"I know. I—"

"I've got one question for you."

She'd retreated too often in her life. She spread her feet slightly. "And you think I owe you an answer? You think I owe you an explanation? Well, I don't. So don't bother asking. I won't answer that question."

"*That* question? You don't know what my question is."

"Yes, I do. You want to know why I didn't stop—" She searched for a word innocuous enough not to reignite memories. "Why I didn't stop *things* last night."

"That's not my question."

"*Right.*" She went full throttle on sarcasm. "Then what is?"

She saw the trap then, but he'd already sprung it.

"As long as you asked, I'll tell you. What I want to know isn't why you didn't stop kissing me last night—or last fall. It's why you *started.*"

"Why I started? There were two of us on that couch last night."

He raised a hand. "That's for damned sure. There were two of us. Just like last fall. And I want to know how it got to be two of us, when most times you make sure you're as far away from me as possible? I've got ideas about why you keep me on the outside of that locked door of yours. But why would you open the door even those cracks, when you're so good at keeping it closed and locked and bolted? That's my question, Jessa."

Her mind raced as fast as her heart. What did he mean he knew why she kept him outside a locked door? And what did he mean about her *letting* him in? He made it sound as if she'd wanted those nights to happen, made them happen. Her guard had slipped and he was there. Period. End of story.

"I told you—I don't owe you an ans—"

"You're right." He stepped forward, not quite touching her. "You don't owe me an answer. You owe one to yourself. So think about it." He brushed two fingertips to her temple, then slid his hand into her hair and cupped her head.

Maybe she was lulled by the softness of his voice or the gentleness of his touch. Maybe she was expecting the restraint of last night.

She wasn't ready for his mouth covering hers so completely, his tongue sliding into her mouth so easily, his rhythm demanding a response so blatantly.

The passion held back last night surged through her, arced between them like lightning.

She held on to him. She responded to him. She kissed him with power and need. His body was against hers, the chest that had pillowed her cheek now pressing her tingling breasts, making her want to move against him, answering the rhythm.

And when he ended the kiss, giving her a long, hard look before striding off to the cabin, he left her knowing she wanted him every bit as much as he wanted her.

Aunt Philly used to say a man who kidded himself took in only a fool. Cully had long prided himself on not being caught in that particular trap. But there was no denying he'd been kidding himself about Jessa Tarrant.

He'd told Boone he didn't need any more complications, and she qualified as a major one, but his plans to keep her at a distance had been nothing more than a fool fooling himself. She was under his skin, in his dreams and on his mind. It was not a comfortable state.

All of which left him unusually grim when he drove

Travis to the shop on that sunny Monday morning. His mood took a turn for the worse when he spotted a knot of spectators and two sheriff's department cars in front of Jessa's shop.

"What's happening?"

Travis's question from beside him were the boy's first words this morning. Practically his first words since they'd gotten back from the hospital.

"I mean to find out."

By the time he parked in front of the tiny video store two doors down from Jessa's shop, he could see a gaping hole in the glass transom above the main shop door and a slash of blue down the wall behind the cash register. Cully put the gearshift into Park with unnecessary force and jerked home the parking brake.

He spotted Jessa immediately. She was talking to Tom Milano, who had a comforting arm around Rita Campbell. Deputy Kasper was taking notes. Jessa's words were not loud enough for Cully to distinguish, but the tone was low and even. She was pale and she had her arms wrapped around herself as if to hold her ribs together.

Cully made himself scan the gathering around the door rather than go immediately to her. He recognized several owners of nearby shops from their worried will-it-be-me-next expressions. He knew Dax Randall and his son, Will, from the ranch next to the Westons. And, off to one side, he was not the least surprised to discover Denny Sorenson and two of his hangers-on. After mentally cataloging the remaining unfamiliar faces for future reference, he walked slowly toward Jessa's group.

The crunch of glass under his soles alerted her. She looked up, and for an instant, he thought she would move into his arms. The way she had the night her tire was cut. The way she had the night before last on the Westons' couch.

Instead, she hugged herself tighter and turned to the

sheriff. But Cully had seen the warmth of relieved pleasure in her eyes.

"Grainger, glad you're here." Sheriff Milano stretched out a hand to shake, keeping his left arm wrapped around the plump shoulders of Rita Campbell. "Tried to call you at the Westons', but you'd left."

Still looking at Jessa, Cully shook his hand.

"Are you okay?" he asked her.

"I'm fine," she said. "Everyone's fine. It happened before anybody got here."

"When?"

"'Bout an hour and a half ago," Milano supplied. "Plenty of light, but early enough nobody spotted our window breaker."

He could hear Travis talking about Jessa's stalker. *He messed up her garbage, broke windows and cut her tires....* Then something else. But the important thing was he could swear in any court in the land that an hour and a half ago he was having one devil of a time trying to roust Travis from bed and into the shower. The boy couldn't have been involved in this. *Thank God.*

But the relief didn't unsqueeze another knot in his chest. *So who was doing this?*

"The alarm—"

"Oh, it went off, but the night dispatcher's new and he was making himself some tea and the kettle was going off, so he didn't hear it right off. He didn't know how long it was going before he called Kasper. Soon as Kasper saw what was what, he called me. Jessa was on our heels, and pretty soon others started showing up to get town opened, and then word spread fast."

"Nobody saw anything?"

"Nope. But it looks like whoever it was threw a quart can of paint through the glass. It hit the wall behind the register and broke open. That's what the blue's from. How 'bout takin' a closer look? Kasper, put out the word we're looking for anybody around Bozeman Road at the right

time. Somebody mighta seen something without knowing
it." Milano squeezed Rita's shoulders before releasing her,
then started toward the shop's door.

Cully studied Jessa a moment. "I'm sorry 'bout that
quilt."

Her eyes widened, and he thought he saw tears form,
but she only nodded as he headed after the sheriff.

Cully was the only one to have said anything about her
quilt. As far as she could tell, the only one who had noticed
the drenching smear of blue paint across it.

The photo of her and the Westons also was covered in
blue and beyond repair. But she could get another copy of
the picture from Cambria; the quilting was irreplaceable.

She'd found it in an antique store during a school trip
to Philadelphia. The colors had faded and the fabric had
worn. But it seemed to her those were badges of endur-
ance. Scraps of fabric from a skirt had joined a kerchief
and a shirt sleeve and a shawl to start a second life in a
new design. They were no longer scraps but part of a
whole, thanks to the patient skill of a woman no doubt
long dead.

Jessa blinked back tears.

"This is a shame, Jessa." Dax Randall spoke from beside her.

"Yes. But no one was hurt. That's the important thing."

"You don't expect things like this to happen in Bardville."

"No, you don't."

"Look, Al at the hardware store has a piece of plywood,
and we've got tools in the truck, so as soon as the sheriff
says, Will and I'll cover the hole."

"Thank you, Dax. That's very kind of you—and Will
and Al."

"Okay. We'll get the plywood now."

Dax shifted from one foot to the other, then gave her a
quick, hard hug that surprised her so much she nearly lost

her balance when he released her abruptly and strode to his truck. She found herself smiling for the first time that day at the awkward, heartfelt sign of comfort from Dax Randall.

"Sheriff," she called, "can we clean up this glass?"

"Sure, sure. You go right on ahead. We'll be takin' the paint can, but I can't think of a reason in the world for you not to dispose of the glass. Can you, Cully?"

Cully was staring after the Randalls' pickup, heading toward the hardware store. Instead of answering the sheriff, Cully walked toward her.

"Who was that?" Cully indicated the departing truck with a jerk of his head.

"I introduced you to him a couple weeks ago here in the shop, remember? It's Dax Randall."

"As a matter of fact, you didn't. The man introduced himself. What I want to know is who he is."

"He's a rancher. Owns the place just beyond the Westons. You've met Will at the Westons'. And you probably met Dax's sister, June Reamer, who rents the cars at the airport. She's real nice. Very friendly."

She was babbling and she knew it. She felt unsettled. Mostly because of the broken window and the unpleasant memories it stirred. But she couldn't deny some of her off-balance feeling came from Cully's uncharacteristic curtness.

"Yeah, I remember her." But he would not be turned from the subject. "What is he to you, Jessa?"

"He's a friend."

"A friend," he repeated flatly. "That's all?"

"Yes, that's all. Why, you should have heard Cambria going on the other day about how Dax would be crossing multiple state lines faster than the speed of sound if he thought I was interested in him as anything other than a friend."

He didn't return her smile. "Are you?"

She saw no reason on earth she should clarify her relationship—more precisely her lack of relationship—with Dax Randall. No reason to reassure Cully Grainger, for heaven's sake. So she truly couldn't understand it when she opened her mouth and a firm, calm "No" came out. She even added, "I am not interested in Dax as anything other than a friend."

Cully relaxed. "Good." He started back to where Sheriff Milano waited, then stopped and faced her. Without any hurry he took off his sunglasses and looked directly into her eyes. "That's real good. Because you should know that I am."

"Interested in Dax?" she countered weakly.

Her heart hammered so hard, so fast her lungs burned as if she'd been running miles.

Cully grinned. Slow and hot. "Not hardly. Not damned hardly."

Then he was gone. And she was left to tell herself she wasn't shaken and her pulse wasn't skittering. He wasn't serious and he wasn't dangerous.

Lies, all lies.

Jessa was sitting on the desk, with one foot on the chair seat, and talking on the phone when he entered her office that afternoon. He started to back out, but she waved him in. She finished her conversation quickly, hung up and asked, "Have you found anything?"

"No. I want to talk to you." He moved forward, almost touching her knee. Another half step and he would be standing between her legs, a reverse of their positions the day she'd told him about being stalked.

She swung her legs around and slid off the desk, gaining space, as she always did. "Oh?"

"You might've heard I'm going to Washington to interview for a private security job. I'm leaving in the morning."

"Yes, I heard. I also heard it was considerably more prestigious than you're making it sound."

He shrugged. "While I'm there I want to look into that Glenn Kaye guy."

"Cully, that's—"

"I can do it without your permission, Jessa, but I'd rather have your okay."

"Cully—"

"Say okay, Jessa. That's all you've gotta say. It's a precaution. To make sure he's been where the officials think he's been this past month."

She looked at him so long and so hard he wished he hadn't taken his sunglasses off when he'd stepped into the dim office.

"Okay."

He expelled air through his teeth. One hurdle cleared. "Good. Then you could help me out by giving the prosecutor a call and telling him you want me to see the file."

She frowned. "Is that really necessary?"

"I can't say necessary. I could probably get the information another way, but it'd make things a lot faster. And," he added, "I wouldn't make as many waves."

"All right." She didn't like it, but she was going along. Although her next question had a sharp enough edge to cut a thinner hide than his. "Anything else I can do for you?"

"Not a thing," he said cheerfully. But at the doorway, he changed his mind. "No, wait. There is one more thing."

Two strides brought him back to her. He had her encircled in half a heartbeat and his mouth on hers a moment later.

Her lips parted. Maybe only from surprise. He hoped not.

He slid his tongue into her mouth, finding her flavor, delving into it. He set a rhythm. Her tongue met it, took it up.

Tightening his arms, he brought her against his body

and felt her hips rock against him in an echo of the rhythm their tongues kept.

He thought another instant of this would be too much. He knew a lifetime of it wouldn't be enough.

He ended the kiss when his mind held only one blazing image—carrying her down to the floor and making love with her right here and now.

He held on to her, trying to cool his raging body without giving it what it craved, humbled by the recognition Jessa was trembling against him.

When he could, he walked away without a word because he'd said it all.

Chapter Twelve

"Hey, Jessa. How're you doing?"

She jolted as if the words were a pronouncement from the devil at the edge of hell instead of a greeting from Boone Dorsey Smith in the produce section of the Bardville Supermarket.

"I'm fine, just fine." She wasn't fine. She was edgy, nervous and tired. And she had Cully to thank for it. If hormones had been radioactive, she'd have glowed in the dark since he'd walked out of her shop twenty-four hours ago. "Did you get sent shopping so Cambria can rest?"

Perhaps if she kept her head down in concentration on selecting peaches, Boone wouldn't comment on the dark circles under her eyes. That would make him the only one. Rita, Sheriff Milano, Maureen Elliston from the café, June Reamer, Doris Mooney and every other customer who had ventured into Nearly Everything today had something to say. Even Travis had said something about her being in a bad mood.

"More like I got sent shopping so Irene can sit on Cambria to keep her still."

"Sounds like Cambria. That's a good sign." She replaced a nearly ripe peach and picked up one the size of a grapefruit.

"You don't want that peach, Jessa. Take the smaller one. Smaller peaches are less likely to be mealy."

She put down the extralarge and added the smaller peach to her bag. "I didn't know you were an expert shopper, Boone."

"I wouldn't say expert." He followed as she pushed her cart on to the tomatoes. "Cully's Aunt Philly used to take the two of us to the market when we were waist high. She'd say a woman shouldn't rely on a man for her money and a man shouldn't rely on a woman for his food. That way neither would starve."

"A wise woman."

"Oh, yeah, Aunt Philly was quite a woman. She was Cully's great-aunt—maybe his great-great-aunt. I can't ever remember her without white hair. She had eyes just like Cully's." He looked at her to see if she understood. "She used to claim some people tried to burn her as a witch when she was young, but she loved a good story. She wore white tennis shoes all the time. To church. In snow. Even wading in the stream in the heat of summer. White tennis shoes and a cotton skirt. When it got cold, she'd wear three, four skirts together, but always white tennis shoes.

"If she'd been a little younger, I suppose she would have taken in Cully and the other kids permanent. As it was, if things got too rough, they'd go to her tiny place up the ridge. I sure wish Aunt Philly had been around when Manny died."

She picked up a tomato, looked at it blindly, then put it back and turned to him.

"Boone, Travis has said a couple times that Cully barely

stayed for the funeral. He's bitter about that, and if Cully could explain to him—''

"He won't. Fran—Travis's mother—told Cully she didn't want him around. She never cared for him and Manny being close, and she did her best to keep Cully at arm's length from them. To keep peace, Manny let that happen. Then, when he killed himself, Fran blamed Cully. Said he wasn't around when Manny needed him. Said Cully failed him—when Cully was dying inside already. Said a lot of other things that made me want to take the woman's neck and...'' Boone shook his head. "God, when I went looking for him the morning after the funeral, he was still at the cemetery. Just sitting there. Of course, when Fran wanted Cully to take on Travis, all the things she'd said were forgotten. And if you think Cully's going to tell Travis those things, you don't know him half as well as I'd hoped.''

Under his probing stare, she put her head down and wheeled her cart into the next aisle, stacked with pasta, rice, vegetables, juices and soups. Boone came along, his cart conspicuously empty.

"I'm worried," he said abruptly.

"About Cambria?" With her hand on a can of tomato juice, she turned in alarm.

"No. The doctors say she's fine, she says she's fine and she's acting like herself, so I'm not worried about her. I'm worried about Cully. You know he left for that job interview? I'm sure they want him for the job—they just have to sell him on it.''

"Yes, he mentioned it. Travis, too." If grumbling, snide comments about his uncle's hotshot spook job qualified as mentioning. "But why worry? You said you're sure they'd offer Cully the job.''

"That's why I'm worried.''

"But—"

"They offer, and what happens if he accepts?"

"He moves to Washington and takes a prestigious, well-paid job."

"And ends up miserable."

"I'm certain Cully—"

Boone trampled on her words of certainty. "Have you ever seen a man who's spent sunup to sundown working in a hot sun, a man who's sweated out, fall into the cool, clean waters of a swimming hole? That's what it was like watching Cully in police work.

"The most content I've ever seen him were those first few months in Atlanta. Before he got so disappointed by flaws in the system. He's focused on them and how he doesn't fit instead of how he does, and it's got him twisted up about law enforcement. But away from it, he's like a man without water."

"If you believe that, you're in the best position to try to talk him out of making the move."

Boone went on as if he hadn't heard her stiff words. "Or what if he rejects the job for the wrong reason?"

Enough of this fencing. "What would be the wrong reason, Boone?"

"You might be, if you're not looking at the same long road he is."

It was blunt and not totally unexpected, but it rocked her. "I have no influence over whether Cully takes or doesn't take this or any job."

Boone's tone was gentle when he finally spoke, as if delivering shocking news to a heart patient. "The hell you don't."

"Boone, I know you care about Cully. And you mean well, but he has never said a single thing to—"

"Cully doesn't say much. Sometimes he says the least about what he feels the most."

Did Cully feel something for her? Desire, yes. She couldn't deny she returned it. But more? Even if he did, what was the use?

Maybe he wasn't the rigid man she'd thought. Maybe

she'd been wrong, or he'd changed. But her past hadn't changed. And his future hadn't changed.

"I...I don't know what to say, Boone."

"I'm not the one you should be saying anything to, anyway. Cully is." He started to turn away, then stopped. "I just... I feel bad. I know you wanted things to work out between Cambria and me, and I always appreciated that. And here I am, warning you off Cully. I just don't want to see him hurt more. He's had enough."

Cully headed straight to Jessa's house from the airport. On the way, however, the lights of a sheriff's department car strobed in his rearview mirror. He pulled over and got out, leaning against the rear corner of the four-wheel drive while he waited for Sheriff Milano to lever himself out of his car.

"We 'xpected you back couple days ago. You can't make up for being two days late no matter how fast you drive, Grainger."

"Give me the ticket and I'll be on my way."

"Is that any way to talk to a man who wants to say hello?"

"Hello." Cully straightened. "See you later."

"Now, hold on there, Grainger. You weren't reckless and I can't say as you endangered anybody, but you *were* driving over the speed limit...."

"Fine. Give me the ticket."

"For a Southern fella, you're in an awful hurry, Grainger. Somebody'd think you were going to see a woman."

Cully dropped back to his resting spot. Tom Milano wouldn't wrap this up before he was good and ready.

"I am."

"That's good. Jessa Tarrant's a fine young woman. And I suppose you're off to tell her all about your trip back East. 'Bout things you heard when you interviewed for that important job with the big security firm, most likely."

"Yeah."

"Things you picked up that didn't have to do entirely with that job, too?"

"Could be."

Milano nodded. "That's what I thought."

"I might tell her a few things I learned about you, too, Tom."

"Me? Now, what could you tell her about me?"

"Oh, I could tell her you not only went to Quantico, you shot what they call a possible on the range—hit every damned shot. I might tell her they've talked to you about writing up a course on rural policing."

"Not till I retire. I keep telling 'em," Milano protested.

"Which you have put off twice."

Milano's gray eyebrows popped up. "Well, now, you do have friends. I suppose you understand all about everything, eh?"

"I understand even less. Why'd you hide away in Bardville?"

"I thought we had this clear." The sheriff sighed. "I chose to go where I could serve people and live my own best life. Strike any chords with you, son?"

"Why should it?"

"Because I've been watching you, Grainger. If you gave yourself half a chance, if you relaxed enough to trust yourself, you'd be real happy in a place like this. In a job like this."

"Sheriff—"

"Don't be wasting time flappin' your jaw with me. You've got a woman to see. You'd best get on with it. Specially since you're two days late."

Travis answered the knock at Jessa's front door because they both expected Pete, who was giving him a ride to the Westons'.

Travis had been putting in his regular hours at the shop, even with Cully gone. Today he'd seemed particularly withdrawn and blue. He'd never admit it, but she suspected

Travis had felt deserted when Cully extended his stay in Washington. Worse, Travis had gotten the word through a message relayed by Irene Weston.

Maybe Travis missed Cully.

Maybe she did, too.

On impulse, she'd invited Travis to have supper with her. It might not have been such a treat for the boy, except her next-door neighbor's yellow Lab mix had had puppies a few weeks before. The appointed time for Pete to come by had rolled around quickly.

Having just put their dessert plates in the dishwasher, Jessa came out of the kitchen prepared to hear Pete Weston. Instead, she heard the low drawl of Cully Grainger.

"Hey, Travis."

"Oh. It's you."

Jessa arrived at the front door in time to see a frown darken Cully's face as he stepped inside and drew off his sunglasses. "Yeah, it's me. What're you doing here?"

"I'm not stealing anything if that's what you're thinking."

"I didn't—"

The Westons' aging four-wheel drive pulled up and a horn sounded.

"Gotta go. Thanks for supper," Travis called over his shoulder as he bolted out of the house.

Cully stared after him before turning to her. "Well, that was a real touching welcome."

"What did you expect?" Anger welled up in her. Anger for Travis's pain, but also anger that her heart beat sharper and her breath came faster because Cully had walked in a door. "You can't leave him behind like so much excess baggage and expect him to long for your company."

"I don't think of him that way."

He sounded so wounded her tone softened despite herself. "How do you think of him?"

"He's my blood. He's a bit of my brother. But... But he's not Manny, either," he added slowly, as if discovering the truth only this moment. "He's...himself." He shook his head and half smiled. "Spit and vinegar. A mouth on him like nobody's business. But he's got courage, too."

"You like him." She was confirming what she saw and heard.

"Sometimes."

"You love him."

"Yeah."

"Then be honest with him. He'll know if you're not, and he won't trust you. Why did you stay away longer than you'd said you'd be? Travis needs to be able to count on you."

"Travis can count on me." Suddenly irritable, Cully added sharply, "And why the hell do you think I stayed longer?"

"I don't know. It doesn't make sense, and I don't understand it—I don't understand *you*."

"That feeling's entirely mutual."

"Now what does *that* mean?"

"It means," he answered with exaggerated patience, "I took longer in D.C. because I was trying to clear my head of a certain dark-haired female, who's been turning me around so fast I could make the Olympics as a skater doing one of those—" he twirled his forefinger in the air "—twisting things."

"Oh."

"Oh?" he echoed with a snort. "Is that all you've got to say? It wasn't exactly the welcome I'd hoped for from you, either."

He took one step toward her; she backed away two.

"It's not that simple, Cully."

"Simple? What the hell's been simple?"

"It's just... There are things—"

He held his hands up. "Wait. Let's back up. Let's sit down, and I'll tell you a story I heard in D.C."

"A story?"

"Yeah, a story." He gestured toward the couch. She considered taking the chair, but it would seem a petty, cowardly gesture after the past few weeks. She sat, and he joined her, leaving a foot between them. "A story I heard from another cop. I had dinner with a guy I knew in Atlanta who's with State Department security now. Turns out another guy in his outfit started as a cop in a Washington suburb. He had this case a few years back. Seemed a woman was being stalked."

She folded her hands. It would have been the gesture of calm she meant it to be if her knuckles hadn't been white.

"A professional woman," Cully went on. "Sharp. Smart. Attractive. This stalker crossed paths with her when he was fixing computers in her office. Instant obsession. The woman tried to handle it on her own a long time, longer than she should have. Until a friend of hers talked her into going to the police."

"This is a boring story, Cully," she said tightly.

"You think so? I didn't when I was hearing it from this fellow. 'Course, the really interesting part's coming up."

"You *happened* to run into Thomason?"

He raised one eyebrow. "I never said the guy's name was Thomason. But, no, I didn't *happen* to run into him. I did some digging, and I used a connection to meet him. I didn't ask any direct questions about you, Jessa. I told you before I left I was going to look into that guy who stalked you."

"I thought you meant if Glenn Kaye was meeting his parole officer, going to his job, things like that."

"I did check that. And what the prosecutor told you over the phone is true. Kaye's been going to his appointments. He's had no unexplained absences. No gaps of time that would've let him hop a plane and get here."

"Why don't I feel better?"

"Because it's still somebody, and we don't know who."

The man certainly didn't sugarcoat situations. "I guess you're right."

"I am. I was also right to find Thomason. I learned a lot of interesting things."

"You must have heard hundreds of more interesting cases. Women get stalked all the time."

"Wouldn't say all the time. But they're not real rare. What *was* rare was what Thomason had to say about the vic—the woman's father in this case."

She looked at her hands with great attention, as if their shape might change before her eyes.

"It impressed Thomason," Cully said. "He said the father was a cop, and he was a real SOB to this woman, his own daughter. He said he called the father, partly as a professional courtesy, partly on the off chance of the stalking having some connection to the father being a cop. Said the father's first question was if his daughter had been raped. When Thomason said no, the father seemed to lose interest in her welfare—if he'd ever had any."

She flinched.

"The father told Thomason his daughter had been a troublemaker as a teenager. The father urged Thomason to check what she could've done to stir up this stalker. Thomason said when he hung up, he felt mad. But when the envelope arrived a couple days later from Philadelphia, he said he felt dirty. The woman's father had sent her juvenile records. When Thomason went home that night he said his kids could've held a riot and he wouldn't have minded."

She said nothing for a long time. When she did, it was still with her gaze focused on her hands. "Why did you tell me this?"

"Because we've had too many secrets between us, Jessa. I didn't want more. And because it explains a lot of things."

"What does it explain? That I was stalked? You knew that. That I didn't have a great relationship with my father? Big news. A lot of people don't. You for one."

"It explains a lot," he repeated stubbornly.

"Like what?" she challenged.

"Like why you took such an interest in Travis. Like why you always see his side. Like why you didn't think he should be held to the rules. With a father like that, it makes a hell of a lot more sense."

"Don't read so much into it."

He ignored that. "Like why you're not fond of cops. Like why you have so much trouble trusting men."

"I don't—"

"The hell you don't." He said it loud enough to drown her words. Loud enough to leave a hush when the echo faded. He pushed a hand through his hair, down the back of his head, and rubbed at his neck. "God, I'm not saying I blame you. A stalker's enough to make any woman leery of whether the next man or the one after is going to be a wacko. But your father sounds even worse."

"Oh, so now you understand all about me?"

"Not all. More. I understand more. If I understood it all, I'd understand why you're so afraid of me knowing."

She opened her mouth to deny it, then stopped. She *was* afraid. She was afraid of his knowing *her*.... The recognition of it froze her.

"But hearing your history did raise a question for me," Cully went on. "A major question."

"What?" she asked automatically.

"You've fought me on Travis, because you've been thinking I'm like your father. No—don't deny it. It's real clear, even to this country boy, Jessa. But what I gotta know is if you truly think I'd treat Travis the way your father treated you?"

Her answer was immediate, stark and strong. As vivid as the memory of Cully standing beside his nephew, hand on his shoulder, beside Cambria's hospital bed. Making the boy face the consequences of his actions. But not deserting him. Not denying him support and love.

The truth swept over her in a wave of cold, then heat. Because it wasn't the answer to one question. It was the answer to a hundred. To the questions she'd been asking

herself since Cully had taken those first long strides across
the Westons' yard a year ago, and she'd started running.

She'd fallen for Cully. She'd sensed the possibility from
the start, and she'd feared it. She *was* afraid of his knowing
about her, afraid of his getting inside the door he'd said
she was so good at keeping closed. Even more afraid of
wanting to let him inside, because if she *wanted* him inside, it opened her to so much more hurt, so much more
pain....

But how could she remember the possibility of her own
hurt, when she saw so much in Cully's eyes right this
moment?

He had opened himself to judgment—and he waited to
hear the sentence.

She reached up to touch his cheek with her fingertips.
"No," she whispered, then added more strongly, "no,
Cully, I don't think you'd treat Travis that way. I know
you wouldn't."

Unguarded, his extraordinary eyes stared into hers. Then
he closed them slowly while he reached up and covered
her hand, molding her palm to the ridges and hollows of
his cheek and jaw.

When he opened his eyes, they held a new light. He let
his gaze slide to her lips, and the light triggered an answering fire in her.

Desire.

In desire's fire, the past became ashes and the future
was a smoke not yet risen from mistakes not yet made.
Desire was now.

Cully gave her time to pull back, closing the space between them so slowly she couldn't wait. She put her other
hand up to bracket his face and met his kiss more than
halfway.

Her thumbs, resting under his jaw, absorbed a leap in
his pulse so strong she gasped as they came together,
mouth to mouth. He plunged into her opened mouth and
met her second gasp.

She wanted to touch him, everywhere. And to be touched by him. Unfamiliar urgency guided her hands as she jerked at buttons, tugged at sleeves and snatched at material. His skin was heated, smooth over bands of muscle that shifted and twitched at her explorations.

She was mostly in his lap, her hip pressed against his groin, the heat and power of his desire apparent even through layers of cloth.

He opened her blouse, his big hands brushing against her skin; she didn't want him to stop, yet thought she might cry with impatience. His hand delving under the plain cotton of her bra made her buck and moan. When his thumb at last brushed across her aching, hardened nipple, she knew she'd been waiting for this since long before he'd touched her in the Westons' den.

Arching her back, she asked, and he answered. He bent his head, circled her aureole with the tip of his tongue, then put his mouth over her nipple and drew on her.

Pleasure flooded up her back and down to her core. It covered her completely. She was spinning with it, but not drowning. How could it be drowning when she kept throwing herself deeper and deeper into the sensations and kept reaching higher and higher?

"Wait, Jessa." He held her away from him, resting his forehead against hers. The moist warmth of his breath touched her bared breast. "Give me a minute."

"Okay." She'd give him anything.

"Slow down." He drew in a breath. "Okay?"

"Why?"

"I don't want to stop. I don't want it to get so I *can't* stop. Understand?"

Yes, she understood. But he didn't.

"Can you stand up?"

He muttered a curse. "Jessa—"

She stood and extended her hand, not bothering to cover herself. What there was to see was what he had discovered in her. How could she hide that from him? "I'm not throwing you out. I'm taking you to bed."

His eyes narrowed as he studied her face. Slowly, he put his hand in hers and stood.

She led him toward her bedroom. The short hallway seemed to grow longer and the moment they'd carved out between the past and the future smaller with each step. She tightened her hold on his hand.

"Jessa." He stopped at the doorway. Turning her so her back rested against the door frame as it had eight months before. Bringing her back to where she'd been and making her face the moment again. "Are you sure?"

"Yes." Wonder colored her answer. "I'm sure. I want to make love with you."

Cully swung her up into his arms, and two long strides took him to the bed. Setting her there, he drew his wallet from his pocket and removed three packets. He put them on the nightstand and waited, as if for her to comment, perhaps criticize. She had no criticism for sanity.

He wasted no time removing the rest of his clothing, then starting on her last barriers.

He was long and lean and powerful. A man fully aroused.

Jessa wasn't naive. She'd slept with men. She'd had a few relationships. Sane, orderly relationships with a measured pace and civilized pattern. The first few dates with a perfunctory kiss good-night. More dates with a little more. A period of increasing activity. And then, after a special dinner and carefully chosen wine, the first time in bed together. A considered decision, reached gradually. Always at night, with the lights out.

Nothing with Cully had been predictable or measured.

The setting sun poured fiery light through the sheer curtains, leaving no shadows to hide in. Even if there had been, Cully wouldn't have let her stay there.

He lay beside her and took her hands, molding them around his hot length. "I won't hurt you, Jessa."

With fingertips and palm, tongue and mouth, he sought out her secrets and insecurities.

He rubbed his stubbled chin across the stomach she thought too soft.

He licked and sucked the inside of the elbow she'd given no thought to at all.

He plumped and massaged the breasts she dismissed as too small.

He guided and slowed the fingers she worried were too unsure to draw on a condom.

He stroked and admired the legs she wished were longer.

And he showed her how to wrap around his narrow hips.

"I want you, Jessa."

"Yes."

He tried to press into her gradually, but she didn't want that. She shifted under him, deepening the angle. It was amazing. Incredible. He was *inside* her body. He filled her, stretched her. She wanted more.

"Jessa, I can't…hurt you. Go slow."

"No." Smiling, eyes closed, she drew him deeper.

"Ah, Jessa," he whispered.

She curled her nails into his flesh and felt his constraint snap.

"Look at me."

She answered his harsh demand, seeing what she had already known—she had unleashed his urgency. She met it, driving up as he thrust into her. Then again, and again.

Not measured. Not sane. Not civilized.

Feeding on his urgency and fueling it. Higher and higher again.

Seeing it all reflected in his eyes. Knowing he saw it in hers. Wondering what else they had unleashed, as he plunged again into her body and she cried out, and began the swirling, dizzying return. And knowing when he crossed the boundary, his body taut and still as he shouted her name, then collapsed, to cover her.

* * *

He knew the instant she awoke. With her cheek on his shoulder, his arms wrapped around her and her leg resting between his. Twilight caressed the rumpled bedcovers and the creamy skin of her buttocks.

He waited for her to start, to pull away, to tense.

She nestled against him and sighed.

He breathed again, drawing in jasmine and peace.

"Tell me about it," he murmured against her hair.

She moved to her side, pressed against him, running a hand over his ribs. She smiled, slow and contented. "I didn't think you'd be the kind of man who'd need reassurance on his performance, Cully."

"Not that. Tell me about your father and the stalking."

Her smile fled and she settled on her back. "There's nothing to tell."

"Jessa—"

"You heard it, Cully. What Thomason told you, that was it. He called my father. My father asked if I'd been *messed with*—his phrase. Then my father asked what I'd done wrong to cause this."

"He and your mother didn't offer any help?"

"What could they have done that the police couldn't do?"

"They could have taken you home, or been with you—"

She laughed without amusement. "Believe me, I was a lot better off with Cambria."

"But—"

"No more." It sounded harsh. "Please," she added more softly. She touched a scar low on his side, below his waist. "What's this from?"

"Broken bottle."

"When you were a kid?"

"No. Army. A bar fight."

"A bar fight?"

She sounded so scandalized he chuckled. "Breaking one up, not participating."

"Oh."

She bent over and kissed it. Then kissed around it, and pretty soon Cully wished he'd been scarred in every one of the dozen bar fights he'd helped break up in his career.

But even as they made love again, it didn't ease the tight fist lodged in his chest. The fist holding the knowledge that Jessa was a long, long way from really trusting him.

Chapter Thirteen

He'd left during the night. Sometime after midnight, pressing his forehead to hers. "I've gotta go. Travis is alone in the cabin."

Now, with her eyes closed against the early-rising sun streaming into her bedroom, she could smell his scent. Smell their lovemaking.

She jumped out of bed, suddenly unwilling to stay where his imprint marked more than the pillow.

She'd showered, thrown on her robe and finished mixing a pitcher of orange juice, when she spotted a tall form through the filmy curtain over the back door's window.

"C'mon in, it's open!" she called out nearly in time with the knock.

The door immediately opened. Cully frowned at her. "You shouldn't leave your door unlocked. Anybody could walk in."

"That's why I leave it unlocked, so just anybody can walk in. The way you did."

"I'm not just anybody."

"Oh? You're not?" She looked up at him and grinned a little, not entirely sure of her ability to banter.

Then she swallowed. Those intent eyes of his zeroed in on her. And his intentions were clear. They had nothing to do with banter.

She'd shared her bed, her body and portions of her soul with this man. She didn't regret it, and she knew with a certainty seldom experienced that she could trust him with what she had shared with him.

That didn't stop her from feeling awkward when she faced him in a sunny, old-fashioned kitchen, wearing only her silk robe and the freshness of a recent shower, while he wore jeans, shirt and an expression of absolute hunger.

She turned her back to him and gave the pitcher of orange juice sitting in the sink another vigorous stir.

Cully came up behind her. She knew that more from the warmth against her back than any other sense. He slid a large hand under the hair at the back of her neck, and her nerves sizzled with the remembrance of what else his hands could do. Then he touched his lips to the vulnerable skin there, and her entire body hummed. His tongue followed, then his mouth covered the dampened area and he sucked gently.

"Am I?" He kissed the left side of her neck, and her head tipped to the right.

"Are you?" she repeated dazedly.

"Just anybody." He kissed higher, under the point of her jaw, his tongue tracing a pattern so heated she thought it might remain forever on her skin. "To you."

His hand curved around the right side of her neck, then over her jaw, until his fingertips brushed her lips, as if he wanted to feel as well as hear her answer.

"No."

"Good."

She barely heard the word. He turned her in his arms,

lifted her onto the counter to the left of the sink and moved between her legs, to kiss her.

Something behind her kept her from sliding back from the insecure edge of the counter. An appliance, she thought vaguely. They could stop this and move whatever it was, or move themselves into the bedroom... She wrapped her arms around Cully's neck and forgot about it.

The tie of her robe came undone under his hands. His shirt was opened and discarded under hers. Her skin flushed and heated under his fingers. His pulsed and hardened under hers.

He slid his tongue against hers, long and deep thrusts. Changing the angle, he shifted his hips deeper into the vee of her legs.

Tough denim over tougher muscle, bone and sinew rubbed against her delicate flesh, sensitized from the night's lovemaking. The sensation was so intense she arched her back, upsetting her precarious balance. She slid forward, almost over the counter's edge, stopped by Cully's body.

"I'm going to fall."

"I won't let you."

Only his hands on her hips held her steady.

"I don't think we can do this, Cully."

"Don't think we can or don't want to try?"

"Don't think we can." She said it quickly, honestly, before she could think about it.

"Oh, yes, we can, honey. If you'll cooperate."

"What do you want me to do?"

His grin dipped toward evil. "Reach into my pants pocket."

She slid forward, drawing a groan from him, then wiggled her fingers between the pocket and the jeans proper.

A deeper groan came from Cully. "Uh, maybe that wasn't such a good idea."

"Here, let me—" She took her fingers out and bent

forward to use both hands to unbutton, then unzip, his pants.

"With that kind of cooperation this isn't going to last long," he warned gruffly.

"I'm only trying to…" Her words died out as she slid her fingers back into his pocket. This time with enough leeway for her to reach a foil packet there.

"And you're succeeding." He imparted that information through clenched teeth. "Let me…"

He did, despite her help.

With murmurs and touches they found the perfect balance. An instant of quiet union, which departed unmourned under more urgent moments. He filled her, again and again. Until she gave up all concern for balance or gravity or reality, because the world was spinning too fast to hold on to anything…except him. And he carried her back to safety. With kisses and touches of her own, she urged him on, until he shouted her name, head back, spine rigid. She welcomed him and held him.

Jessa groaned as he laid her on the unmade bed a short while later.

"Did I hurt you?"

"Not you." She rubbed her rear end. "I think I'm going to have a bruise that would be hard to explain. If anybody ever saw it."

As he dropped down next to her on the mattress, he rolled her onto her side and took a look at the affected area. "Hmm, there is some redness. It closely resembles the shape of a handle. My advice is not to let anyone see it—at least, not anyone else." He dropped a light kiss on the sore area.

"I will never look at that toaster oven the same way. I might never look at a kitchen the same way."

"Good. That's what every man likes to hear—that his lovemaking has changed a woman's outlook on life. Or on one room, anyway."

She kissed him quickly on the lips. "Oh, you've definitely succeeded there." She kissed him again, more slowly.

He responded, then held her slightly away from him.

"We have to talk, Jessa."

For a moment she was absolutely still, then she drew back, pulling the sheet around her. "Oh?"

"You might not believe this, Jessa, but I came back this morning to talk." He grinned. She didn't. "Not that I didn't enjoy the diversion."

She grabbed an oversize sweatshirt from the nearby chair and pulled it over her head, then she drew on a matching pair of sweatpants. Frowning, he studied her back, now completely covered.

"Something wrong, Jessa?"

"I'm wondering what you wanted to talk about, now that the diversion is past."

He didn't like the sound of that. He stood and pulled on his jeans. "I wanted to tell you so you heard it from me—the security firm, the one I interviewed with, offered me a job."

"Oh."

It was about as neutral as a word could get. Not happy, not sad. Hell, it was barely interested.

"Is that all you've got to say?"

"What else do you want me to say?"

"Whatever you're thinking."

As calm as ever, she replied, "I'm thinking it sounds like a very good opportunity. One you will need to give careful consideration."

He still didn't much care for her tone, but he couldn't pass up that opening. "That's what I wanted to talk to you about."

"Oh?"

Damn, he was coming to hate that syllable.

"Yeah. I thought we could go away this weekend. Cambria told me about a place in the Big Horns. We could do some hiking. It should be pretty up there this time of year. Cambria and Irene said the wildflowers are blooming up there." The closed lines of her face relaxed slightly at that. "It sounds like a good place to go and do some thinking. I'd like you to come with me."

The moment of softening passed. "Cully, no one can help you make a decision like that. You're better off going alone."

"I don't want to go alone. I want you there. I want to—"

A knock at the front door stilled them both. Jessa started from the room, but Cully was faster and strode down the hallway ahead of her.

"You shouldn't be answering the door—"

"It's my house." She tried to slip past him as they neared the front door; he blocked her. "This is ridic—"

"You don't know who it might be. With the stuff that's been going on—"

"If you'll let me look, then I *will* know who it is."

"It's me!" came the shout through the door. "Sheriff Milano!"

Jessa grimaced at Cully as he retreated to the living room to give her room to open the door, which she did with a jerk.

"What is it, Sheriff?"

"'Morning, Jessa. Beautiful day, isn't it?" He stepped inside as if he'd received the most gracious of invitations. He smiled at Jessa, then looked over her shoulder. "Ah, good, I sort of guessed you'd be here, Cully."

Hands on hips, Jessa shifted her glare from the sheriff to him and back. "Why would you guess that, Sheriff?"

An expression of utter innocence settled onto Tom Milano's features. "Why, because his car's out front, Jessa."

Cully firmly suppressed an urge to grin. "What did you want to see me about, Sheriff?"

"Well, I heard you got offered that job."

Despite his growing admiration for Tom Milano, Cully

felt a surge of annoyance. "Guess I shouldn't be surprised you heard already. Hell, you probably knew before I did."

"Could be," Milano said complacently. "What I want to know is what you're going to do?"

Cully was aware of Jessa's tension. "I don't know."

Milano slapped his palms on his thighs. "Good! Now, that's real good to hear. Because that means I can say my piece."

"I've never known you not to say your piece."

"That's true, but it's a lot more pleasant when I'm not spittin' into the wind, like I might've been if you'd already settled your mind on taking that job."

"There are a lot of good reasons to take that job."

"There're reasons—I don't know how good. Not stacked up against a man doing what he's meant to do with his life."

"Tom, being a cop's been your destiny and you've made a good life of it. It's not mine. I've got the scars to prove it."

The sheriff snorted. "Only scars you've got are ones you've inflicted on yourself from being pure stubborn. But I've seen a change in you these last weeks." He looked at Jessa from under his brows. "Sort of like a pair of boots getting broken in. I do believe you're learning, Grainger. And a man who can learn can do anything. Could even find a spot in the finest little town on the face of this earth. Not a paradise, mind you, but a place that gives back more than it takes. A man can't ask for more than that."

He settled his worn hat on his gray hair. "I'd best get going. Ida Tronsit's reported another alien landing in her side yard. That's the most hopeful woman I ever have encountered." With his hand on the knob of the front door, he turned back to them. "You talk it over with Jessa here."

"I've been trying," Cully said wryly.

The sheriff took no notice of that. "She's got a good

head on her shoulders, and a good heart, even if she gets a mite stubborn about holding on to hurts too tight.''

Milano appeared not to recognize the warning signs as Jessa straightened and tensed.

"I'm hoping we can go up into the Big Horns for a couple days," Cully said hurriedly. "Shepherd's Inn."

"That's a fine idea. Been there a time or two myself. They got fine, wide beds there. Just the thing for...uh, talking.''

He departed to Cully's muffled chuckle and Jessa's attempt at indignation. But Cully had caught the laughter in her eyes.

The door hadn't fully clicked shut behind the sheriff, when the phone rang.

Jessa started toward it, but Cully held her arm. "Wait. Say you'll come away with me this weekend. Please.''

"But—"

"We need to get some things straight, and it's clear we can't do that here.''

She looked at him while the phone rang a third time. "Cully, I—''

She broke off, and he'd have given all of the exorbitant salary he'd been offered to read her mind at that instant.

"Okay, Cully. I'll go with you.''

Jessa awoke in the predawn darkness of that Sunday morning deeply uneasy—uneasy because what had awakened her from a sound sleep was Cully's absence from the bed.

They'd shared a bed one night, and already the knowledge of his leaving it reached her through her sleeping senses and brought her fully awake.

Each of the two nights after Cully's return he'd left her bed to go to the Westons' cabin so Travis wouldn't be alone. For this weekend, Travis was staying in the Westons' guest room until Cully and Jessa returned Monday morning.

Travis had been moodier than ever since Cully's return from the East, not even showing much pleasure at getting permission to attend a pool party Sunday evening at Theresa Wendlow's house.

When Jessa and Cully had arrived at the inn Friday evening, they'd had a fire in the fireplace against the chill mountain night. They had made love twice, and had slept in a tangle of legs and arms that should have kept her awake all night. Instead, she'd slept heavily and dreamlessly.

It was clear Saturday morning Cully had not.

He'd become increasingly quiet and withdrawn as the day wore on. He talked only in snatches, and then always about what they saw as they drove and hiked around the green lushness of the mountains.

By nighttime, Jessa fully expected him to make some excuse for them to go to bed at different times. Instead, he had held her and made love as if his existence depended on it.

Now he stood at the closed French doors, ignoring the chair beside the bureau to lean against the frame, staring out toward the charcoal black sky pinpointed by stars.

Jessa sat up. He made no sign of hearing, yet she was certain he knew she was awake. She rested her chin on her drawn-up knees and studied the lines of his back, bare down to his low-slung boxers.

"Trouble sleeping?" she asked quietly.

"I slept."

"Not long." He didn't argue. "Your muscles are tight. I can see that from here."

He turned his head enough that she saw the slight curve of his mouth. It wasn't in amusement. "Why're you surprised? You keep telling me how rigid I am, and I don't think you meant it as the kind of compliment most men would like to hear."

"Maybe I thought Tom Milano was right."

"About what?"

"That you've changed the past few weeks."

He was quiet a moment. "Would you like me to have changed?"

"It doesn't work that way, Cully. You've got to be the one who wants the change."

"Wanting's not the hard part." He shrugged, as if to ease his shoulders' tension. "If wanting was all it took, I would've had you in my bed a long time ago."

She pulled on her robe and came around the bed to stand behind him. She spread a hand at either side of the valley of his spine and slid them up. A groan, deep in his throat, told her when she'd reached the tightest muscles at the top of his shoulders. It was a stretch for her, but she kept kneading.

"I would've had you in my bed a long time ago," he repeated, then added, "and I would've changed a long time ago."

"You would have?"

"I'm not stupid, Jessa." He dropped his head forward, slightly muffling his words. "I've seen trees that don't bend when the wind comes along. They stand up fine against the small wind, but a big one comes and they crack like an icicle."

"That won't happen to you," she said quickly.

"It's happened to better men than me. Besides," he said in a new tone, "I'm not sure any sane man could pass up the money they're offering. It'd mean security and then some. Not just me, but for Travis and... I gotta look at the future. What if I turn this down and try going back to being a cop and I can't bend any better than before? What kind of future would that be?"

"But, Cully—"

"No more."

His stillness shattered as quickly as his mood. In one motion he turned, pulled her to him and sat on the chair, holding her in his lap. One hand at the back of her head guided her mouth to his. He parted her lips with his tongue and kissed her deeply.

When the kiss ended they were both breathing hard.

Her pulse upped another notch when he maneuvered her position so she straddled him. His plans were clear. So was his desire.

"I like this robe."

"Do you?"

"Yeah." He slid his hands inside the veed neck, then stroked across her collarbone and up, until his hands cupped her bare shoulders with the material of the robe gathered over his forearms. "I like it even better off."

"Cully, I'd like to go home."

Jessa's request Sunday evening didn't surprise him.

He'd been bad enough company for a saint to wish him to hell.

He'd wanted her here; he'd needed her here. Only, her being with him didn't change the fact that he didn't have all the answers or that he darkly suspected he didn't have all the questions.

The strength of the passion and caring between them surprised him. At times, it unnerved him. The next instant, he wanted to drown in it. It was a hard lesson that, no matter how strong his feelings for her, for the moment, his uncertainty was even stronger.

"Okay."

He turned into Jessa's street and heard her gasp from beside him.

Light poured from the windows and open front door of her house. Two marked sheriff's department cars strobing their rooflights and two unmarked cars with bubble lights on the dashboards lined the curb. Clusters of neighbors, several in bathrobes and slippers as befitted ten-thirty on a Sunday night, stood on the sidewalks and nearby lawns.

Cully's first concern faded as he noted the absence of rescue vehicles, ambulances or fire-fighting equipment.

He pushed back a string of mental curses as he guided Jessa up the front steps with a hand under her elbow. She hadn't uttered a sound since that gasp.

"Grainger, glad to see you."

Tom Milano stepped aside in the front hallway, and Cully saw what he'd expected to see—his nephew, trying to look defiant and succeeding in mostly looking scared. Behind Travis, a half-gone fifth of whiskey and a dozen beer bottles ranging from empty to nearly full stood on the coffee table, side table and floor.

Jessa sank into the straight chair nearest the door.

Cully looked at Travis. "What happened?"

The boy kept his gaze on a fascinating square of white wall and his mouth shut, so Milano spoke up.

"Got a call from neighbors about a disturbance. They said Jessa wasn't home, but somebody was in the house. Our arrival started a stampede over the back fence. We caught a couple in the next block, but most of 'em got away. This 'un was caught trying to lock the back door 'fore he left, and Charlie Sorenson—that's Denny's cousin—was puking his nine-year-old guts out in the back bushes, so he wasn't real hard to track down."

Cully nodded. He was so disappointed he thought he might follow Charlie Sorenson's lead.

While they'd been talking, two deputies had come from the back of the house, apparently checking that everything was secure and shutting off lights. Milano waved them out. Soon the strobing lights went out and the cars drove off. Outside was returning to a normal Sunday night.

"I figure the best thing," Milano went on, "is to sort this out in the morning. After everybody's gotten some sleep."

"Okay. Thanks. Good night."

After shaking the sheriff's hand, he turned to Travis.

"You were supposed to be at Theresa Wendlow's pool party."

"That's for kids. Bunch of babies paddlin' around in the water? Who needs it?"

"So you broke into Jessa's house—"

"Didn't break in. Used the key from the shop."

Cully overrode the sullen mutter. "You stole her liquor, made a mess of her house and got a nine-year-old puking drunk. That's real adult. That's—"

"What do you care?" Travis yelled. "Go fly off to Washington and be a hotshot and leave me alone."

"I'm not going to leave you alone." Not even Cully was sure if it was a promise or a threat.

"Why not? You've got your big-deal job. You'll be guarding millionaires and making sure they don't get kidnapped. That's what Boone said, so you won't have to worry about a kid having fun."

"That job has nothing to do with you—"

"Right, because you're going to dump me. Who's the next member of the family to get stuck with Travis, huh? Another uncle I don't know except from stupid stories? Or are you planning on sending me back to my mother? Well, good luck."

Travis turned his back and Cully was reaching a hand out to bring them face-to-face again, when a guttural sound of pain jerked them both around to Jessa. She stood with her arms wrapped around herself. She was shivering and pale…Cully had only seen one person more pale, and he didn't want to think about that.

"Jessa—"

She didn't even seem to see him. She was totally focused on Travis, yet Cully had the chilling certainty she didn't see the boy. "Are you trying to ruin your life?" she cried. "Is that what your plan is? Are you trying to turn us against you? You've had opportunities. You've been given chances. You've had things other kids would die to have. You're throwing them back in our faces. Are you trying to prove you're not worth anybody loving? Are you?''

Travis's eyes were wide and shocked.

"Do you have any idea," she started again, her voice trembling with the same shocks shuddering through her body, "how one stupid act as a kid can affect your whole life? Can change it forever. In ways you can't even imagine."

The last word came out a broken whisper. She spun around and ran out.

"Jessa!"

Cully took two steps after her, then stopped and marched back to Travis. Even if he could catch her, it might be better to let her collect herself—to let her draw some covering back over the raw edges she'd exposed. In the meantime, he had another matter to settle.

"Whether I take that job or not, you're stuck with me, kid. Do you understand that? For good." He dragged the boy into a hug. After an initial instant of surprise, Travis resisted all the way, until Cully's embrace became half punishment, half reassurance. "For good and for bad. And let me tell you, Travis, tonight was damned bad."

Cully wasn't entirely surprised he found her in the back section of her shop. Not in the office, but sitting on the top step to the dark loft.

What did surprise him was she didn't say a word about how he'd gotten in. Until she figured out he had a spare key to her security door, he wouldn't raise the subject.

"Jessa?" he said softly.

She raised her face. She hadn't been crying. Maybe it would've been better if she had been. He had the feeling she wasn't really seeing him, any more than she'd been seeing Travis at the house more than an hour ago.

He'd taken Travis back to the cabin, told the Westons what happened, made sure the boy was asleep, then rigged a bell that would alert Irene Weston if Travis opened the cabin door. Then he'd gone looking for Jessa.

"Oh, God, I totally blew it," she whispered. "I can't believe I lost it like that with him. I said I'd never do that. I swore I'd never be like that, but the first push, and I went right into the mode."

"Jessa—"

"I've been giving you all this grief about the cop mentality and treating Travis like a criminal, and look what I did. I acted like one transgression was the sum of his existence. Like that's all that mattered. He'll never trust me again. He has no reason to trust me again. God, I can't even trust myself—"

"Jessa," he interrupted firmly. "Give yourself a break. If Travis wants second chances, he better learn about giving them as well as getting them."

"But—"

"No buts. You were scared and worried and disappointed. You flew off the handle and yelled at the kid. It's not something to beat yourself up about."

She looked at him—really looked at him this time. "You didn't. Fly off the handle, I mean."

He sat on the step next to her. "I've had a lot of practice. I've been scared and worried and disappointed about Travis so long—and before him about Manny and the others—I feel like a man training for one of those hundred-mile runs. You haven't been in training long, so it's not surprising you sort of pulled a muscle."

Her lips twisted. The expression was more rueful than amused, but it was a hell of a lot better than self-condemnation. "Is that what you call it?"

"Close enough." They sat side by side in silence. He took her hand. "This have something to do with your father being a cop?"

She looked down toward their linked hands a long time before answering. "Yeah. He was a third-generation cop.

So he was truly a cop all his life. Being a cop *was* his life.''

"Your mom?"

"Oh, Mom accepted that. In fact, she probably knew the code book better than he did. They'd lived that way, the two of them, for so long that when I came along—a total surprise—they just fit me in, too."

"Sounds like you thought about this a lot."

"Not on my own. I saw a counselor. Toward the end of the stalking. Cambria pushed me into it, and I'm grateful. It got me back on track."

"And let you figure out stuff about your family."

"Yes, but— Look, it's not a big deal. I didn't have the hard childhood you and Boone had. I had nice clothes and toys and didn't have to work after school unless I wanted to."

"When did it change?"

"What makes you think it changed?"

"Give me some credit, Jessa. You never talk about your parents. You never visit them. You never volunteered that your father was a cop. It's pretty obvious."

"I forgot you're the great detective." She smiled. He didn't. "You're right. It changed. I was sixteen, and in full teenager mode. Only, I'd never rebelled. My father had rules and I followed them, by God. As long as I did, I was the perfect daughter. The one he bragged about at the precinct. The one who never got in trouble in school, who got good grades, who didn't wear a lot of makeup or hang around with the wrong kids. The one kids at school viewed as a dull Goody Two-shoes. Oh, and the one who wanted so badly to be accepted. To be part of the group that was cool and fast and a little dangerous."

She glanced at him, perhaps expecting condemnation.

"Not many people get past that age without wanting that."

"Yeah, well, I wasn't satisfied with just wanting it. I decided to get it."

She lost momentum, and he gave her another nudge.

"What happened?"

"I had a party. At the house, when my parents were gone. Strictly against the rules. I knew it, and I did it anyway."

"Like Travis." He understood her reaction now.

"Yeah. Like Travis."

He waited, but she said nothing more. "That's it? You had a party when your parents weren't home?"

"Not quite. It wasn't only the kids I knew who came. Word about the party spread. I didn't realize it until people started showing up, people I never would have invited. I couldn't keep them out. And I couldn't stop them from drinking my father's liquor and using drugs. Right in the den, where my father's awards hung. I told them they couldn't do that. They ignored me. I put the liquor away, then a throw pillow caught fire, and after I put that out and went back to the kitchen, the liquor was open again. God, it was a nightmare.

"Then the cops came." She smiled, bittersweet. "At least that cleared out the place. The trouble was, then I saw what a mess it was and the cops saw the evidence of underage drinking—and the drugs. It wasn't my friends. It wasn't people I'd invited, but that didn't matter." She sighed. "They contacted my father and held me until he and Mom got back the next day."

He muttered a curse.

"Not in a cell," she added quickly. "In the office. I remember sitting in that hard wooden chair feeling stiff and nauseated with lack of sleep and nerves, and wishing I could stay forever, because then I wouldn't have to face Dad."

Silent, she stared off into the past.

"What happened, Jessa?"

"He had me charged with possession. The patrolman who'd been the first one to the house tried to talk him out it. Dad wouldn't hear of it. He told the judge I should get no leniency because of my age or because it was my first offense. He said I should have it on my record so the world would know what kind of person I was. The judge didn't agree. But it didn't really matter. Not to my father. By the time he walked into the police station that Sunday, he'd decided I'd crossed the line from being a good daughter to being a bad daughter—and nothing will ever change his mind.''

"If you talked—''

"You don't think I tried?''

"What about your mother?''

"That day at the station, I remember her crying and asking over and over, 'How could you?' She didn't say much else. She wouldn't have gone against my father in any case.''

"So what happened?''

She shrugged. As a gesture of unconcern it failed completely. The pain in her eyes made him feel as if he were bleeding.

"They fed me. They clothed me. They never trusted me again. I worked like a fiend in school. Got a college scholarship and left home.''

"Did you see your parents?''

"Not much. Christmas usually. I'd spend other holidays with friends' families. They came to graduation. I think they were even proud of me then, in their way. Since I came to Bardville, the Westons have been my family.''

He cursed her parents, comprehensively and imaginatively.

"You've been blaming yourself, Jessa. You need to put the blame where it belongs—on your parents, though from the sounds of it they weren't much in the way of parents. They were wrong to treat you the way they did, and it's time you stop blaming yourself. Your father—''

"My father was a product of his own upbringing and his occupation. Of all people, you should understand that, Cully.''

"You can make all the excuses you want for him, but no cop—no man—should act the way he did. Especially not a father. And why didn't your mother stick up for you and protect you?"

She shook her head sharply. "Her world had collapsed in twenty-four hours. She thought she had this perfect daughter, this perfect family."

"How about your world? You were a kid. She was an adult. And your mother. She had responsibilities to you. She—"

"Just because your parents weren't responsible, don't lay the same blame on mine. They were responsible. They clothed me and fed me and educated me—"

"And stopped loving you because you made one mistake. That's not my idea of love. No parent should desert a kid. Not mine and not yours. I've seen your sympathy whenever my childhood comes up. Well, save some for yourself. You got one hell of a raw deal. Your parents should be—"

"Don't judge them. Don't you judge them." She clenched her hands into fists. "That's just like you. Look at a situation, decide who's right and who's wrong and start passing judgment. You don't want to be just the law. You want to be judge and jury, too. Hell, you probably want to be executioner. *Your idea of love?* You're the most judgmental person I've ever met, and let me tell you, I was raised by a champ when it came to judging."

In the silence that followed, she did not look at him. She didn't need to look to be aware he was drawing his legs back, putting his palms on the wooden step and levering himself up. He stood slowly, each movement measured and controlled. He gave no sign of distress, hurry or discomfort. No indication his heart might be hammering painfully at his chest the way hers was.

"How about you, Jessa?" She looked up at that low question. "It seems to me, you judge everybody innocent—no matter what the evidence says. Everybody except yourself. And me.''

"I'm not judging. You're the one who's always judging people. And always finding them lacking, just like—''

"Just like your father? *Just like your father.* That's it, isn't it? That I'm just like your father. That's what you've been thinking all along.''

"I told you before—''

"I want to hear it now, Jessa. Do you see me like your father or not?''

Like him or not. Either or. Yes or no. Black or white. All or nothing.

The phrases pounded in her brain. But she'd learned well over the years how to keep the screaming in her head from showing. She sat motionless, schooling her expression to neutrality. It had gotten her through the final years under her parents' roof. It had gotten her through being stalked. It would get her through this.

It had to.

"I guess that's my answer.'' He went down two steps, then stopped and turned to face her. "I don't know if I'm like your father in some ways or not. But I can tell you this, Jessa—I wouldn't ever turn my back on any child of mine the way he did to you. And I'll also tell you, I won't keep paying for his sins against you. If it would fix things for you, I would. But it won't. Because that's a sin that won't ever be forgiven until you face it.''

After the echo of his words and then his footsteps faded, she continued to sit there, even after a tear splashed on the back of her hand, followed by another. And another.

"Iced tea?'' Jessa's offer was as cool and polite as the words she'd used to invite Cully inside when she'd answered his knock at her front door at noon Wednesday.

"Thanks.''

She said nothing as he followed her into the kitchen. She took down two glasses from the top shelf of the cabinet over the toaster oven. Without looking at him, she filled each glass, then led him into the living room.

He sat in the center of the couch. She took the chair.

"Seems to me this was where we started, wasn't it, Jessa?"

His own voice sounded raspy to him. She didn't answer, simply continued to look down at her glass.

"I've been meaning to tell you…" Cully stopped, cleared his throat and started again. "I took the quilt from your shop. A friend knows this woman at a museum in D.C. and she said she'd look at it, see if it can get fixed. There's no promise, but—"

"Thank you."

"You're welcome. But that's not why I came. I thought you should know—I'm going to be leaving, and I'm taking Travis. I'm going to see about getting custody of him."

Silence.

"Jessa—"

"Where?"

"Washington. I'm taking the job with the executive security company. I just sent the fax accepting. I'm going to the cabin to pack now. I'm on the afternoon flight for Denver, then North Carolina, to see Travis's mother. I think she'll give me custody. Then I'll find a place for us to live. I'll come get Travis in a few days, then we'll head east for good. I told them I'd start in two weeks."

He thought she wouldn't answer. He was certain she hadn't wanted to, because when her words came, they seemed to rush out, refusing to be stopped despite her. "Oh, Cully, don't do that."

"It's a good job. It'll be a good life."

"It's not the right life. Not for either of you."

"Why not?"

"It'll be bad for Travis. You'll be traveling. You'll be gone a lot. He needs you around."

Cully had thought the silence would kill him. Two full days. Not a word from her. He'd grimly accepted that he'd destroyed whatever chance they had. All he could do was tell her he was leaving. At least, he'd thought, it would end the silence.

Now he wasn't so sure words were any better.

"I'll get someone to look after him. Someone good with kids."

"That's not enough. He needs you."

They stared at each other.

How about you, Jessa? Do you need me?

She looked away.

"It'll be bad for you, too, Cully. You don't want that job."

"I'd be a fool not to. It's great money. There're a couple dozen folks in law enforcement who would give their eye-teeth and their pensions to get that job."

"Then you're a fool, because your heart's still in being a cop. I've listened to you and I've watched you these past weeks with Tom Milano, and it's so clear. Police work— public police work—is what you love. That's where your heart is, no matter what your head's telling you."

Silence. Again. As if they both waited for something. Something that didn't come.

"We don't always get what our heart wants, though, do we, Jessa?"

He stood and left.

He *had* been waiting. Waiting for her to give him one more reason not to take the job. Waiting for her to say the words that would stop him from taking this afternoon's flight. Waiting for her to use the one argument that would keep him here.

Waiting for her to say what she'd never said—that his taking the job would be bad for her because she wanted him to stay.

She washed their glasses by hand, even though there was room in the dishwasher.

As long as she didn't think, didn't feel, she'd get

through this the same way she'd gotten through the past few days.

Leaving.

She'd tried to hold on to the safety of silence, but Cully hadn't let her. Now she had to find the safety again.

The monotonous, routine movement of washing the glasses wouldn't jar her cocoon of frozen calm.

He was leaving.

Leaving.

As she dried the second glass numbness melted under the first tears sliding down her cheeks.

Leaving.

Would he have stayed if she had asked him to?

She'd wanted to ask him to stay. She'd wanted to beg him not to leave on this afternoon's flight. But then what?

I don't know if I'm like your father in some ways or not...I won't keep paying for his sins against you. If it would fix things for you, I would. But it won't. Because that's a sin that won't ever be forgiven until you face it.

He was right. She needed to face the feelings and reactions to what had happened with her parents and even with the stalking. She'd hoped by pushing them aside she could make them go away. But they hadn't gone away. Instead, they'd surfaced again and again. So she'd pushed them down deeper and deeper. But it still hadn't worked. Not even after fifteen years.

Wasn't it about time she tried another approach?

And, after she'd done that, perhaps it would be time to consider Cully's other words.

She wiped her hands, dried her eyes and blew her nose. Then she went searching for the family photograph album she knew lay at the bottom of a box of old memories.

Chapter Fourteen

"Uncle Cully, can I go to the Randalls' for—"

Cully looked up as Travis stopped dead at the threshold of the cabin's bedroom. He dropped the shirt he held into the open suitcase, then faced his nephew.

"I'm going to Washington, Travis. I've got a flight out in a few hours."

The young face before him shifted into its old, sullen lines. "Yeah. Well, tell the president I said hello. Hope your plane doesn't crash and they don't lose your luggage. Maybe you'll get an Arnold movie. See ya—"

"Travis. We've got things to talk about."

"Nothing to talk about. You're going to Washington. Big deal."

"It is a big deal to me. It might be to you, too. Sit down."

For several long, slow ticks of the clock, Cully thought Travis would refuse. He'd bolt and run. Then, with a jerk of his shoulders, he moved across the room and dropped into the upholstered sliding rocker in the corner with enough force to set it in motion.

His belligerently angled chin proclaimed, *You got something to say? C'mon and say it.*

"I'm going to Washington to see about a place to live. Before I do, I'm going to stop in North Carolina."

The boy stilled. "Why?"

"I'm going to see your mother. To talk to her about you."

"You think she wants me back?" His laugh grated with pain, not humor. "You're in for a surprise. She's all hot to trot for that new guy and he doesn't want me around, so she doesn't. It isn't going to do you any good trying to talk her into it. You think she'll take me back?" he repeated, like someone probing a painful tooth.

Cully pushed the suitcase to the middle of the white bedspread and sat at the end of the double bed, hooking one arm over the iron bedstead.

"No, I don't. I'm not going to try to talk her into it, either."

Surprise made Travis look younger than twelve. "You're not?"

"No." Jessa had said to tell the boy the truth, to tell Travis what he thought and felt. Here went nothing. "I'm hoping I can talk her into having you stay with me. Permanent."

"You?"

"Yeah, me. Is that so hard to believe?" He waved off his own hasty words before Travis could respond. "Look, Trav, I want to have you live with me. To have custody of you. I'll find a house around Washington. Someplace with good schools and kids your age."

The boy eyed his uncle with a mix of hope and skepticism. "I get in trouble all the time."

"Not as much as before. And you can keep doing better. I'll help you."

"What about Jessa?"

"What about her?"

"You and her," Travis said impatiently.

"That's between us, Travis."

"But..."

"I'd suggest if you have anything you want to get straight with Jessa or anybody around here, you'd better do it soon." Travis stared at him, obviously trying to gauge what he knew. Cully stared back. "Okay?"

His nephew swallowed. "Okay."

They'd crossed some threshold with question and answer, though Cully was damned if he knew how they'd done it or exactly what it meant. Still, he found he needed to clear his throat before he could go on. "Good. Now, how do you feel about living with me?"

"Does it gotta be in Washington?"

"Looks that way." Cully's mouth twisted slightly. "A lot of people put in a lot of hard work and pay a lot of money to live in Washington."

Travis dismissed that. "Politicians. I'd rather stay here."

"You didn't like it here to start, either, remember? Besides, Washington's where the job is."

He thought his nephew might argue. Instead, Travis held his tongue and stared at him. Sitting still and letting the boy look his fill, Cully would have preferred arguments.

Finally, Travis demanded, "Why?"

"Why what?"

"Why do you want me to live with you?"

"We're family, Trav. You're my brother's son. I—"

He's my blood. He's a bit of my brother. But he's not Manny, either. He's...himself. Spit and vinegar. A mouth on him like nobody's business. But he's got courage, too.

You like him.

Sometimes.

You love him.

Yeah.

"I love you, Travis."

The boy stared back at him with disbelief. Cully couldn't blame him.

Be honest with him. He'll know if you're not, and he won't trust you.

"I do love you, Travis. You make me angry. You disappoint me. You scare the devil out of me. You exasperate me. I probably do the same to you. But I see good in you, and I'd hate to see that go to waste. And I love you."

Travis's eyes brightened and he blinked. "Dad used to say stuff like that to me."

Cully swallowed, but managed a smile. "Who do you think taught him?"

"Do you miss him, too?"

It was one of the bravest questions Cully had ever heard. "Yeah, I do. I miss him a lot."

"I'm going to Washington with my uncle."

Jessa looked up from restocking car polish and upholstery cleaner. "I thought he left yesterday."

"He did. I mean for good. When he starts the job there and everything."

Jessa put a price sticker on a can of polish and handed it to Travis. He put it neatly on the shelf.

"He's going to North Carolina first to ask my mom for custody."

"What do you think of that?" she asked carefully.

"She'll say yes."

There wasn't much to grab onto in his flat answer, but she tried. "What do you think about living with Cully?"

He shrugged. "Okay, I guess."

Jessa imagined what the answer would have been a few weeks ago and smiled to herself.

Her smile faltered when he pulled something from his pocket and held it out to her. It was a red pocketknife.

"Rita said you're, um, gonna do inventory soon, counting all the stuff in the store. I thought you'd better count this, too."

She studied his face, as he looked everywhere but at her.

"Okay," she said slowly. "Why don't you put it away? You know where it goes."

He darted a look at her, then away. "Okay."

When he returned, he was humming. She applied price stickers and he put away cans in companionable silence for several minutes.

"We talked about my dad—me and Cully," Travis announced.

"Did you?"

"Yeah. Before Cully left. When he asked me if I wanted to live with him. Cully misses him. You know, they were really tight when they were kids."

"Yes, I did know that." She started to say more about how Cully felt pain over Manny's suicide, just as Travis did, when something in his face stopped her. She wondered if he even remembered she was next to him.

"You'd think he'd be pissed, wouldn't you?" Travis said.

"Who?"

"Cully. You'd think he'd be pissed off his brother killed himself and left him. I mean, they'd been real close their whole lives. They were supposed to love each other. They'd gone through a lot, and then his brother just *killed* himself and left him. I wouldn't do that if I had a brother. Not ever. I'd be pissed if I were Cully."

Despite a tightened throat, Jessa said, "Yes, I'd think that along with being very sad, Cully would be angry, too."

Travis nodded at the confirmation. "Yeah, me, too."

"Are you, Travis?"

He froze, one hand wrapped around a can of Special Won-Coat Wax. "Me?"

"You have a right to be angry, too. Just like Cully. Angry that your father left you."

"He's dead. What's the use of getting pissed? It'd be pretty sick."

"No, it wouldn't. It isn't sick for Cully to be angry, and it wouldn't be for you, either. Actually, it makes a lot of sense."

"It does?" He slid a stubby thumbnail under the orange sticker and started to pry off the price she'd put on.

"Yes. Your father left you, just like he left Cully. That gives you both the right to be angry. You can be angry at somebody and still love them. I suspect that's how you feel about your mom, too."

"She's had a rough time. It's real hard for her, being the widow of a cop—"

"Travis." She hadn't bought this before; she bought it even less now. "Remember all the times Cully talked to you about accepting responsibility for your actions? And you remember how he made you see Cambria in the hospital and tell her you were sorry?"

"Yeah."

"Well, that applies to adults, too. They have to take responsibility for their actions. And they have to take responsibility for the consequences of their actions. Even parents—maybe especially parents."

"What does that mean?"

"It means you have a right to be angry at your dad for leaving you that way, Travis."

No parent should desert a kid.

Cully was right. No parent should desert a child. Not by suicide. Not by drinking. Not by abandonment, whether physical or emotional. She could hear Cully's voice, hear his anger and pain. On her behalf. She concentrated on that voice, even as she went on, "No parent should desert a child, Travis."

Not mine and not yours.

"Not yours and not mine."

"Yours?" Travis looked up.

"Yes, mine."

You got one hell of a raw deal, too. Your parents should be—

Should be what? She wanted to ask him, but Cully was gone. He'd return, but only long enough to pack his belongings and pick up Travis. Then he'd leave for good. *Should be what, Cully?*

"Are you pissed at them?"

She looked into the young-old eyes of the boy beside her. A softer blue than Cully's, they still had an intensity that was pure Grainger. They demanded truth.

"Yes. I am. I'm very pissed at them. I have been for a long time. Only, I didn't know it." Until Cully made her see it.

"How could you not know it?"

"Well, I tried to pretend I wasn't angry at them. And I was so good at pretending I convinced myself, too. I guess I was afraid if I was angry at them, something bad would happen."

"But it already happened, or you wouldn't be pissed at them."

"Good point, Travis. Very good point." She hoped her eyes did their own share of truth demanding. "How about you, Travis?"

"You mean being pissed at my dad?"

"Yes. You know, Travis," she said gently, laying her hand over his restless one, "the worst has already happened, like you said for me. Your dad committed suicide, and he left you. That doesn't mean he didn't love you. Just like being angry at him doesn't mean you don't love him."

"He shouldn't've done it." Tears choked his words.

"No, he shouldn't have. He shouldn't have done it to you." Or to Cully. Or to any of the others who loved him.

"He shouldn't have—" He slammed the can against the edge of the shelf. "He shouldn't have—" A second time. "He shouldn't have." The third time the cap flew off. Travis slammed the can down again. "He shouldn't have."

When the tears overcame him, she wrapped her arms around him and rocked them both back and forth.

Now both she and Travis had to learn to forgive their parents.

Jessa was glad the next day was quiet in the shop. It gave her a chance to start inventory. She would continue after closing. Rita had volunteered to stay, but Jessa refused. She wanted the monotony and the solitude. It would give her more time to think.

Travis's anger had been in the open, though not aimed at his parents. Hers had been buried more deeply...or maybe not.

Maybe she'd simply transferred it. Mostly to Cully—probably because she was so attracted to him, and anger counteracted that.

By connecting Cully with her parents, especially her father, she'd taken out a lot of anger on him.

She thought of the family photographs and the memories they'd stirred. She remembered a stern man. Unsmiling, unbending. A man who didn't teach lessons, but passed harsh judgments.

No man could be more different from Cully Grainger.

He'd grabbed onto the rules to hold himself above water when he was a kid. He thought that was what had saved him, not realizing his own strength deserved credit, too. Sure, he needed to learn to let go of the rules some in order to know his own strength. But he'd already started. He was like a man who didn't know for sure his leg had mended until he put aside his crutches. Only then would he realize he could stand—and bend.

The one thing she never wanted Cully to bend on was wanting her.

Cully would be back tomorrow. She'd meet him at the airport.

* * *

"We've got to run into the bank, Travis. You want to come or stay in the car?" Boone asked.

"I'll stay here."

"Okay. We won't be long."

Boone went around the car and opened the door for Cambria. Before she got out she twisted to look at Travis.

"Are you sure you don't want to come in?"

"Cambria," Boone said before Travis could answer. "We won't be gone above a couple minutes. We can't be, because the bank's closing any minute, and even if they let us hang around, we'd be late for meeting Cully's flight."

His uncle had called the first time after he'd left North Carolina and gone to Washington. His mom had agreed to give Cully custody. Travis had cried a little, alone in the spare room in the Westons' house. He was glad nobody knew, because that was stupid. He didn't want to be with his mother and Darryl. Cully was real strict, but he wasn't a butthead like darling Darryl.

Then his uncle had called today, saying he'd found a house to rent sooner than he thought and was flying back today. Boone and Cambria had agreed to pick him up. Travis decided to go along at the last minute.

"I'll stay here," he repeated.

"We'll be right back."

Cambria seemed so intent on reassuring him that he wondered if she'd seen the same figures around the corner he had.

He'd been tempted to go with her and Boone into the bank and avoid this meeting. But his dad had said the things you avoided were the ones that turned around and bit you. He'd been remembering things his dad had said a lot lately.

He was out of the car, slouched against the side, when Denny Sorenson and three buddies sauntered up.

"Hey, Grainger, haven't seen you around lately."

"I've been out at the ranch. Haven't been in town much."

"What, they cut those apron strings they had you tied to?"

"No apron strings."

"That's not what I hear. I hear that witch who owns the shop's been like a mother to her widdle baby boy Travey."

Travis looked at Denny Sorenson and realized how big a jerk he was. "Give it up, Sorenson."

Denny didn't seem to pick up on either the disdain in the words or how much his star had fallen with Travis.

"Don't have to give it up. Because I've got it all figured. She won't mess with me again."

Denny's grin and the tittering of the three other boys made Travis uneasy. "Whaddya mean?"

"I mean, that Tarrant witch is going to find out in about an hour—she can have as hot a time in ol' Bardville as back East."

"What are you going to do?"

"Don't look all innocent. You gave me the idea."

Travis looked from face to face, and then he knew. "You're going to set a fire."

Denny grinned widely. "Don't wet your pants over it, Grainger. It won't be a big one."

"We're going to torch the shop," a boy named Bill said, his voice skidding through an octave in his excitement. "Denny's going to cut the alarm."

"You'll get caught," Travis said.

Denny waved that off. "Who's going to catch us? Milano? Besides, we're waiting until the shop closes. This hick town closes up at sunset, so nobody'll be around until we're long gone, just like when I broke the window, only this time there won't even be an alarm for those idiots to ignore. By the time that joke of a fire department catches on, the Tarrant witch will be sure her stalker's back." He laughed. "That oughta keep her from poking her nose in my business."

Denny sauntered away, and the other boys followed. Travis stared after them.

A fire. In Jessa's shop.

Cully would kill him.

And how would he explain to Jessa about telling Denny about the guy who'd stalked her? She hadn't said it was a secret, but he wasn't a baby. He knew she'd been telling him something special. Something she hadn't even told Cully about until later. He'd heard Cully talking to Boone about that.

It slipped out when he was drinking that stuff Denny had brought to the theater. It hadn't tasted good, but Denny kept saying Travis was Jessa's pet, as bad as Pete Weston or Will Randall. Pete and Will weren't so bad. They'd been pretty nice to him, especially since they were so much older and all. But Travis hadn't said that to Denny. Instead, he'd started telling them about that guy who'd stalked Jessa.

It wasn't his fault Denny had done those things to Jessa. Cutting her tires and throwing her garbage around and stuff. He hadn't done them. He'd only heard about them afterward—when Denny bragged about them last Sunday night at Jessa's house. Travis squirmed at that memory.

He'd wanted to show everybody he wasn't a kid. He'd wanted to show he couldn't be ignored. Getting into Jessa's house had seemed like such a cool idea when he planned it.

But it hadn't felt cool. And when Denny started talking about the things he'd done to Jessa, Travis had almost felt as sick as that jerk Charlie Sorenson. At least those things Travis hadn't known about until afterward.

This time he knew what was going to happen.

A fire in Jessa's store.

Cully would kill him.

It wasn't his fault.

A fire in Jessa's store.

* * *

Despite himself, Cully's gaze went beyond Boone, Cambria and Travis, awaiting him inside the one-room terminal. Absently, he answered Cambria's questions about the trip, then listened to Boone's updating on his progress with their house.

No reason on earth he should have hoped Jessa would show up. If she'd wanted things to be heading down another path she would have said so long before now.

"You got a plane to catch, Travis?"

Cambria's question brought Cully's attention back to the present in time to catch his nephew's nervous start.

"What?" Travis looked at Cully, then jerked his gaze away.

"The way you keep checking your watch I thought you had someplace special to get to," Cambria said.

"No, I..."

From the past weeks with Travis, or from years of police work, or both, Cully's instincts came to full alert. "What's wrong, Travis?"

"I, uh, I gotta tell you something."

When the boy came to a full stop, Cully prodded him, fighting an inexplicable urge to shake the words out of him. "What?"

"They're going to set a fire in Jessa's shop."

Travis ran the words together so fast it took Cully a moment to separate them into something that made sense.

"Denny Sorenson?" Cully demanded. Travis stared back mulishly. "And you knew about this?"

"No," Travis said quickly, defensively. "I just found out. They said it's not going to be a big fire, and nobody'll get hurt because nobody'll be there after closing today. So it's not so awful. Only it's Jessa's shop, and—"

"Today?" Cambria's strained echo drew every eye. "Travis, are you sure it was today?"

"Yeah."

"Oh, God. The store's not empty. Jessa's doing inventory after closing today. Jessa is in there."

It was a nightmare.

Smoke and confusion and shouting. The fire truck had arrived in front of Nearly Everything, and volunteers kept showing up on the run. Some had the hose laid out and were hooking it up to the water supply. Stan Elliston from the café was wielding a fire extinguisher just inside the broken front door.

But nowhere could Cully see Jessa.

"Jessa!"

His shout turned a head in the crowd, but it wasn't Jessa. It was Rita Campbell. She was up-front, trying to shout something to Stan Elliston, but the hand cupped to his ear indicated he couldn't hear. Seeing Cully, she pushed aside firefighters and spectators alike to reach him.

"Cully, Cully! She's in there! Jessa's still in there!"

"Where?"

"She was doing inventory and—"

"I know, dammit—where!"

"In back. Probably upstairs. I told Tom..."

She said more, but Cully didn't hear. He was running. He rounded the corner into the alley behind the store at a full-out run. He heard footsteps behind him he guessed belonged to Boone.

The alley was a more controlled scene of confusion. Two men in full firefighter regalia were looking at the security door Cully had installed, while Tom Milano stood behind them, issuing orders.

"Grainger! You got the key to this contraption or are they gonna have to break it down?"

"Jessa?" Cully asked as he dug for the key in his pocket.

Milano shook his head. "No sign. You open the door, and these boys can go in and find her. Your backup alarms worked just fine, so we got here real fast."

The key slid back the bolt, and the door swung open, emitting a billow of smoke and heat.

"Get back, Grainger. And let these boys do their jobs."

"The hell with that." He jerked free of a restraining hand and stepped inside.

Chapter Fifteen

"Jessa!"

He stopped inside the door, trying to adjust to the eye-stinging, vision-blurring smoke.

"Jessa!"

"There it is!" The firefighters plunged past him, focusing on the leap of flames that seemed to come from the base of the stairs. Half a carton was eaten away by the fire, so its label read only "St. Valen". A stack of red paper hearts stored inside burst into flame with a rushing sound.

"Cully?"

He spun around. She wasn't there.

"Jessa! Where are you?"

"Upstairs."

He jerked his head back and saw her crouched, peering at him over the bottom rail of the loft balustrade.

"Cully, you shouldn't be here until tomorrow."

"Neither one of us should be here," he said darkly. "The damned building's on fire."

"I know. The bottom of the stairs are bad. I've been looking for a rope or something to climb down."

Cully glanced at the firefighters to his left. They'd backed up a couple of feet from the base of the stairs, moving closer to him and the door.

"No time. Jump. I'll catch you."

"No. It's too far. I'll hurt you."

She didn't even consider he might fail, and if he did, she could be badly hurt. But he couldn't think of failure.

"Jessa—"

"No!"

Her face was dimmer in the smoke. Desperately he looked around. A wooden crate by the door would put him a couple feet higher.

"Get ready to jump, Jessa." He lunged for the crate and shoved with all his might.

When he looked up, Jessa was already climbing over the loft balustrade.

One corner of the crate was under her position. That would have to be enough. He climbed up on it, as close to her as he could get.

"Jump!"

She didn't answer. Instead of jumping, she slowly lowered herself by her arms until she was barely hanging on to the bottom rail. He reached up. But even with her stretched full length and his six feet four inches, he had only a tenuous hold around her calves.

"You have to let go, Jessa."

She looked over her shoulder and down at him. He thought he caught a faint smile. "I know."

He kept his hold loose, using his body to help balance and guide her. The two of them stumbled back; his heel caught in the crate's wooden edge, and they went over.

He landed hard on one knee on the floor, but kept his other foot under him and kept Jessa mostly upright. Not even waiting to see how she was, he hobbled out of the building, half dragging, half leading her into the relatively smoke-free air of the alley.

"It's Jessa!"

"He's got her!"

"Cully found Jessa!"

"She's okay!"

Shouts went up around them, but Cully didn't pause until they'd reached a far corner where two buildings joined. It wasn't completely private with the firefighters going in and out of her shop and onlookers trying to stay out of their way, but it would have to do.

He cupped her smudged face between his palms.

"Are you all right?"

"I'm okay, Cully. I'm okay." She was coughing and laughing and crying at the same time. "I'm okay. I have so much to tell you—"

"Shh, shh. You should have oxygen." He looked over his shoulder toward the rescue equipment parked at the alley entrance. A tug on the front of his shirt immediately brought his attention back to her.

"No oxygen. I'm okay. Really. I have to talk to you."

"Not now, Jessa. Not yet." He put his arms around her, then dropped his forehead to hers. The relief surging through him left him weak-kneed.

"Cully..."

"Don't say anything, Jessa. Just let me hold you for a while."

He turned her all the way into his arms, feeling the reality of her flesh pressed against his. There was nothing better in this universe.

She tipped her head and her lips touched the side of his neck, above his collar. Beneath the acrid smoke, he could smell her sweet, soft jasmine.

"How long is a while, Cully?"

Until you make me let go. "Just a little longer, Jessa."

He forced his tone to sound teasing. "God, you're impatient, woman."

"I think I've been incredibly patient waiting for you."

His heartbeat stuttered, then took off as if he were being chased. "Waiting for me?"

"Yes. To tell me you love me."

He pulled back, not entirely sure he'd heard right. He saw in her face he had. "I do love you, Jessa. And I'll do whatever I have to to keep us together. I'll work for Boone—I'll raise cattle—I'll sell insurance—I'll pump gas. It doesn't matter—"

"Of course it matters—"

"Jessa, I love you. That's final. Loving you and Travis are the only things in my life that can't change. So, you don't want a cop? I won't be a cop anymore."

"I couldn't ask that of you, Cully. I know how much that means to you."

"Not as much as you do."

"Cully, will you shut up and listen? I don't want you to change—not professions, anyway. I hope you'll keep adding shades of gray to your vision, but I don't want you to change what's here." She put a palm over his heart. "I love you."

He immediately covered her hand with his, pressing her palm flat. "Your father…"

He said no more, but she understood. "Do you know, I was going through pictures the other night and you don't look like him at all."

"Jessa—"

"You're not like him, Cully. He served only his code, never people. He never made allowances for people. You're a totally different man."

"But—"

"Listen to me, I've been thinking about this. It's not that I don't trust you. It's that I don't trust myself."

"But—"

She covered his mouth with her hand. "Shut up and

listen. This is what happens. I start thinking I can trust you, but then I start thinking how wrong I've been before. I mean, I trusted my father—I adored him—and look what happened. So I don't trust my judgment. But you've got doubts about yours, too. I know you do. That's why you think you need the law and all the rules so much—because you're not sure you can find your way through right and wrong without all the clear-cut answers. But I'm sure you can. And you're sure I can trust you. Aren't you?''

He pulled her closer and pressed his lips to her hair. ''Absolutely.''

She eased back enough to see his face. ''See, I figure a lot of people don't trust themselves in some way or another. But we're a lot better off, because we trust each other. If you trust me and I trust you, we'll be fine.''

She put her arms around his neck to draw him down to where she could kiss him hard.

''Hey, you two. We already got one fire to put out here.''

Tom Milano's drawl ended their kiss, but they each kept an arm wrapped around the other as they turned to face the sheriff, Rita, Boone, Cambria and a miserable-looking Travis at the head of a clutch of townspeople. Beyond them, the firefighters had shifted from high speed to more measured movements, indicating they had the fire in hand.

Jessa used her free arm to receive hugs from Cambria, Rita and Boone. Then she reached out and hugged Travis, too.

''It's my fault,'' the boy blurted, on the edge of tears.

''Your fault?''

''I told them. I shouldn't have, but it came out, about you being stalked and what that guy did. I didn't mean to, but I should've known better. And it was wrong to tell anybody, specially Denny Sorenson. It's my fault. Like with Cambria and Midnight. And I'll do whatever you say. I'll work for you as long as you say. I'll pay you back for every penny of what's burned.'' He gulped, flashed a look

at his uncle, then considered the tips of his battered shoes.
"Unless I'm in jail."

"You're not going to jail." Jessa pulled the boy back
into her arms and gave Cully a stern look over his head.

"We'll talk about that later, Travis, but I don't see you
going to jail." Cully patted his nephew on the shoulder as
the boy straightened. Then Cully's tone hardened as he
turned to the sheriff and continued, "But there are some
who should be going to jail. There's good reason to think
Denny Sorenson's behind this as well as the other inci-
dents. Travis's statement should be enough. It's your duty
to arrest him and follow through with—"

"Well, now, it so happens Deputy Kasper radioed in
that he'd found Denny Sorenson a bit ago with his clothes
fairly reeking of gasoline. He's taking the boy to the jail,
and that's where I'll head next." The sheriff's gaze slid
away from Cully. "But as to the following through, that
won't be my duty. Not entirely."

"What do you mean it won't be your duty? That kid's
dangerous. If the courts don't—"

"Guess you didn't hear I put in for retirement." It was
clear, even with his face averted, the sheriff was grinning.

Above a surprised buzz from the people surrounding
them, Cully asked, "When?"

"Yesterday. Effective with the election of a new sheriff
come November. I want plenty of free time to share with
my new bride."

"Rita! You and Tom are getting married?" Jessa
stepped from Cully's embrace and hugged her clerk again
as the older woman nodded. "You never said a thing!"

"Well, you've had so much on your mind and I didn't
want to worry you about finding a replacement, not until
I knew for sure. But Tom didn't know for sure until yesterday after talking to a friend of his in Washington who
works for some big security firm and knows Cully. And
this man said Cully didn't seem all that happy about the
new job, so…"

She trailed off and looked from one face to another, apparently suddenly aware of currents passing between the two men facing each other at the center of the interested circle.

Jessa stepped back to Cully, slipping a calming arm around his waist. He put his arm around her, but still glared at Tom.

"Sheriff Milano, you manipulating, interfering—"

"No, no, don't go starting the testimonials. There'll be plenty of time before November. Besides, all I did was ask an old friend for an honest opinion. And even if you did thank me like you should be doing, I wouldn't believe a thing you had to say. Not after the way you've run me ragged with that gol'durned computer." Tom rubbed his chin. "Though, if a man like you were looking to stay around these parts, sheriff of Shakespeare County wouldn't be half-bad. 'Course, you'd have to register right quick for the election."

Cully's arm tightened around Jessa, his gaze not leaving the other man's face. "I don't know—"

Sheriff Milano didn't wait to find out what he didn't know. "Madge has the forms. She'll expect you first thing Monday."

With that edict, he tipped his hat to Jessa and went back to where his deputies were securing the scene. But there were other voices eager to second the sheriff's mandate and more hands to shake. Stan and Maureen Elliston from the café and Al from the hardware store and Wanda from the library and June Reamer, Doris Mooney and Henry Poole. They all thought Cully would make a fine sheriff, and were happy to tell him so.

Boone clapped him on the shoulder and pumped his hand. Cambria reached up on tiptoe to kiss his cheek, then gave Jessa a hug, a rather awkward embrace since Cully wasn't willing to do more than slightly loosen his hold on Jessa's shoulders.

When Cully brought his eyes back to Jessa he met hers, huge and dark in her pale face, but steady.

"What about you, Jessa?" He pulled her to him. "You think I'd make a good sheriff?"

As if by magic, the other people around them slipped away.

Jessa didn't even seem to notice. She nodded, the movement a brief friction of the top of her head against his chin. Then she tilted her head back, and he had her eyes to fall into once more.

"I think Bardville would be incredibly lucky if you stuck around permanently. Me, too. If you want to. Do you want to?"

He wanted to give her an answer right then, right there, in a manner that would scandalize even unflappable Tom Milano. But even more, he wanted to get this right.

"You trust me to take care of you?" he demanded.

"No. I trust you to help me take care of myself."

He considered the distinction. Could he live with that? Hell, yes. He fought down a grin.

"And vice versa?"

She nodded. "That's a deal."

She pulled away enough to stick out her hand for a shake. He dragged her back into his arms and kissed her so long, so deep and so hot they were within a hairbreadth of scandalizing Sheriff Milano after all.

As it was, they reached her house, but not her bedroom. Then, with clothes scattered across the rug, they exchanged vows in a language deeper than words.

Epilogue

"**D**on't you think we should be getting out of bed?"

Jessa stretched, and Cully was immediately less interested in getting out of bed, even though it was five in the afternoon and they'd occupied that particular piece of furniture for nearly four hours. Outside, it was a wind-whipped raw day. Inside, it was two people in love who'd stolen an afternoon off after a very busy stretch. It was the first Tuesday in November.

The damage to the main shop had been minimal and Jessa had reopened quickly. Stock in back, the holiday decorations and the loft stairs had to be replaced, and the place required industrial-strength scrubbing to erase smoke and char marks.

Denny Sorenson was in a juvenile facility downstate. His younger accomplices were still doing community service. The library stacks and public grounds had never looked so good.

There had been no charges against Travis, but Cully

instituted a private "community service" program, and a lot of Grainger elbow grease went into the smoke removal at Nearly Everything. Travis hadn't been cheerful, but Jessa considered his being resigned to his fate a big step forward.

"Why should we get out of bed?" she asked Travis's uncle.

"Because the polls close in a couple hours."

"No reason for me to get out of bed."

"How about your civic duty?"

She rolled onto her stomach. "I already voted."

"Oh, yeah?" He kneaded her shoulders. "When?"

"Mmm. This morning. On the way to open the shop."

"I avoid that time. That's when the commuters vote."

She laughed. "Not many commute the way you're thinking and there isn't much of a rush hour. Better learn these things about the people you're going to serve and protect after today."

"That's presuming I get elected sheriff."

"Don't be a pessimist. With Tom Milano's blessing I don't see how you can miss. Even if you are an outsider."

He grimaced. "Thanks for reminding me."

"I wouldn't worry, Cully. Not only do you have Tom's backing, you've shown you're putting down roots by enrolling Travis in school here. And you turned down a glamorous, high-paying job back East to run for sheriff. That counts for a lot."

He allowed a slow grin to spread across his face. "And if they don't elect me sheriff, they'll never figure out the customizing I did to the department's computer system."

Jessa raised up on her elbows to look at him. "You didn't."

His grin deepened. "It's much more efficient—as long as you know how to run it."

"And only you know how to run it?" She shifted to her side.

"I'll teach 'em."

"That's presuming you get elected."

"Now who's the pessimist?" He ran his knuckles along her exposed side. "By the way, who'd you vote for?"

"Uh-uh, I'm not telling. That's why they have private booths and call it a secret ballot."

"I'm not asking for the rest of the ballot. Just sheriff."

"Uh-uh," she repeated.

"Oh, yeah?" He ran his knuckles along her side again, this time pressing where she was most ticklish. She squirmed and tried to slide away. He followed. "We have ways to make you talk."

"That's not fair," she said, gasping, left breathless by the tickling and another, very different, involuntary reaction stirred by the rubbing of his naked body against hers.

"Who said anything about fair? I figure a guy who's about to bring up an important issue is entitled to a vote of confidence."

"Vote of confidence? I thought you wanted to know my vote for sheriff." She quit struggling, launching a counterattack by wrapping her arms around him and drawing him close enough to plant a hot kiss to the right side of his chest. She had the satisfaction of equalizing their oxygen deprivation.

"Both. I want both. But don't you want to know the issue?"

"I'm not sure I do."

He cupped her head between his palms, holding her so he could see her face. "I love you, Jessa. I want to marry you. I want the world to know we're together, no matter what. I want to know *you* know it. I want it legal, official and religious. I want two rings and a honeymoon. And I want—"

"What about the election? We said we'd wait until—"

"You said that. It just confuses the issue. What we decide has nothing to do with the election. It only has to do with you and me. If we have that, then we'll deal with whatever happens. If I lose the election we'll figure something. I can freelance security. Go to Denver a couple weeks a month or look in nearby counties. But first we have to decide about us." He touched the pad of his thumb to her lips. "It's time, Jessa. Are we going after forever or not?"

He stared into her eyes. Knowing she was looking into his, seeking answers to questions, seeking reassurance to fears that only time and their hearts could give. The real question was if she had the faith—in him and herself—to take the leap.

"Yes. We're going after forever."

His heart hammered at his chest as if he'd been holding both his breath and its beat. He kissed her on her lips. Almost chastely. Certainly the most chastely they'd ever kissed with the two of them naked in bed.

"I love you, Cully."

"I love you, Jessa." They kissed again. Not so chastely. "There's one more thing to talk about."

"What?" She nuzzled at the joining of his shoulder and neck. He wanted to drop his head back and howl.

"Not *what*. *When*. When do we get married. Thanksgiving?"

"Thanksgiving? You're crazy. That's three weeks."

"When did you think?"

"Spring."

"Christmas," he countered.

"Valentine's Day."

"New Year's."

She opened her mouth, then closed it a moment. "Okay. Ring out the old year, ring in the new life."

"Sounds good." He kissed her eyelid, her nose, her chin, her throat, her collarbone. Each kiss less chaste than the one before.

"Mmm, very good. *Oh.*"

Which is why Cully Grainger slipped in just before the polling place closed, and why he cast the final vote of a landslide election for the new sheriff of Shakespeare County, Wyoming.

* * * * *

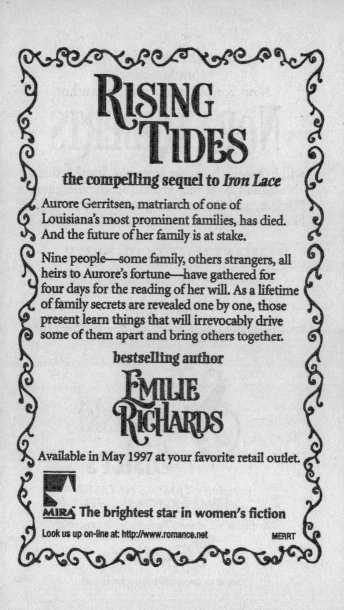

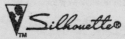

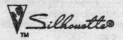

New York Times
bestselling author

Jennifer Blake

Laurel Bancroft has been a recluse,
isolating herself from a town that
has branded her a murderer. Now,
convinced people have finally
forgotten, she is ready to resume her
life. She hires Alec Stanton to help
redesign her garden. But as their
relationship grows, so do the threats
from someone who wants Laurel to
return to her seclusion and give up
her younger lover. Someone who
hasn't forgotten that night so many
years ago.

GARDEN
of
SCANDAL

Coming into full bloom in May 1997
at your favorite retail outlet.

MIRA

Silhouette

SPECIAL EDITION ™

Watch as three sisters fall in love
with the men of their dreams
and walk down

The Bridal Path

A delightful new Special Edition trilogy by **Sherryl Woods**

Sara, Ashley and Danielle. Three spirited sisters raised on a
Wyoming ranch by their strong-willed widower father—and
each one nothing alike. Feisty Sara is a rancher through and
through who wants to follow in her father's footsteps.
Beautiful Ashley is a rebel model who doesn't want to settle
down. Warmhearted Danielle is a homemaker who only
wants to find a husband and raise some children.

A RANCH FOR SARA
(Special Edition #1083, February 1997)—
Sara fights for her ranch and her man.

ASHLEY'S REBEL
(Special Edition #1087, March 1997)—
Ashley discovers love with an old flame.

DANIELLE'S DADDY FACTOR
(Special Edition #1094, April 1997)—
Danielle gets a family of her own.

Don't miss a single one of these wonderful stories!